THE WAGES OF SIN

THE WAGES OF SIN

J.M. Gregson

severn House

This first world edition published in Great Britain 2004 by
SEVERN HOUSE PUBLISHERS LTD of
9–15 High Street, Sutton, Surrey SM1 1DF.
This first world edition published in the USA 2004 by
SEVERN HOUSE PUBLISHERS INC of
595 Madison Avenue, New York, N.Y. 10022.

British Library Cataloguing in Publication Data

Gregson, J. M. (James Michael)
   Wages of sin
   1.   Peach, Percy, Detective Inspector (Fictitious character) - Fiction
   2.   Police - England - Lancashire - Fiction
   3.   Prostitution - England - Lancashire - Fiction
   4.   Detective and mystery stories
   I.   Title
   823.9'14 [F]

   ISBN 0-7278-6055-0

Typeset by Palimpsest Book Production Ltd.,
Polmont, Stirlingshire, Scotland.
Printed and bound in Great Britain by
MPG Books Ltd., Bodmin, Cornwall.

*To all the ladies who helped me
with the research for this book!*

One

This would be the end of her first week of doing it for money.

She still didn't like to call it 'on the game', still didn't wish to acknowledge to herself the reality of what she was doing. She thought of it as a temporary phase; as a means of raising the money necessary to her independence; as something a future husband would never need to know about.

She was still very young.

She'd been petrified by the man she'd met on the first night, the man who'd held her chin in his hand and snarled fierce words into her face from no more than six inches. But she hadn't seen him since then, though she'd looked fearfully over her shoulder for him each time she'd been out.

This man didn't look dangerous. Well, nothing like as dangerous as that man who had clenched her face in his gloved hand and spat his contemptuous words into her terror-stricken face. That man had been a nutter, for sure. The girls said you got a lot of nutters in this game, but most of them were harmless.

She mustn't let this man know how new she was to this, mustn't let him sense her nervousness. You had to remain in charge of the situation; treat the punters as schoolboys, Karen had said. If you dictated the terms, told them what to do, you kept control, so that they couldn't take advantage of you. Always remember they were desperate for it, or they wouldn't be here: that way you would keep the advantage. They were probably just as nervous as you were about the transaction.

This man didn't look nervous. When you are only seventeen, you aren't good at ages, but Sarah guessed that he was

1

in his late twenties. He had sharp features, with a growth of black stubble around his chin and the back of his cheeks. His black hair was straight; perhaps it would have benefited from a wash, but it was parted neatly enough. She didn't know much about men's clothes, but she fancied his had been expensive when they were new, though they were indisputably shabby now. He might have been good-looking if he hadn't looked so hunted, with his red-rimmed eyes and his anxious glances over her head towards the door of the pub.

But to Sarah Dunne late twenties seemed old, and there was a staleness about the man that she couldn't quite define, but couldn't make herself ignore, however much she tried. She hadn't yet the experience of life which would enable her to recognize a user of hard drugs.

In any case, it didn't matter whether he was good-looking or not: she was much too nervous to be attracted to anyone.

She ran her fingers round the top of her glass, willing herself not to lift it and down the gin and tonic in one to give herself the courage she needed to carry on with this. She longed to feel the alcohol burning her throat, warming her chest, giving her back the confidence which seemed to have drained away. Instead, she said, 'You're not from around these parts.'

He looked at her sharply, and she realized she had broken one of the rules. You didn't ask them about themselves; above all, you mustn't give them the impresssion that you were prying. They came to you for sex, but sex that was anonymous. They might be inadequate in their own lives, and sometimes it paid you to think of them like that, to give you the confidence to handle things. A little contempt could be useful, but you must always conceal that contempt to the men who were paying to be between your legs.

Or in other places. They had bizarre demands, some of them. Listening to the older women, she had been filled with horror, which she had fought hard to hide beneath her sniggers. She'd keep this one to straight sex, she told herself firmly. But if he started asking for things like the golden rain she could hardly tell him she'd never done that, could she?

2

He'd laugh in her face, or wherever else he was at the time. More important, he might refuse to pay. And she needed the money: how she needed the money.

He pulled his attention back from what was going on behind her in the rest of the saloon bar and gave her a crooked grin. 'No, I'm not from round here. You are, though, aren't you? I can tell by your accent.'

Sarah Dunne was absurdly discomforted by his words. For an instant, she was back in school, with the teacher making her repeat what she had said without 'talking Lancashire'. She thought she had been speaking to her pick-up in a neutral accent, and here he was spotting her as local from the few phrases she had uttered. 'Yes. I was brought up not far from here,' she said.

He looked down appreciatively at the swell of her thighs where the short, cheap skirt ended. 'And very well brought up, too, I'm sure.' He reached forward and put his hand on the hem of her skirt, letting his fingers caress the soft flesh with gentle appreciation.

She managed to avoid tensing the thigh and snatching it back from him, as she had thought she would do when she had imagined this gesture in the privacy of her room before setting out. She even managed to rock her leg a little beneath the fingers, in an answering erotic movement.

The response was easier because he did not look into her face, but kept his eyes upon his hand, as if he could control both its actions and her minimal movements of response by the intensity of his attention. Sarah sipped her drink, gave him a little smile of encouragement when eventually he looked up at her, as she had known he must.

He didn't seem a bad bloke, really.

He smiled quickly at her, then transferred his attention back to the scene beyond her, to the noisy conversations she could hear but not see as she sat facing him across the small round table. Apparently what he saw reassured him, for she caught a tiny nod of satisfaction before the grey, red-rimmed eyes came back to her face and he said abruptly, 'How much?'

It was like a slap in the face. But he wasn't to know how few were the times she had done it for money. And he'd done her a favour, really: she knew you had to tackle the subject of money early in any transaction; you couldn't negotiate, once the punters had got themselves aroused. She glanced automatically down at his crotch, but there was no sign yet that Percy was calling the tune.

'It's fifty,' she said firmly. 'And that's for straight sex. I only do straight sex.'

Sarah was going to throw in her spiel about the rate for blow-jobs, but she saw that he was nodding. 'So do I!' he said, with a laugh which never properly developed. 'So that's a relief for both of us!'

It was, really. She smiled and allowed herself another sip of her drink.

But he lifted his whisky and downed it in one. 'That's settled, then. Let's get going.'

He hadn't even asked her name. But that was all right, she decided. There wasn't supposed to be affection in this, so why pretend that you were going through the motions? It was better this way, for her as well as him. She downed her own drink in a parody of his gesture, then said, 'You'll have to leave straight afterwards. I don't have clients staying overnight.'

'Suits me.' He was on his feet, pushing his arms into his well-worn leather jacket, leaving her to pull her coat around her as well she might. There was no squiring here: just a straightforward financial transaction.

Now that the moment was here, her anxiety came back with a rush. Surely he must realize at some stage how seldom she'd sold herself like this before? And what would he do then? Make fun of her? Refuse to pay her the price they seemed now to have agreed?

Her knees seemed to have deserted her in her hour of need. They trembled so much that she had to hang on to the back of the chair he had just left as he turned his back on her and made for the door. She shut her eyes and pushed herself forward in his wake, wondering if her legs would support her, or plunge her face downwards on to the grubby carpet.

It was all right. After the first faltering steps, she moved normally, catching her man up at the door, taking his hand

4

as he moved out into the street and the sudden cold of the night hit them.

He held her hand until they had moved no more than five yards from the door of the pub, whose orange lights seemed suddenly warm and attractive in the darkness behind her. Then he dropped it abruptly, looking not at her but up and down the street, as if he feared there would be someone waiting for him here.

Sarah Dunne surveyed the street in her turn, her gaze automatically following her companion's. It looked to her deserted. The flagstones glistened, wet with the thin drizzle which had been falling when she went into the hotel. It was fine now, but the wetness threw back the glare of the lights from high above them. They could see for a hundred yards and more down the street before the row of terraced houses curved gently to the right, and there was not a soul visible.

November the fifth had been and gone a week ago, but half a mile away, somewhere on the edge of the town, a belated rocket soared and burst into a dozen brief comets, startling them both with the sharp crack of its explosion. She found that she was gripping his arm quite hard, and had to force herself to release the tightness in her fingers.

It was that relatively quiet hour before the pubs finally shut and deposited winter revellers upon the chilly streets. Sarah found herself wondering whether there might be hidden presences in the shop doorways which lined this side of the street. Her companion's nervousness was communicating itself to her, when she had quite enough of her own.

'It isn't far,' she said, and he looked sharply back at her, as if for a moment he had almost forgotten her presence and what they were about. He smiled down at her, forcing himself to relax, and, as his features softened in the weird white light from the lamp, he reminded Sarah Dunne of her father. She wasn't ready for that thought, and her stomach churned anew with it.

Her head swam, but he put his arm round her shoulders, then slid it down to her waist and marched her in step with him along the street. He looked into each doorway as they passed, checking that they were empty. Her heightened awareness

5

seemed to stretch distance as well as time. The road they must turn down to reach her bed-sit loomed like a cavern of darkness, still a hundred yards away as they reached the bend in the road. 'How far now?' he asked urgently.

'Not far. Along that street over there and then the second on the left.'

'Further than you said. I haven't much time, you see.' Still he didn't ask her name. He slowed, then stopped, snatching a look behind them towards the distant amber windows of the pub, far enough away now for them to catch no sound from it. 'I haven't much time, you see,' he repeated. He was almost apologetic, and she felt a sudden shaft of sympathy for him.

It was going to be off, she knew it was. Whatever the reason, he was going to renege on their deal. She should have known it couldn't be as easy as this. Yet the only emotion she felt was relief.

Then he said, 'How about a quicky in the car? I'll give you twenty-five and you can be back at work in no time.'

Sarah knew should refuse him, she knew that. Insist on the fifty they had agreed or nothing. Give him a mouthful of obscenities for the insult he was offering her. Stalk away on these ridiculously high heels, if he wouldn't play fair with her. But his compromise offer came almost as a release. She said simply, 'All right. If you're in a hurry, it's all we can do, I suppose.'

He lengthened his stride, as if he had known she would agree. She wondered for the first time just who he was, what background he came from. She had been too preoccupied with her own anxiety to think about her client so far. But that was all right. When you were on the game, you didn't ask questions about your customers, if you knew what was good for you. One of the rules of the game, one of the things they paid for, was anonymity.

She was on the game now, she thought, with a little spurt of excitement. She had the money from her first jobs, and the first week would soon be over. Tonight would be the end of the initiation rites.

His car was in the shadows, beside a group of unlit lock-up

garages. The clouds must be lifting, for here, without the street lights above them, she could see a few stars, small and white against the navy sky above the rooftops of the mean houses. He looked swiftly around him, checking again that there was no one here to see them, then turned the key and threw open a rear door of the big old saloon.

The back seat was musty with disuse. She noticed that he had both of the front seats forward, to allow the maximum room in the back of the car. Perhaps this is what he had planned all along. She caught him looking around again before he almost threw himself into the car beside her and slammed the door shut.

His arms enveloped her in the clammy darkness. 'Money first!' she said firmly. 'We always insist on that. And you've got to use a condom.' She was surprised at her boldness.

But he didn't argue. He grunted, fumbled into some inner pocket of his jacket, and produced notes. 'A twenty and a five,' he said, and held them against the damp rear windscreen of the car, so that she could check them in the dim light. She couldn't see enough to be sure, but she said, 'That's all right, then!' and tucked the notes hastily into the pocket of her jacket. He turned away from her, cursing under his breath as he struggled with the condom.

Then he was on her, urgent, breathy, his strength immensely greater than hers with the compulsion of his need. She was glad she had worn the stockings; they said you had to do it because the men found them such a come-on, but in the cramped space here tights would have been another encumbrance. He said nothing, not showing even the semblance of affection she had expected. It was better really, she told herself; there was no need for her to pretend to be enjoying the exchange.

Sarah felt as if she was sitting on some viewpoint above and watching the loveless struggle on this fusty couch. It did not last long. The man came with a short, gasping climax, and she held him hard with her arms, grateful that there seemed no need for her to simulate orgasm. Then, as their breathing slowed, she eased herself slowly apart from him.

It was over.

She had got the punter's money. She hadn't thought it would be like this, in the back of a cold car with their breaths condensing on the windows. But it hadn't been long or complicated, and she had twenty-five pounds to show for it; her hand crept to the pocket of her jacket and found the notes still there.

Perhaps the man took the movement as a sign of her anxiety to be away, for he eased himself upright beside her and said. 'It's all right, love. You can go whenever you like. I need to get away myself.'

Sarah Dunne grinned at him in the darkness, grateful that he was not going to ask her how it had been for her. Perhaps this was how it usually was when men paid for it; perhaps they neither expected you to fake an orgasm nor to praise them afterwards. And you got money as well! Impulsively, she leaned forward and kissed her benefactor on his forehead.

He grunted what might have been a thanks, then flung open the door. 'Have a good weekend, love. And take care! I must be away.'

It was a dismissal. He was round at the other side of the car and into the driver's seat without another look at her. She had scarcely time to snatch her pants up from the floor and slam the rear door shut. The car's engine roared into life as she moved uncertainly over the uneven ground on her high heels. The big car moved swiftly past her and back to the street they had left, its headlights briefly brilliant on the wet cobbles left from a vanished age.

Sarah took a deep breath and pulled her scarf up over her chin and her jacket tight about her slim shoulders. This last encounter of her first week had been easier than she had expected. She hadn't envisaged it happening in the back of a car, with the foetid smell of disuse in her nostrils and the man not troubling even to know her name. But he hadn't hurt her, hadn't asked her to do any of the things which lurked among those secret fears she could scarcely formulate. And she had her money: her fingers felt yet again at that reassuring paper in her pocket.

She could take a short cut back to her bed-sit from here, get herself a shower and a warm drink in front of the telly.

She was finding her feet in this lucrative game – that was the important thing. There'd be more and better pickings to come in the weeks ahead.

She thought she heard a footstep behind her as she strode through the back entry. She didn't see anything when she looked fearfully back over her shoulder, but it was too dark here to discern anything clearly. She wished now that she had taken the longer way home, beneath the high, comforting lights of the street.

She tried to hurry, but the tightness of her skirt and the highness of her heels did not allow speed, especially over the uneven cobbles which had been laid a hundred and thirty years ago and never altered since those palmy days of the old cotton town. She was certain this time that she caught the noise of someone behind her. She would have called out, but her voice was stilled in her throat. Fear dropped silent as a cat on to her back.

She didn't stand a chance. It was the scarf which was the instrument of her downfall. Strong hands pulled it from behind her, so that it snapped down from her chin to her neck as if it had been a steel cord. In twenty seconds she was dead, her throat crushed by the scarf as her limbs thrashed briefly and hopelessly at the damp air.

The arms which lifted Sarah Dunne's body found it surprisingly light.

Two

It was Monday morning and Chief Superintendent Thomas Bulstrode Tucker was feeling depressed.

He had endured a trying weekend with his wife, Barbara, who was built like a Wagnerian soprano and just as bellicose. She had carried him off to her parents' house and he had been forced to make conversation instead of watching the television. That was unreasonable enough, but Barbara had required him to address the family at large upon his most recent triumphs in detection.

As these didn't exist, he had been sorely taxed. Modesty was not an option with Barbara hanging upon every word of his heroic tale, but Tucker was a man of limited imagination and his well of invention soon ran dry. He had looked forward to Monday morning as a welcome deliverance.

That was another mistake. These days there was no relief for him at work. His role as Head of the CID section in the Brunton police had always been a nominal one: he was an expert at seizing the praise for his staff's successes and dodging the brickbats for their failures. For eight years, the system had worked well: Tucker had basked in far more adulation than abuse, since the Brunton clear-up rate on serious crime was as good as any in the country.

The man his staff knew as Tommy Bloody Tucker had been Superintendent Tucker the super-sleuth in the eyes of the public. He was a good front-man: urbane, silver-haired, immaculately uniformed, ready with a quote for the media and a smiling acceptance of their plaudits for his latest brilliant piece of detection. His superiors knew what the real story was, of course, but that was the system. If you carried the rank, you collected the rewards.

The other side of the coin was that if things went wrong it came back to you like a load of wet sewage. And in the last year, things had been going seriously wrong at Brunton CID. It had all happened since Superintendent Tucker had been promoted to Chief Super. It had been no more than his due, as far as Barbara was concerned, and she had trumpeted the promotion loud and long at coffee mornings and among the ladies attached to the men who attended Tucker's Masonic lodge.

The snag was that Tucker had had to ensure that Detective Inspector Peach had been promoted at the same time to Chief Inspector.

Percy Peach carried the bumbling Tucker upon his sturdy Atlas shoulders. He was a thief-taker, a cop respected by cops, a cop whose reputation among serious villains carried much further than the patch of town and country in north-east Lancashire where he hunted down killers and fraudsters.

It was inconceivable that Tommy Bloody Tucker could make Chief Superintendent without taking Peach, the man who had preserved and enhanced his reputation for so many years, up the ladder with him. So Percy Peach, coppers' copper and villains' scourge, had been promoted to Chief Inspector, a rank supposedly abolished but still found useful by police promotion boards.

The snag from Tucker's point of view was that he was deprived of Peach's services in CID. The police rules said that anyone promoted to Chief Inspector should spend a year in uniform. It was daft, but there was no escaping the rule. Tucker consoled himself with the fact that he would at least be rid of the taunts of the egregious Peach, who exploited his usefulness to his chief quite shamelessly.

The paradox for the Superintendent was that the man who had made his reputation for him, the man who had made police committees purr over his efficiency, had also made his daily life a misery with his insolence. Well aware that Tucker could not afford to transfer or demote him, Percy Peach had amused himself by seeing just how far he could go in baiting the man who in theory directed his working life.

It had been nice to be rid of him. Detective Inspector

11

Collins, the man who had taken over from Peach, had been pleasingly obsequious. For a little while, Tucker had thought how splendid it would be to be get rid of Peach for ever.

The euphoria had lasted less than a month. Collins and the other inspectors demanded day-to-day direction, and Tucker was no good at that. He told them they must use their initiatives: his job was to maintain an overview of the situation. So they took their own decisions, and made mistakes, which came back to him. He tried to rally the troops with inspirational addresses, but they attended dutifully and then asked awkward questions about responsibilities.

So, as things went from bad to worse, Tucker gave them bollockings: he'd always fancied himself as rather good at those. They listened sullenly, without the interruptions Peach would have made. But the bollockings had no effect. The CID men below him played things by the book, and Tucker was required to do the job he could not do. He was forced to direct investigations instead of maintaining his lofty overview, and he made embarrassing mistakes.

It was very nearly a year now since Peach had left the CID fold. He could be out of uniform and back in the CID soon, but Tucker was determined to do without him. He would work his way through to retirement without that unique form of mock-obsequious insolence which was Peach's forte, whatever the cost.

On this grey and gloomy Monday morning, when the November cloud hung low over the drab old cotton town, that cost seemed considerable. There was a sheaf of statistics comparing the Brunton crime clear-up rates with those of other areas in the north-west: it made melancholy reading. There was a memo from the Chief Constable which was no more than a terse command to see him at eleven thirty that morning to review these figures.

There was also a query from the custody sergeant as to whether he should release the four men being held in connection with an Asian/British National Party punch-up in the town centre early on Sunday night. 'We've got to charge 'em or enlarge them, and their briefs are getting lippy,' that grizzled officer told him succinctly, and stood waiting for a decision.

'Hold them a bit longer. I've got DCs out in the town trying to get witnesses to the violence,' said Tucker importantly.

'The Asian brief's asking to see you, sir,' said the custody sergeant implacably. 'Says if we're holding them any longer he wants to know the reason why, and he wants to hear it from the top man. Says if they're not out of the slammer by ten thirty he'll be claiming racial discrimination on behalf of his Paki clients.'

'We can't have that,' said Tucker unhappily.

'No, sir. Shall I tell that lippy lawyer you'll be down to tell him the reason why we're holding his men?'

Tucker squirmed in his big leather chair, stared unhappily down at the centre of his huge executive desk. 'Let them go,' he said almost inaudibly.

'Very well, sir. And what about these National Front lads? They're keeping shtum as yet, but they've got tattoos bigger than their IQs, if you ask me.'

Tucker mused unhappily, wondering how he could inject energy and enthusiasm into his troops. 'What those cocky young sods need is a good grilling, Sergeant. They don't like being locked up, you know, and it makes them nervous in the end. They might even break down and confess, with skilled interrogation.'

'Yes, sir. I can see that. Will you be down to question them yourself, sir?'

'No, of course I won't. I've far more important people to be dealing with than petty thugs.' Tucker gestured vaguely at his vast expanse of empty desk.

The custody sergeant followed his gaze and paused. 'All the experienced CID staff are out and about, sir, on your orders. The National Front brief's getting a bit stroppy as well, you see, sir. Bright young feller, unfortunately – knows that even thugs have their legal rights. He's been wondering aloud about whether some of their wounds might have been inflicted in custody, rather than in the fight last night. Even muttering about wrongful arrest, though I don't think he can make that stick. Don't suppose you'd care to have a word with him, sir? Put him right about the law and where he stands, from your detailed knowledge?'

'No, I wouldn't. I'm far too busy to go tangling with young lawyers still wet behind the ears. Oh, I suppose you'd better let them go, if that's really the best we can do!' Tucker cast his eyes to heaven theatrically at the incompetence with which he was surrounded.

The custody sergeant went back down the stairs and did what he'd known he would do all along: he released the men involved in the weekend fracas with no more than an official caution. It was inevitable, without a better case to offer the CPS, but at least he had played it by the book and made Tommy Bloody Tucker take the decision.

It proved to be the wrong decision, from the Superintendent's point of view. When he saw the Chief Constable at eleven thirty, he was told that there was to be a firm policy on all racial violence. Trouble was to be nipped in the bud at source by decisive police intervention. 'So let's make an example of these ruffians who got involved in last night's violence,' said the CC. 'Let's show them who's in charge of this particular manor.'

Chief Superintendent Tucker had to confess they'd been released. 'The custody sergeant was insistent,' he said. 'I was reluctant to let them go, but I didn't think we'd enough for the Crown Prosecution Service to take on the case.'

This time it was Tucker who was on the wrong end of the bollocking. Chief Constables used phrases like 'surprised and disappointed' and 'marked decline in the efficiency of the CID section' and 'very disturbing figures' rather than the more basic language further down the ranks, but both men realized that this was a severe bollocking.

When Tucker described it as such with a sickly smile, hoping for some conciliatory words to end the meeting, the CC responded with a curt, 'That's good, then. A bollocking it is. At least we understand each other!' and dismissed him without a smile.

Chief Superintendent Tucker went back to his office and sat with his head in his hands. He was too upset even to do the calculations about his pension with which he usually consoled himself on such occasions. There were far too many days like this to endure before his retirement. They stretched away interminably before him in his imagination, like the rows of Banquo's heirs in Macbeth's vision of the future.

It was all very well his staff being obsequious, but there was no one around equal to the task of carrying him.

He was contemplating lunch when the news came in of a serious incident, a bank raid in Clitheroe. The masked gunmen had got clear away with a large but so far undefined sum in used notes.

There was also a body by the railway line in Pleasington, on the other side of Brunton: possibly a suspicious death.

Thomas Bulstrode Tucker swallowed his pride and reached for the phone. 'Get me Chief Inspector Peach!' he said grimly.

The day was so gloomy that the early winter dusk was mingling with the night by the time the children got out of school at four o'clock.

The cars had their lights on and, as the boys came through the school gates, the street lights came on abruptly above their heads, making what little remained of the daylight even less apparent. There was a thin mist of drizzle in the air. It was a depressing evening, even for twelve-year-old boys newly released from the classroom.

Tommy Caton had his red hair cut very short. It had seemed a good idea at the time, almost as short as the cuts he saw on some of the footballers he watched on television, but now he felt a chill about the back of his scrawny neck that he could not acknowledge without losing face. On this bitter evening, he would have welcomed the balaclava helmet that his gran had knitted for him and which he had treated with such derision as soon as she had left the house.

He flapped his thin arms and tried to banish the cold by the energy he put into his shrill cries to his companions, as they trotted through the familiar streets towards home. There were a dozen of them at first, but the group became smaller as boys and girls peeled off at each street junction to go to their homes.

Tommy lived furthest from the school, and presently there were just he and Jamie Betts left, kicking a battered lager can to each other across one of the town's few remaining cobbled streets and pretending to be racing down the field for the Rovers.

15

They had known each other for almost as long as they could remember, these two. They had gone through junior school together and been delighted to find themselves together in the same first-year class at the comprehensive.

A sour-faced woman at the door of one of the mean brick terraced houses called them noisy little beggars and told them not to play football in the street. Tommy picked the can up and they got to the corner before pulling horrid faces in concert at the closed door of the woman's house. They didn't shout anything: they were getting too near home to take risks.

Tommy dropped the can again when they got round the back of the houses, on a patch of unpaved ground where a mill had been felled and not yet replaced with new buildings. There was no danger of cars here. All they had to do was avoid the puddles of grey water in the potholes of the uneven surface. Tommy wove a swift path between the water with the can at his feet, shouting his own excited commentary: 'And it's Damien Duff on the wing for the Rovers! He beats one man! He beats another! And he gets his cross in as he reaches the goal line!'

He flicked the ball at right angles as he came to the wall at the end of the waste ground, and Jamie Betts met it expertly on the half-volley, yelling, 'Goooooaaal!' in that long drawn-out roar of triumph they shared with the crowd at the Rovers' matches on Saturday afternoons.

'You put it over the bar!' said Tommy, panting with bright-eyed excitement from his sprint down the wing.

'Top corner. Goalie had no chance. Nearly broke the net!' Jamie swung his right foot in happy remembrance of the strike. 'Good as Alan Shearer, that one was!' They were too young to have seen the folk-hero with the Rovers, but they saw him still on television.

'I reckon you just missed. It wouldn't have gone in there if you'd hit the goal,' said Tommy. He pointed towards the broken door of a decrepit hut in the corner of the site and the black hole where their tin had disappeared.

'I was aiming for that!' claimed Jamie, with the prompt and shameless improvisation which comes naturally to twelve-year-old boys. But he already had a grasp of the diplomacy that could end arguments. 'It were a smashing centre, though, Tom. Right on to my instep as I came in on goal.'

They went forward together to retrieve the can which had become a football. It was almost dark now, and Tommy Caton paused for a moment before ducking into the cave of blackness beyond the broken door. You couldn't say you were frightened by a bit of darkness: fear was for girls. All the same, he made sure that Jamie Betts was following him as he went into the hut.

Jamie was right when he claimed to have caught his shot just right. The can had gone well into the centre of the hut. They could see it gleaming dully as their eyes grew more accustomed to the gloom.

But there was something else, too. A sweet, heavy smell. Not a pleasant smell. The panting boys sucked the odour deep into their lungs, even as they gasped that they did not wish to do that.

There was something beyond them, against the rotting boards at the far end of the shed. Something which had human form, but which lay with its limbs oddly disposed upon the floor, as if it was not human after all, but some life-sized puppet which had been dropped here. It had a skirt, and legs protruding below the skirt which were lifelike, and yet had no life at all.

Tommy did not want to touch it. He saw a hand reaching out towards the thing in the dimness, and it took him an instant to realize that the thin fingers belonged to him. Those fingers were still cold, but the flesh they touched below the skirt was much colder: cold as any marble.

The boys found they were in each other's arms, clutching each other briefly for comfort in a way they would never have believed possible before they came upon this terrifying thing.

Then they were out of the hut, running frantically back across the derelict site and towards the sanctuary of the lights and the street beyond, their lungs screaming their terror at what lay behind them in the hut.

Their lager tin lay forgotten beside the corpse of Sarah Dunne.

17

Three

'Come in, Percy! Do sit down! Tell me how life has been treating you since our paths had to diverge.' The Chief Superintendent was at his most effusive.

Bloody 'ell, thought DCI Peach. He's calling me Percy. Better be careful here. Tommy Bloody Tucker wants something. He sat down cautiously in the armchair towards which Tucker had waved an expansive arm. 'Can't grumble, sir. Variety is the spice of life, they say – especially police life.'

'You're looking well, Percy, I must say. Very well.' Tucker eyed his man up and down as Peach regarded him warily from the other side of the big desk. Tucker wasn't used to seeing this man in uniform. The dark cloth emphasized the contrast with the white of Peach's round bald dome, which was also set off by the neat black fringe of hair around it and the jet moustache and eyebrows. The pupils in the eyes below those mobile eyebrows were almost black: they were Peach's most valuable asset in interrogations, those piercing black eyes. They seemed to penetrate the defensive armour of people who argued with him, but gave nothing away about the thoughts of the powerful, stocky man behind them.

'I'm feeling well, sir. Very well. Happy with my lot in my new section. Carving out a new and better career path. And I trust you're well too, sir. Maintaining your usual perceptive overview of CID, I expect. Bringing your usual powerful presence to the direction of serious crime? I'm sure you are, sir. Of course, I'm not really in touch with CID matters, but I hear how things are going from time to time. Your reputation goes before you, as you might say.'

Thomas Bulstrode Tucker felt the interview slipping out of his control, even at this early stage. He had expected this bouncy little sod Peach to be desperate to get out of uniform and back into plain clothes and CID work, as people normally were. And here he was saying he was happy where he was. And making remarks about CID which were most suspicious.

Tucker peered over the gold-rimmed half-moon glasses he had donned for the occasion and tried to assert himself. 'The CID section has been progressing pretty well without you, Percy. Going from strength to strength, you might say.' He tried not to notice the black eyebrows rising higher than seemed possible in the forehead beneath the bald pate. 'However, I'm always looking to make a strong team even stronger. I like to think that's one of my virtues, not being content to sit upon my hands just because things are going well.'

'No, sir. I used to tell the lads and lasses in CID in the old days, "Don't think the man upstairs is just sitting upon his hands, because he won't be."' Peach nodded several times over this gnomic utterance, as if remembering old, forgotten, far-off things.

Tucker was thrown. 'Yes. Yes, I see. Well, as I say, I want to reinforce my team. And I would regard you as providing that additional strength, Percy.'

'Very gratifying, sir.' And it's still Percy, so watch your step here, lad, he thought. 'I don't quite see my way to coming back to CID at this moment, sir.' He had been counting the days until he could get out of uniform and back to serious villain-taking, but he thought he'd keep that thought to himself.

Tucker's jaw dropped most gratifyingly. 'But – but I thought you'd surely be grateful—'

'Grateful, sir? Well, of course, I'll always be thankful to you for what you've taught me. I learned some interesting things from you, over eight years. But it seems that I have a future in Traffic Policing, sir.'

'Traffic? But surely—'

'Expanding field, they tell me, sir. Governments keep spending more money on motorways, but congestion grows ever worse. The man who can keep traffic moving in this part of the world will carve himself out a reputation, they tell me. Not that you haven't got quite a reputation your-self, sir.'

Tucker glared at him suspiciously. Then he thought of the Chief Constable's acidic comments and pressed on. 'We were always a good team, you and I, Peach.'

'Not for me to say, sir.' Peach allowed himself a winsome smile; he felt happier when he heard Tucker lapsing back to his surname.

'Well, we were. An effective combination.' The Chief Superintendent tried to keep the irritation out of his voice. 'That was recognized by the powers that be. Without me, you'd never have made Chief Inspector, you know.'

'I'm well aware exactly how much my promotion owed to you, sir.'

Tucker glared at him, but Peach's countenance was impassive, his eyes firmly fixed on the wall behind his chief's head. Tucker had planned this as a lordly offer, but it seemed to be turning into a plea from him. He said rather desperately, 'Well, I think the time has come for you to resume your duties in CID, Peach. I shall be making arrangements for you to do so.'

'Beg pardon, sir, but shouldn't you discuss my future career path with me, at the end of my year in uniform?'

'I – I suppose I should, if we played things by the letter of the law. But you were never one for playing things strictly by the book and—'

'Stickler for it now, sir. Perhaps it's the result of a year in uniform. Perhaps that's why I decided that my future path lay in Traffic Policing. Quite consoling, the book seems, sometimes. Like the rules of golf, sir. They always say you can use them to your advantage, if you know them well enough, don't they?' Peach smiled innocently into the increasingly reddening face beyond the desk.

Tucker did not want to get on to the subject of golf, where he had never got beyond the tyro status in many years of effort and Peach had reached a single-figure handicap five years after giving up cricket. 'Look here, Peach, we need you here. And you must surely realize that CID is your natural métier.'

'Need me, sir?'

'We need your experience. Your insights. Your natural talent as a thief-taker.' Tucker tried not to speak through clenched teeth. He had intended to patronize his man and admit him back into CID as a great personal favour; he could scarcely believe that he was now saying these things.

Percy beamed at him with a delight which was almost that of a child. 'Wonderful to hear you say these things about me, sir, needless to say. I believe your judgement is a little clouded by your natural affection for me, but I'm very touched, all the same.' He spent a couple of seconds trying hard to look very touched. 'But it's not quite as simple as you suggest, unfortunately. It is hardly modest for me to relay it, but the Chief Superintendent in Traffic has been saying equally complimentary things, you see. I'd more or less decided that my future lay there.' Even if he had actually decided that he would be out of Traffic like shit off a shovel during the very first minute after his year in uniform was concluded, there was no need for Tommy Bloody Tucker to know that.

Tucker said feebly, 'You'll have more or less a free hand here. The arrangement you always liked in the old days.'

The system which suited you, whereby you didn't dirty your hands but took all the credit, you mean, Thomas B. Tucker. Percy Peach pursed his lips, shook his head sadly over the brilliant career he was giving up in Traffic, and said doubtfully, 'I suppose I'd have to take DS Blake back as my sergeant?' Percy, who had just spent a night of bliss in bed with the delectable Lucy Blake, had no intention of working with anyone else, but he might as well have her imposed upon him as a burden.

Tucker was prepared to concede anything now to get his man. 'Not if you don't want to have her. I know how put out you were when I had to allocate you a female detective sergeant in the first place. I'm sure that we could arrange for you to have someone else assigned to you if that is—'

'Wouldn't be fair, sir, that. Politically incorrect, it would be, nowadays, for me to discard a female officer who has always been entirely satisfactory.'

'But within the privacy of this room, you and I know that

21

you are a man's man, Peach, happy working in the rough camaraderie of a male ambience. I'm sure if I explain the matter tactfully to DS Blake—'

'No need to do that, sir, I assure you.' Peach held up a hand magisterially, demonstrating his penchant for traffic control. 'I wouldn't dream of causing embarrassment. We must move with the times.' He stiffened his back, moving into the martyr mode which Tucker had rarely seen in him, and said in a lofty, neutral voice, 'I shall be happy to resume working with DS Blake.'

'Well, I suppose that would cause the minimum of disruption. It's good of you to look at it like that, Peach.' Tucker stood up and offered his hand. 'Welcome back to CID, Percy.'

Percy Peach got out quickly, once his forename was used again. As he went down the stairs from Tucker's penthouse office he dropped his martyr's mode and punched his fist into the palm of his hand in triumph. It was good to be back.

It didn't take Peach long to get rid of his uniform. He shook himself like a dog coming out of cold water when he was back in his smart grey suit.

And he felt the old, familiar excitement returning as he approached the scene of a serious crime. He could scarcely conceal his eagerness as he put the regulation white plastic bags over his shining black shoes and prepared to go through the break in the plastic tapes and into the shed where the mortal remains of Sarah Dunne had been found.

There was a light in here now, a strong beam from the naked bulb illuminating the scene which darkness had made even more fearful for Tommy Caton and Jamie Betts. The heat from the bulb seemed to accentuate the smells of the place as well as throwing it into pitiless detail. The smell from the body mingled with the smell of the rot at the base of the shed, as if the decaying timbers of the hut sought to emphasize the human decomposition they had entombed.

Jack Chadwick, the Scenes of Crime Officer, exchanged the briefest grins of greeting with Percy Peach. It was over a year since they had last worked together, but they behaved as if it were yesterday. Peach went and stood wordlessly for a moment, looking down at the corpse with its awkwardly posed limbs. Beside him, DS Lucy Blake crouched and looked closely at the dead face, as if drawn by the invisible bonds of gender into a final, useless intimacy.

'It's a suspicious death, I suppose,' she said hopelessly. It was a last gesture to the dead girl she had never known: there would surely have been less pain in a death from natural causes or suicide, whatever the mental anguish involved.

'It's murder,' said Jack Chadwick quietly. 'She was strangled.' He lifted the scarf the police surgeon had already loosened away from the throat with his ruler, showing the ugly red-black marks of constriction around the young throat.

The unmarked face looked more frightening with the contrast of the livid marks in the white flesh of the unlined neck. But Peach had eyes only for the wounds. 'No signs of thumb or finger marks, Jack,' he said gloomily, as if he were accusing Chadwick of making things difficult.

'No. The police surgeon reckoned she was probably killed by simple and rapid tightening of the scarf, though he gave us the usual guff about having to wait for the PM report.'

The pathologist arrived at that moment and the policemen went outside to look at the approach to the hut, affording the dead girl a privacy she could never appreciate whilst the forensic examiner took rectal temperatures and conducted his minimal brief examination on the site before the body was removed for the detailed science of the post-mortem investigation. Lucy Blake remained in the hut; she had still not managed to become blasé about death in the approved, self-protective, police manner, though she knew that Peach would want her to get whatever she could from the medical man at this early stage.

She found herself looking away automatically as the man lifted the clothing of the dead girl. He said softly, 'We can't hurt you now, love. We want to find who did this, you see.'

Lucy was startled for a moment. Then she realized that the pathologist was speaking to the corpse, not to her, as if apologizing for the liberties he had to take, the indignities he had to inflict in the causes of science and detection. He spoke as if she was a child, but a living child. Lucy was pleased and a little moved to hear it: it was a human contrast to the man's necessary detachment, an acknowledgement that what lay beneath his hands had been a living human being, with a person's reactions and emotions.

'Did she die here?' asked Lucy tentatively.

'Impossible to say, yet,' said the man without looking up. He switched his dialogue back to the corpse. 'Just let me move you a little, love. Gently does it.'

Lucy Blake let a few seconds pass before she said, 'Any idea how long she's been dead?'

He grunted and at first she thought he was not going to answer. Then he said, 'She's been here some time. There's extensive hypostasis throughout the body. Do you see?'

Lucy looked unwillingly. She saw his ball pen pointing to a slim thigh that was very white on its upper surface but dark blue in the inch above the floor, where the blood had sunk in the many hours since the heart had stopped pulsing it around the limbs. She nodded, not trusting herself to comment. After a moment she said, 'Is there much rigor?'

The pathologist looked into her face for the first time, wondering how much these young, unlined features had seen of violent death. 'It's not as advanced as you might expect. But if she's been here since she died, in the temperatures we've had this weekend, it would take a long time for the processes of rigor mortis to be complete. It's not a very reliable guide to the time of death, you know, rigor.'

Lucy seized her cue. 'So you think she's been dead for some time. Days, perhaps?'

The pathologist smiled at her. Professionally, he wouldn't commit himself to anything yet: he was experienced enough and had appeared often enough in court to have the spectre of a clever defence counsel who was out to make a fool of him perpetually at the back of his mind. But he was here to help the police, and the only service he could offer to this poor dead girl who sprawled so pathetically behind him was to point the way towards her killer. So he said, 'You'll have to wait until I've had her on the table for anything more definite. Even then, it will be informed speculation: time of death is notoriously difficult to establish, when we're not on the scene immediately. But this girl's been dead for some time: the body temperature has dropped virtually to that of the environment.'

'A day? Two days?'

He smiled into the white face beneath the striking dark red hair, so anxious for information, so eager to get on with the hunt for the killer of what lay behind him. 'I couldn't stand up and state this in court – not yet anyway – but I'd say she'd been dead for two or three days. That's an informed guess: it could even be longer than that; it's as cold as a fridge in here, and cold preserves. But probably not less that a couple of days.'

'Thank you. It will help us with the door-to-door enquiries when we set them up. We've no idea who she is yet.'

They turned automatically and looked down at the white face, smooth as carved alabaster upon a tomb. He said, as though reluctant to trample a little more on that face's privacy, 'She'd had sexual congress not long before death.'

'You mean she'd been raped before she was strangled?'

He shook his head. 'I can't say that, yet. You'll understand that I have to disturb the body as little as possible here. When we have her on the slab, we'll be better able to see whether penetration was violent, whether there was much, or indeed any, resistance to intercourse. All I can tell you at the moment is that there are traces of sexual fluids evident in the genital area.' He stood up. 'That sounds like the meat wagon arriving now. I've finished my site examination. The sooner she's removed, the sooner we shall be able to give you the benefits of a full post-mortem report.'

He sounded glad to be briskly professional again. And he was right about the vehicle arriving. With swift, practised hands, the slim body was slid into a plastic body bag and placed in its 'shell', a plain fibre-glass coffin. Thus concealed from the prying eyes which still lined up behind the plastic ribbons on the edge of the area, the corpse was borne away from the shed on the derelict site.

Lucy Blake reported to Peach on her exchanges with the

25

pathologist as they returned to Brunton Police Station in the Mondeo. At least they now knew that she had been dead for some time, possibly since before the weekend. But it was back at the station that DS Blake discovered what she thought was the most depressing fact of all about the dead girl.

No one had yet reported anyone of her description as a missing person.

Four

Lucy Blake was glad to spend that Monday evening with her mother. It took her away from the dour, narrow streets and cheap and grimy brick houses of the town and back to the more innocent country world of her childhood.

Her mother's cottage, in the village at the base of Longridge Fell, was within ten miles of the sordid shed in the industrial area of Brunton where she had knelt beside the decaying body of that still anonymous dead girl. Yet in the feeling it conveyed of a safe and wholesome security, this place might have been on the other side of the world.

It was a stone cottage with a neat, cheerful garden at the front, at the end of a row which made up one of the three lanes in the small village. These had been humble dwellings for farm workers when they were built, but the small houses had been skilfully placed. When the winds howled in from the Fylde coast on its western side, these dwellings seemed to curl themselves up in the lee of the hill, letting the winds sweep over their sturdy slate roofs.

Agnes Blake had been widowed for ten years. She was sixty-nine now, but still hale and independent enough to work part-time in a supermarket in the neighbouring Longridge. She looked forward to her daughter's visits more than she would ever have admitted. Although the old place had central heating these days, Agnes had lit a fire two hours before Lucy's arrival, so that flames now licked cheerfully up the chimney. And the face of the woman Agnes still saw as a girl glowed pink and healthy, as she nestled cosily into the chair in which her father had once sat and told stories to the wide-eyed child upon his knee.

'I never see you in your uniform now, our Lucy,' said

Agnes as they sat with their cups of tea after the meal. 'Used to look very smart, you did, with the dark blue and that hat.'

Lucy grinned: she didn't remember her mother saying that at the time. 'I don't wear the uniform now, Mum. Except on formal parades. I told you, that's part of being in CID.'

'And are all these murders and stabbings and rapes I read about part of CID too? You lead a dangerous life for a young girl, our Lucy.'

'Not as dangerous as you think, Mum. Most of it's routine and boring, petty burglaries and the like, but you don't read about that.' She thought about the stark, accusing face of that dead girl earlier in the day, the face she could never mention here.

'I can't imagine life being boring with Denis Charles Scott Peach.' Agnes was the only woman who was determined to make use of Percy's real forenames, because he was named after her favourite of all cricketers, Denis Compton. 'I bet your Percy's as quick on his feet in the job as he was when he batted in the Lancashire League. He gave up cricket far too early, you know.'

'So you keep telling me, Mum. But everyone tells me he's quite a good golfer now.'

'Golf!' Agnes managed to squeeze all her contempt into a single exclamation mark.

'And he's thirty-eight now.'

Lucy expected a comment on the difference in their ages, for she was ten years younger than Peach. But Percy had been an unexpected and total success with her mother when she had brought him here, so that, despite the golf, he could do no wrong in her eyes now. His cricket had helped, but so had a softer and more compassionate strain in Percy.

Lucy had not seen much of this side of her lover at work, where his hard-man image was so important to him and to others. He had hit Agnes Blake's wavelength immediately and instinctively, and Lucy's mother and the man she saw as a son-in-law had remained in perfect tune with each other ever since.

Agnes looked up now at the photograph of Percy, dapper

in his cricket whites, which she kept beside the older one of her husband on the mantelpiece. 'Time you were making an honest man of him, our Lucy. He won't let you down, you know, our Percy.'

Lucy felt an absurd shaft of jealousy at that 'our Percy', that reminder that her mother now saw him as one of the family. She regarded him as solely hers, wasn't sure that she wanted to share him, even with this loving mother who, she knew, was lonely for much of the time she was away. She said vaguely, 'There are complications, Mum.'

'Nothing you can't sort out, I'm sure. He loves you, does Percy. I can see that from the way he looks at you.'

Lucy was disturbed by the mention of the word love: you didn't talk about such things across the generations, not in Lancashire. The fact that Percy 'wouldn't let her down' was the code for that; there was no need to go breaking the old taboos. She said, 'I didn't mean complications in our relationship. I'm talking about things in the job. We wouldn't be allowed to work together, if we were married. We wouldn't even be working together now, if the powers that be realized we had a serious relationship going.'

'Relationship!' Agnes visited the word with almost the degree of contempt that she had given to golf. 'You should be thinking of getting married, our Lucy. Happen thinking of having bairns.'

Lucy smiled affectionately at the older woman. Emotion always brought out the Lancashire in her mother's talk, the accent and the expressions she had striven to subdue. She'd be talking of them 'living over t' brush' soon. What made it more difficult for her to argue was that there was a lot of truth in what the older woman said: Lucy felt her biological clock ticking steadily, saw her school contemporaries with growing broods, and was occasionally envious of them.

She said resolutely, 'I enjoy my job in CID, Mum. I'm told I'm quite good at it. I don't want to give it up. And I don't want to give up working with Percy. We work well together.'

'I'll bet you do. Well, I can see the problem, when you've worked hard to get the job you want and don't want to give it up.'

Daughters always see parents as old-fashioned, and there was a much greater age-gap between these two than was normal. But Agnes Blake was seen by her contemporaries in the village as dangerously progressive, with her views on women's rights. Agnes had seen too much potential wasted in her own generation not to be conscious of her daughter's hard-won position as Detective Sergeant in Brunton CID. She was very proud of her Lucy.

Agnes took a deep breath and plunged in boldly to the words she had thought about long and hard. 'But you can't have everything, Lucy Blake. You need to think of yourself at my age now, to consider where you want to be then. Do you want to be a lonely old woman with an impressive career behind you, or a woman with children and grandchildren to keep up your interest in the world?'

Lucy found herself wanting to get up and hug her mother. She didn't, of course. You didn't do that sort of thing in her family and they'd both have been embarrassed. So she said, 'I'd like to be a woman with a good career behind me and also be a mother and grandmother. Surely it shouldn't be impossible for a woman to have both those things?'

'Perhaps it shouldn't, but it might be. You'll have to work it out for yourself. You're the one who knows the situation.'

'All right, Mum. I'll think about it. I'm not quite as blinkered about the future as you may think.' She knew her mother wanted grandchildren more than anything. But you couldn't have kids just for that reason.

But long after she should have been asleep, she lay staring at the ceiling in the room where she had slept as a girl and wondered about these dilemmas which the modern career woman was supposed to shrug off so lightly.

Whilst Lucy Blake wrestled with her problems in the darkened room beneath the eaves of the cottage to which she had been brought as a baby, another man was wide awake, in an urban house.

He had not even thought about going to bed yet. He had not slept well, since Friday night. He found increasingly that he did not want to face that dimly lit, claustrophobic room up the stairs. He sat beneath a powerful light in a large, comfortable armchair, with a television set flickering its unwatched pictures in the corner of the room.

He was thinking about the same bleak stretch of ground, the same cold, dank shed and the same white, dead face which had stayed so obstinately in Lucy Blake's mind.

But not in the same way.

He'd been watching the news whenever he could since Friday night, but there'd been nothing for two days. Been a good idea, dumping her in that shed. He'd looked around the area before Friday, and thought that place might be useful. Some people would be surprised that he was capable of planning like that.

He couldn't understand why he did not feel more cheerful. Most murderers were caught within the first week: he was sure he'd heard that somewhere. Well, it was three days since this one, already, and the police hadn't even got started.

Well, perhaps he should say only just got started. There'd been the announcement he was waiting for on Radio Lancashire tonight, followed by a snippet on the local part of the television news at ten o'clock. Some kids had found a body in Brunton, they said. Police were treating it as a suspicious death. There was no more than that.

This must be his girl's body. He was almost relieved to hear it: he wasn't good at waiting, and he had become quite impatient when there was no news report over the weekend. It was quite exciting to have it out at last: he would be able to lie in bed tonight and think of all those expensive policemen baffled by one man. Him.

Because they were baffled. They hadn't mentioned anyone helping them with their enquiries. And they wouldn't, in the days to come. Or if they did, it certainly wouldn't be him. There'd be more details, as time crawled by. They hadn't even said how long they thought she'd been dead yet. He could tell them exactly when she'd died, right to the minute, if he chose. But he wouldn't, of course.

He couldn't see that the world wouldn't be any the worse for what he'd done. The streets were rid of another trollop. Another bitch who took money for it, from men who couldn't get it any other way. He repeated the phrases he had used on himself through every night since Friday.

There were a lot of them about, nowadays, flaunting their breasts and their legs and their crotches at men they could lead astray. Taking money for it. Hitching up their skirts and taking down their knickers to make money! You couldn't get more guilty than that, could you? Women like that deserved everything that came to them! The world was well rid of women like that.

He found he had got quite excited about it. Sexually excited; he had an erection, which he couldn't use. Well, not really use. He fell again to thinking about his last view of that white, dead face, so mobile during its last brief struggle for life, so still and cold in death as he had carried her into that shed. It seemed important to him that he should recall every fall of her hair, every detail of the unlined features.

Five

Joe Johnson looked like a criminal, to most people who came across him.

The police know that criminals come in all shapes and sizes, that the biggest villains often look the most innocent and straightforward people: that is part of their equipment. But the public have some fairly straightforward ideas about what they usually call a 'jailbird'. Such a man – female criminals are much less sharply etched in the public mind – usually has flat features, short, straight hair, minor scars about his visage, and narrow eyes.

Joe Johnson had all of these. He also had unusual irises in those eyes. They were grey, but the remarkable thing about them was that they seemed completely dead. Watchful, even sharply observant, but dead to all emotion. It was not just that they concealed his feelings; with a little practice, most people can do that, though the writers of fiction do not acknowledge it. It was rather that these eyes gave the impression that no emotions at all took place behind them. It was very unnerving to the people who received most attention from those grey eyes.

And on this Tuesday morning, several people found themselves under that intense scrutiny. When he was making a tour of his business interests, Johnson didn't spare his employees. They were left in no doubt of what he required.

Among other things, Joe Johnson was a successful pimp. Living off immoral earnings, the law called it, but the law was usually stumbling along well behind Joe Johnson. You needed witnesses to bring a court case. But the people who might have put Johnson behind bars were not willing to testify in court about the things he did. He had people who made sure of that. Fear was a powerful weapon, the best of all tools for men who made their money as Johnson did.

He was bigger than this now: he didn't need to go round collecting his money. Most of the time, he sent one of his minions out to do that. But he liked to keep himself in touch; hands-on management, they called it. Besides, he enjoyed frightening the women who worked for him.

There was quite a lot of money due to him after the weekend's activities. Sally Aspin had the notes ready for him. 'Ninety-four pounds,' she said, trying to keep the nervousness out of her voice.

'It's not enough.'

'It's right, Mr Johnson. It's half of what I took, honest it is.'

He looked at her steadily, letting the distaste creep slowly into the flat features. 'Then you're not taking enough, are you? Simple as that.'

She was thirty-eight, looking five years older in the morning light. She had the blonde hair and buxom figure that men usually found attractive. But she was running to seed a little now. Her heavy breasts were sagging somewhat, even in the best, expensive bra she kept for her work on the streets. He was surprised to see no dark at the roots of the hair; perhaps the flaxen shade was natural to her, after all. But the hair had lost the lustre it had shown in her heyday, and the conventionally pretty face was looking heavy-featured now, with the suspicion of a double chin, and deepening lines around the eyes and the mouth.

He would dispense with her soon. She was getting very near her sell-by date, this poor man's pin-up. In a year or so, perhaps, he would replace her with a younger model, and she would be banished from his patch. Meantime, there was a thousand or two more to be squeezed from her ageing body. He said, 'You'll have to work harder. Put your back into it. Use your assets.' He laughed harshly at his own joke.

Sally Aspin wasn't laughing. She'd made herself up carefully, knowing Johnson would be calling for his money this morning. Now she was willing herself not to cry, knowing the tears would ruin her eyeshadow, knowing from previous experience that Johnson saw tears only as a sign of weakness. She said, 'It's hard, coming into winter. They're not as randy as they are when the weather's warmer.'

'Or you're not as tasty as you once were. The other girls still bring in the money, Sal.'

She sought desperately for words which would convince him. It had been easier with her first pimp. He'd been small-time, less relentless. He'd knocked her about a bit, from time to time, but at least he'd been open to argument if she'd had a bad week. And he'd been willing to take payment in kind, had Steve. He'd have a roll in bed with her, knead her ample curves, and go away happy. She wouldn't try paying that way with Johnson: not ever again.

Sally had never found out what had happened to Steve. He'd disappeared. This hard, brutal man had thrust his way into her house and told her that he'd bought out Steve's patch, that she wouldn't be seeing Steve any more and would be paying her dues to him in future. Steve, even with the odd back-hander across her belly or her face, seemed now to represent a lost Eden, when the money had come easy, the streets where she plied her trade had been protected, and they'd even had a few laughs.

Sally Aspin thrust out her pelvis and said with a foolhardy hint at jauntiness, 'They haven't the same money, most of them, not coming up to Christmas. But what they have, Sally will have out of them!'

'Will she indeed?' He smiled a mirthless smile and took her chin into his hand before she could shrink away from him, holding her face up towards the light. 'You'll need to convince me of that, you know. The wear and tear's getting to you, girl! The wrinkles are beginning to show. The punters don't like old meat. And there's plenty of kids queuing up to put young meat on the counter for them.'

He was hurting her. She tried to pull her chin away from him, but he sank his thumb and his fingers harder into her cheeks as she tried to withdraw. The pressure distorted her words as she said, 'There's plenty of them want a – a more mature woman. They have more confidence with a woman who knows what's what, some of them.'

It was true enough: some of the shy ones were happier with someone who showed them the ropes, led them on a little. Why then could she not make the argument more convincing, why did she quail before Joe Johnson's harsh, pitiless grey eyes?

He gripped her face harder, digging his nails into the flesh where her chin met her neck for a last, sadistic second before he let her go. 'Is that so? No accounting for tastes, is there? Must be perverts, to take someone like you, given the choice. You'd better get out there and find more of these perverts, then, hadn't you? Up your takings for your Uncle Joe.' He laughed at that thought, stringing his mirth out as he caught her shuddering despite herself.

Then he pocketed his money and went out to his Jaguar. He'd give the poor cow four more months. Perhaps five, if she was lucky. Take her through to the lighter nights, when there were more punters about and the work became easier, and then drop her for some kid. It would give him plenty of time to recruit a replacement.

Best part of the job, that was, recruiting.

The Scenes of Crime team discovered a few things during their detailed examination of the bleak site where the body had been found. The most important one was that the girl had not been killed there.

There were footprints around the puddles, in the damp cindery waste where a mill had once stood. Too many footprints. Children played in the area, as Tommy Caton and Jamie Betts had done. More importantly, adults used it as a short cut, on their way to work or home from the pub. There was a multitude of footprints available, once you studied the ground closely. Some of them probably belonged to a murderer, but which ones?

It seemed likely that the girl had been dumped in the shed immediately after she had been killed, for the evidence of hypostasis suggested that she had not lain anywhere else but the shed. That meant that the footsteps which interested them were not going to be the most recent ones, but imprints which had been made at least two days and possibly longer ago than that. And it had rained over the weekend: not the torrential downpours which would eliminate all traces of where people had trodden, but three periods of steady, obfuscating drizzle.

Jack Chadwick, the SOC officer, brought in the forensic boys to take careful moulds of several shoe and Wellington boot prints from near the entrance to the rotting shed. The murderer's might well be among them, but Chadwick had as yet no idea which ones they were.

The women Joe Johnson was visiting were very different in appearance, and came from very different backgrounds. The one thing they had in common was that they were alone in an uncaring, even hostile world. Joe preferred it like that. It made things much simpler, when people were alone.

Katie Clegg was twenty-seven. She had two children, plus an ex-husband who wasn't keen on paying maintenance and wasn't easy to track down. She was a willowy brunette, pretty enough to attract serious male attention. But most of the men veered away when they found she had two children in tow. And Katie was cautious about any lasting attachment: once bitten, twice shy, her friends said, and she was forced to agree with them.

She lived in a small nineteen thirties semi-detached house, pebble-dashed and drab, reaching the age when it needed a lot of maintenance. She was watching at the cheap wooden bay window for Johnson's arrival, anxious to give him his money and have him gone. She didn't want to be linked with a man like that by the ageing eyes which peered out from behind the curtains around her. She was the subject of quite enough local gossip already.

Joe Johnson would not have registered as an intelligent man in any standard test. But he had that instinctive shrewdness in assessing situations which many successful criminals possess. He sensed the nervousness in Katie Clegg immediately and knew that she wanted to be rid of him. So he sat down uninvited in an armchair and determined to stay for a while.

'Thought we should review your activities, young Katie,'

he said unpleasantly. 'Assess your progress and set ourselves future targets.'

He had thought to bewilder her, but Katie Clegg was not unfamiliar with business gobbledegook. She had been a personal assistant to a sales director before her life went wrong. She said without looking at the man in her chair, 'I have done everything you asked of me.'

'So you have, Katie, so you have. So far. And I've done everything to protect you. The law's been kept off your back. No one has interfered with your patch. No other employer has threatened to take over your services.'

He had hesitated fractionally over the word 'employer'; Katie gave an involuntary, bitter smile. 'And you've had no reason to complain about your takings from me.'

Johnson grinned back at her. He liked a feisty woman. It made a change from the defeated demeanour of most of the women he used: like flattened grass, they were. A bit of spirit was all right in a woman. Especially when you held all the trump cards in your hand. He nodded at her. 'You're doing all right, Cleggy.' He lifted the hundred and fifty pounds she had just given him upon the palm of his hand and nodded his satisfaction. 'Might be time to think of a little expansion.'

Kate's face clouded. This was why she feared this man's visits more than anything in her life; more even than police exposure and disgrace; far more than the men to whom she sold herself, who were mostly pathetic creatures. She said dully, 'I'm doing all I want to do. All I can do. Four nights is enough and more than enough. I've two children to look after.'

He smiled up at her, taking his time, taking care to drop his threat so that it would make maximum impact. 'Two children who might end up in care if anyone chose to give the authorities the details of how you support them, Katie. Let's not forget that.'

She found herself holding on to the back of an upright chair for support as her head swam. Someone should kill this man: he was vermin. But no one would. Life didn't work like that. She wanted to pick up a knife from the kitchen and fly at him, but she knew she could not do that. Those round-faced, innocent children in the new school uniforms she had bought for them would be lost without her to look out for them. 'I'm only doing this as long as I have to, you know that.'

He allowed himself a broad smile this time, looking up into the white, oval face, mocking her naivety. 'You might have to do it a bit longer than you think, Kate. It might not be you who makes the decision about hanging up your knickers and suspenders.'

'I'll go whenever I can. I don't intend living like this for a second longer than I have to!' She spoke the words slowly and through clenched teeth, looking not at Johnson but through the window at the dank and dripping garden.

He waited until she glanced down at him, as he knew that she eventually must. 'All I'm saying is that you could earn yourself a little more, Katie Clegg. Maybe even keep the extra completely for yourself, as a generous bonus from a grateful employer. I might be prepared to take my extra commission in bed, from a looker like you.'

She clenched the back of the chair with both hands, feeling sick as the full implications of his words sunk in. She said as carefully as she could, 'I'm not available, Mr Johnson.'

He laughed, then stood up unhurriedly. 'Funny attitude for a tom to take, that. Just trying to put a little more cash in your pocket, young Katie. I'm sure you could use it.'

'I can manage. Maybe I'll get some maintenance, next month.'

'And maybe you'll see a herd of flying pigs. But I wouldn't rely on it.'

He took his leave of her on that. Little pep talk would keep her up to scratch. And he wasn't joking: he wouldn't mind an hour or two in the sack with the delectable and feisty Katie Clegg.

It was the uniformed police, pursuing the dull but necessary routine of house-to-house enquiries, who came up with a possible identification for the dead girl.

The information shot quickly up to the top-storey office of Chief Superintendent Tucker and straight down again to the desk of DCI Peach. The information was dodgy, and it would need an identification of the body to confirm it, but the age and the initial description of the girl who had gone missing were right.

She was from Lancashire, but not from Brunton. She came from a village on the other side of Bolton: about twenty miles away. The next of kin seemed to be the parents. There had been no report of a missing person from them. If this was their daughter, someone would have to break the news to them that she was dead.

Joe Johnson's third call was on a nineteen-year-old.

Toyah Burgess was more nervous than either of the others. Or perhaps, having seen so much less of life, she was merely less skilled in concealing her feelings. She was only nineteen, but already an experienced prostitute.

She had the money ready in an envelope on the window sill by the door for him. A hundred and fifty pounds. It was a lot for what he offered her. But she was in no position to resist; it had taken a couple of sharp warnings from Johnson's heavies to make that situation clear to her.

The glint of a knife blade near her face beneath the street light; a huge fist raised for a moment above her small head with its golden hair. No blow struck: they were under strict instructions not to damage the goods which were on sale. And once they started, they didn't always know where to stop, these men: they were not employed for their restraint.

Joe Johnson counted the money slowly. He knew it would be right; these women had more sense than to try to cheat him. But he enjoyed watching the tension build in the young face beside him. She hadn't invited him into her living room, so he looked round the hall. 'Nice carpet. New, isn't it? I must be paying you too much!' He laughed at his witticism.

He didn't pay her at all, she thought. He took money from her: took much more than his due of what she earned by lying on her back for men. And lying in other positions and doing other things too. He didn't know the half of it, this man, with his smooth suits and his scars and his blank, frightening eyes. She said, 'The carpet didn't cost much in the sale. And we shared the cost.'

'Very nice, that, being able to share. Nicer still, if you could up your takings a little. As I'm sure you could, an attractive young beauty like you!' He smiled into the wide, frightened blue eyes, ran his gaze approvingly over the bleached blonde hair, dropping his scrutiny first to her breasts and then to the triangle where her legs met her stomach beneath the cheap cotton dress.

'I'm taking all I can, Mr Johnson. I can't charge them any more.'

'You could get more customers, though, with a little effort. Make a killing while you can, girl, is my advice. Looks don't last for ever. Been talking to one old slag this morning that I'll have to put out to grass before long. So don't you keep sitting on a fortune – get it out and use it, I say!' He laughed out loud at the coarseness of the thought, keeping his eyes still on the triangle of her assets.

Toyah Burgess was young, despite her experience on the game. She was still green enough to think she could ask for concessions from Joe Johnson. She took a deep breath and embarked on the words she had planned before he came. 'As a matter of fact, I was going to ask you if you would consider cutting the rate I have to pay you, Mr Johnson. The percentage of what I take seems an awful lot to pay, for what I get out of it.'

Johnson's smile died very slowly, as if he could scarcely believe what he was hearing. It was replaced by something very different; when Toyah recalled his face in the small hours of the night, as she did several times in the days which followed this meeting, it seemed to have the terrifying savagery of an ogre.

He transferred his eyes back up to the young, fearful, heart-shaped face. 'Think you're not getting value for money, do you, my dear? Pity, that. I keep the competition away from your patch, young Toyah. Even a youngster like you would have to work a lot harder for her money if there were other tarts flashing their fannies around the street! You'd soon find your dainty little quim wasn't in such demand if you had to put it on the counter and let the punters choose, I can tell you!'

He was getting really annoyed now, his voice surging upwards on the rising tide of his anger. Toyah thought he was going to hit her unless she could do something to stem that tide. She said despairingly, 'All right, all right! I was only asking if you could see your way to a little reduction. If you can't do that, we'll go on as we are! Sorry I asked, honestly I am!'

He stilled his breathing, controlled the excitement which had risen in him with her distress. Then he growled at her, 'I hope you do, Toyah Burgess. Because I'd hate anything to happen to you!'

'Happen to me?' She echoed his words stupidly, her fear making her speak when she should have been meekly silent. She knew a lot about men and their sexual demands now, but still very little about the rest of life.

'Yes, dear, happen to you, that's what I said.' He reached out, following her as she flinched away, and took her small chin into the iron grip he had fastened upon the fleshier jowls of Sally Aspin an hour earlier. 'Because it's me who provides you with protection, you know. Protection against the people who prey on people like you. Peddling your pussy might be an easy way of making money, but it can be a dangerous one. Not everyone in the game is as kind and considerate as Joe Johnson, you see. Look what happened to that girl the other night. The one who was dumped in that shed on Dover Street. That Sarah Dunne. I'd hate anything like that to happen to you, Toyah Burgess.'

Toyah wondered how Joe Johnson knew the name of the dead girl.

He held her chin for a moment longer, her pain increasing as his grasp tightened still more. Then he released her, studied the marks his hand had left on her flesh for a moment, nodded twice at her to emphasize his message, picked up the envelope with his cash, and was gone without a further word.

Six

The girl was very nervous. She looked up and down the street before hustling them quickly inside the Victorian house.

They had been fine residences, when they were built, this row, high and proud against the meaner brick of the terraces built behind them for the mill workers. They had retained a gradually eroding grandeur until after Hitler's war, when they had been divided into flats and gone rapidly downhill. In the nineteen eighties and nineties, as they moved past their century of life, the flats had been subdivided again, until most of them were little more than bed-sits. The standard of tenant had declined correspondingly, until the inhabitants were a heterogeneous collection of people, their only common feature being that they did not stay here for very long.

This old-young girl had dark, straight hair and eyes which seemed to have seen much more than the smooth face around them. She took them into a high room, where the ceiling was scarcely visible above a light fitting which hung a good five feet below it. The wallpaper was probably over thirty years old, its fading seventies colours dating from the time when a larger, more gracious room had been divided. The joins where the sheets of thick wallpaper met had been picked apart, low down above the deep skirting board, by some long-departed infant hand.

Lucy Blake took in the crack in the pane of the sash window, the cobwebs building in its upper corners, and tried not to contrast this room with the neat order of her own bright modern flat. She smiled encouragement into the anxious young face and said, 'I'm Detective Sergeant Blake and this is Detective Constable Pickering. And you're Karen Jones.'

The girl scarcely acknowledged her words. 'There was no need for you to come here. I said everything I had to say to that lad in uniform. Get me into trouble, you will.'

'Trouble with whom, Karen?'

The girl shook her head. She was not out of her teens yet, possibly even younger than she looked. 'People like me can't afford to be seen talking to the police. I don't want to go the same way as Sarah.'

'And why should you do that, Karen?'

A shake of the head, agitating the dark, straight hair. It was a refusal to co-operate, not a denial of knowledge. 'You shouldn't have come. You're wasting your time and mine.'

Lucy wondered how she could get this brittle girl to relax. She sat down on the battered sofa, felt Pickering follow her lead, held her peace until Karen Jones reluctantly sat down on an upright chair. Then she said, 'No one will know that you have helped us. The uniformed officers called at every residence in this street. We get together a big team and they ask questions of everyone in the area. It's routine procedure, after a murder.'

The girl started at the introduction of the word, in the way people once reacted to the mention of cancer. She considered Blake's argument, then nodded very sharply, two or three times. 'That's all right, then. But that doesn't apply to you, does it? You're not calling at every house in the street.'

'No. It's our job to follow up anything which might be of interest. We study what the uniformed officers doing the house-to-house enquiries bring in. You were able to tell us who the dead girl was. We're grateful for that.'

'I didn't say I was sure it was her. I just said I thought it might be.'

Lucy went on as smoothly as if the girl had never spoken. 'And naturally we want every scrap of information you can give us. Sarah isn't here to help us herself, is she?'

'No. She's gone. So I can't help her any more, can I?'

Gordon Pickering said gently, 'But I think you might want to help us catch whoever killed her like that, once you think about it.'

He was a gangling, fresh-faced young man, not very much

44

older than Karen Jones, and she appeared to give some thought to these first words from him. She said grudgingly, 'I'd like to see that bastard put away, yes.' Then, immediately defensive, 'But I don't know who did it, so I can't help, can I?' The Welshness she had striven to put behind her when she left the valleys came out suddenly and strongly in the inflection of the last phrase.

Gordon Pickering was persistent as well as surprisingly perceptive: they were among the qualities which had secured him an early transfer from uniform to CID. He smiled into the anxious features and said, 'Sometimes people can help us more than they realize, once we put together what they tell us with what comes in from other sources. And you really won't be putting yourself in any danger by talking to us, Karen.'

Lucy saw the girl responding to his youth and sincerity. It made her feel forty-eight instead of twenty-eight as Karen Jones's face lightened and she said, 'I hardly knew her, really. What is it you wanted to know?'

'Anything you can tell us. We don't even know for certain that Sarah is the dead girl yet.'

Karen's face was suddenly full of a childish terror. 'You don't want me to identify her? I don't want to do that. I've never had to look at a dead body, see, and I don't want to start with this one. Is she badly—'

'We won't be asking you for an identification, Karen,' Lucy Blake intervened firmly. 'We'll need the next of kin to do that: probably one of the parents, when we find them. But you'll understand that we don't want to put any parents through that ordeal unless we've good reason to think this is their daughter.'

Relief flooded into the girl's face and she became a woman again. She gave them a surprisingly precise description of the girl she had known as Sarah Dunne, answering DC Pickering's questions quietly and watching him make a note of her answers. It made them increasingly certain that she was describing the woman whose remains had been dumped on the building site. She concluded with, 'I told the uniformed constable, she came from somewhere over the other side of

Bolton, I think, but I haven't got any address. She never told me that.'

Pickering closed his notebook and looked into the earnest young face. 'And what was your connection with Sarah Dunne, Karen?'

The face which had opened up during her description of the dead girl now shut as suddenly as a book. Karen Jones looked past Pickering instead of at him as she said, 'We was just friends, wasn't we? I told the constable earlier, I didn't know her all that well.'

'But you knew her well enough to give us a very good description. Even to remember some of the clothes she wore. That's very helpful to us, Karen.'

The girl didn't respond. Her face set sullenly as she said, 'That's good then, isn't it? But there's nothing more I can tell you.'

Lucy Blake said, 'Oh, I think there is, Karen. Not much more, perhaps, but that little might be important. You say Sarah was your friend. So I'm sure you'd want us to find out who killed your friend and put him away for a long time.'

They could see the struggle going on behind the old-young, too-revealing features. But her face set into a frown as she said, 'I'd like you to get whoever killed her, yes. But I can't help you. You've had everything I know.'

'Not quite, Karen. Perhaps I should tell you that we know how your earn your living. How you pay the rent for this place.' Lucy Blake looked round the room, with its tiny kitchen beyond a small arch, its door to the cramped bathroom built in hastily a decade ago, its high, grubby walls and dusty curtains. She let her gaze come to rest on the new wide-screen television and hi-fi stack, which gleamed incongruously in their shabby setting.

Panic flashed across the smooth face of Karen Jones as she saw a detective sergeant looking at these things. 'I save up my money. I do a few hours in the Red Lion at lunch times.'

'And in the evenings, you're a hooker. Bringing men back here. Earning enough to pay the rent and buy a few luxuries.'

'You can't prove that.'

Lucy sighed. 'We could, if we wanted to, Karen. But we're not here to harass you. We're here to find out all we can about a dead girl you knew. A girl very much like you. A girl who was murdered.'

'I told her to be careful.' The words were out before she could check them.

'I'm sure you did, Karen. But she wasn't very experienced, was she? You were giving her a few of the tips of the trade, weren't you?'

Karen Jones nodded, her eyes now on a worn patch in the fading Persian carpet, which had graced a grander room than this in its heyday. 'There are places you can't go in this town. Not to work, I mean. Not to pick up men.'

'And why is that, Karen?'

'There are people who control the trade, aren't there? People who keep the best areas for their own tarts. They cut up your face, if you don't keep off. You can't work, without your face being right.'

'And they might even kill a young girl, if they thought they could get away with it. To encourage the rest of you to stay in line.'

She nodded dumbly. Perhaps she felt that if she didn't put that idea into words, if she let the phrases come from the police, she wasn't grassing on the men she feared. The man she feared, to be accurate.

'So you think one of the pimps who control prostitution around here might have had your friend killed?'

Again she nodded rather than put it into words. All she actually said was, 'I can't think who else would have wanted to kill Sarah. She was a good kid.'

It was a belated assertion of her own seniority, a pathetic reminder that this young, vulnerable creature had been a mentor to someone even younger, even more defenceless against the dark forces of this strange half-world she inhabited.

Karen Jones looked fearfully up and down the street as her visitors departed, but was relieved to see no one in sight, as a wan sun lit up the faded dignity of the Victorian facades. Then she went and made herself a cup of coffee and sat down to an anxious review of what she had said to them.

It didn't seem too bad. She hadn't even mentioned Joe Johnson's name.

'We don't even know how long she's been dead yet.' Percy Peach was professionally lugubrious with his chief.

'This is ridiculous, you know. Things moved much faster than this when you were away!' said Chief Superintendent Tucker peevishly.

Peach allowed his black eyebrows to rise expressively beneath the bald pate. 'I see, sir. Bodies were presumably discovered more quickly in the last year, then.'

Tucker stared at him suspiciously. Irony was not his strong point. That left him at a severe disadvantage with DCI Peach. 'I expect they were, yes. Things were generally much tighter when you were away.'

This was manifestly untrue. Peach had skimmed the crime figures quickly and then studied the clear-up rates very closely. Even his experienced eye had been shocked by them: he was holding his own private sessions in the CID section to amend matters; some Inspectorial fur had been considerably ruffled two storeys beneath Tucker's penthouse office. He looked hard at Tucker and said, 'Really, sir. Well, I expect Traffic would still have me back if you think I am a drag on the progress of your section.'

'No, no, Peach, I'm not suggesting that.' Tucker forced the kind of smile we don for the dentist and said, 'Goodness me, you didn't use to be so touchy in the old days. Do come and sit down, Percy.'

Peach sat down with extreme care in the armchair indicated by Tucker's expansive gesture. His first name had been forced through the closed teeth of the Head of CID's wide, artificial smile. Well, Percy didn't want to hear it any more than Tommy Bloody Tucker wanted to say it. He said, 'The girl's been dead two or three days at least. We may get a more accurate time of death from the PM report.'

'Do we have an identification?'

'Probably, sir. One of our young ladies of the night thinks she was called Sarah Dunne.'

'A prostitute?' Tucker's face dropped at the thought.

Low-life murders were always the most difficult to solve. And the least worthwhile: Tucker was firmly of the view that people who dabbled in crime deserved whatever they got. Sometimes it seemed to him a pity that he had to give his full resources to chasing up crimes like this, but he supposed that the law had to be upheld.

'An apprentice prostitute, you might say, sir. None of the female officers who interview the toms when we bring them in has even heard of Sarah Dunne.'

'Once we have an identification, the house-to-house should help us with the time of death. We should be able to establish when she was last seen.'

Peach noted that a year without him hadn't diminished Tucker's talent for the blindin' bleedin' obvious. 'Yes, sir. We've located the people we think are the girl's parents. DC Murphy has gone over to Bolton to break the news and bring someone back for an identification.'

'Good man, Brendan Murphy.' Tucker nodded his approval.

Peach lifted those black eyebrows again, this time in genuine surprise. Tucker was so vague that he rarely knew the names of his staff, and even more rarely the name of someone as humble as a DC. 'I agree, sir. I'm trying to persuade him to withdraw his request for a transfer.'

'He's requested a transfer? Well, talk him out of it, Peach. We need men of his quality. I expect you've been on his back too much. Can't get away with that, you know, in the modern police service.'

Peach refrained from pointing out that he hadn't been around during the last year to be on anyone's back. He had already had a long chat with Brendan Murphy about his transfer request. This had revealed that the man was frustrated by Tucker's bumbling inefficiency and the resultant decline in the morale of the Brunton CID unit over the last twelve months. As an ambitious young DC, he did not want to be working in an indifferent section; he had readily withdrawn his transfer request when he found that Peach was back with the unit. Percy said, 'I expect he'll stay, sir, now that he knows he has your approval.'

Tucker looked hard at the inscrutable round face on the

other side of his desk. 'Well, I shan't delay you any longer, Peach. Get on with it, please. Try to get back to your old standards of briskness and efficiency. The world doesn't stand still, you know.'

'I see, sir. Well, it's good to have your overview of the case. It's been just as useful as it always was. Some things at least don't change.'

Tucker regarded him uneasily. But Peach's eyes were trained on the wall just above his head and his features fixed in a rigid mask. Suddenly it seemed to Tucker much less than a year since he had had a conversation like this. He tried to sound confident, even patronizing, as he said, 'Well. It's one of the reasons they promoted me, I suppose. Some of us have the capacity to see the wider picture, to fit the scene in our own small patch into the wider panorama of crime outside.'

Peach stood up and nodded his agreement. 'And some of us are condemned to work for ever at the crime face, providing the statistics which will fit agreeably into that wider picture. All is for the best in the best of all possible worlds, sir.'

It was always good to leave the old wanker on a quotation: that guaranteed his puzzlement. But Percy Peach was not as unaware of the wider world of crime beyond Brunton as Tucker thought he was. As he went back down the stairs to the real world, he was troubled by the idea which had beset him before he climbed the beanstalk to the land of the evil giant.

Was it possible that this killing was not an isolated crime, but one of a series in a larger pattern? That would mean that the murderer of Sarah Dunne would kill again, if they did not find him.

Seven

It was a bright modern house with lots of windows over-looking neat gardens. Some might have called it dull and box-like, but it was the kind of dwelling for which many people save hard for most of their working lives. It was also an incongruous setting for the news they had to break.

It was quickly apparent that the Dunnes had no inkling of what had happened to their daughter. Brendan Murphy took the initiative: it was the first death the young female constable in uniform beside him had had to break and she was plainly ill at ease.

Mrs Dunne, still unsuspecting, still anxious to break the conversational ice, said, 'That's a real Irish name, isn't it, Murphy? Perhaps you're a Catholic, like ourselves.'

'I am indeed, though I've lived all my life in Lancashire. Mrs Dunne, I'm afraid I may have bad news for you.'

Dismay clouded the bright, open countenance beneath the neat brown hair. 'It's Sarah, isn't it? Has she had some sort of accident?'

'It's worse than that, Mrs Dunne. We're not absolutely certain it's Sarah yet, but the girl we're talking about is dead.' Be as gentle as you can, but don't wrap it up. Don't make it out to be less of a tragedy than it is; there's no way round it. Percy Peach had told him that, and Brendan Murphy listened to Peach as to no one else.

He had got them sitting down before the news, but now Frank Dunne stood up and walked across to sit beside his wife, moving like a man waist-high in water. He was older than his wife, a grey-haired teacher in a Bolton school, a quiet, efficient man with great natural dignity. A man to whom this sort of thing should never happen. But what man anywhere could deserve this?

51

Dunne put his arm round his wife's shoulders, drew her unresisting body against his without looking at her, and said, 'You'd better give us some more details, please, DC Murphy.'

Brendan said, 'There isn't much we can tell you as yet. A body was found in a workmen's hut on a derelict site. A female who answers to your daughter's description. I'm very sorry.'

'A body? On a derelict site?' Rosemary Dunne repeated the words woodenly, as if that might enable her to take in their meaning.

'We're certain now that this girl was murdered.'

Frank Dunne pulled his wife a little more tightly against his side with his right hand. 'Murdered? How was she killed?'

'She was strangled. Apparently with her own scarf.'

Rosemary Dunne's hand flew to her mouth. She gnawed at the knuckle of her index finger, unable to produce words. It was her husband who said, 'And have you got the man who did this?'

'Not yet. But we will do. We'll be asking you to give us whatever help you can with the investigation.'

Rosemary Dunne said, 'But how can we help? We don't even know any of her friends at the college.'

'Your daughter was at college?'

Frank Dunne said with a hint of irritation, 'I should have thought you'd have already known that. She was on a hairdressing and beautician's course at the Brunton College of Technology. She wasn't very academic, our Sarah. And she could have got a similar course in Bolton or Manchester and travelled from home, but she said she preferred the course in Brunton.' He glanced for the first time at his wife. 'I – I think she wanted to get away from home. Establish her independence, show her parents that she'd finished with school and was becoming an adult. It's understandable, I suppose. That's what I told Rosemary when she was worried about Sarah leaving here.'

He was already taking on the burden of guilt for letting her move out into the dangerous world which had killed her, beginning to ask himself the questions which would gnaw at him for the rest of his life.

Rosemary Dunne's eyes were wide and glassy, but she spoke like one in a dream, fumbling for the words she did not want to voice. 'Had she been . . . ? I mean to say, was she . . . ?'

'It seems that she hadn't been raped, as far as we can determine at present.' Brendan Murphy chose his words carefully, anxious to spare them this at least. 'We shall perhaps have more details after the full post-mortem.'

Mrs Dunne nodded several times, as if she might enter the knowledge into her reeling brain by this physical movement. Then she said, with a tiny vestige of hope, 'But you said you weren't certain yet that this girl was our Sarah.'

'I did indeed. But I don't think you should raise your hopes too high, Mrs Dunne.' He wondered how he could give the mother a dampening phrase of realism. Then he decided that it was safest to be straightforward. 'I'm afraid the law requires that one of you should identify the corpse.'

'I'll do it.' Frank Dunne volunteered almost before Murphy had framed the words. 'I'll just get my coat and then I'll drive over behind you.'

'I'm coming with you,' said his wife determinedly. 'I'm not being left at home to go mad with worry.'

Her husband looked at her for a moment, trying to deal with this picture. Then he said, 'All right. We'll go together.'

Murphy said, 'There's no need for you to drive. We'll take you over in the back of our car.'

Frank Dunne argued a little, then accepted the offer. No one wanted to voice the thought that he might be too distressed to drive home after the identification.

Father John Devoy was a Catholic priest who was well respected by his flock, even in these days of religious doubt. He was always welcome in the primary school behind his high stone church, and even after all the crippling revelations about paedophilia among the celibate clergy, the parents were happy to see him laughing with their children.

As he moved about his duties in this largest Catholic parish in one of the most Catholic towns in England, Father Devoy gave no sign of the inner turmoil which rent his soul.

He was forty-three now, old enough to have seen most of the joys and the tragedies of life, but young enough to bustle about his duties with an energy which spread a little of its force among those with whom he worked. Those of his flock who knew him well called him Father John: Devoy was easy enough to say, but it had a faintly Gallic ring, which made it suspect to these sturdy northern folk.

He had been in Brunton for a few years now, after serving his time as a curate in less busy and challenging places. He was cheerful in times of celebration, gravely sympathetic in the face of death, unwanted pregnancies, drugs and the other tragedies which beset his flock. Everyone thought that in due course he would become the Canon in charge of St Matthew's.

The only person who was certain that he wouldn't was Father Devoy himself. People put this down to a natural modesty, a Christian humility which they would have expected of Father John. Only John Devoy himself knew of the splinter of evil which was piercing his soul.

Late on this Tuesday afternoon, Father Devoy took the holy oils and the blessed sacrament into the small, overheated terraced house where a man lay dying of cancer. He heard a last confession in the man's erratic croak of a voice, placed the wafer of the Eucharist on the dry tongue as the man took his final communion. Then he anointed him with the holy oils, touching his lips and eyes and ears, reciting the ritual words of the Last Sacrament over the man who lay with closed eyes on the bed beneath him.

Extreme Unction: the last and most solemn of the Roman Catholic Sacraments. The final solace of the dying. Sometimes Father John, whispering the soothing words over the still form which seemed already unconscious, would have been glad to have this final releasing balm administered to himself.

The woman who was so soon to be a widow was resigned to the death. She was fifty-one, a year younger than her man, full of an energy which was carrying her through the final stages of this mortal sickness up the stairs. She handed the priest a cup of tea and said, 'The doctor came this morning. He's upped the dose of morphine. He says it won't be long now.'

Father Devoy sipped the tea he did not want: you were offered it at every house where you called in Lancashire. He tried to avoid the clichés he had heard too often, but sometimes what people expected to hear was the best therapy. 'He's at peace now, Mrs Fogarty.'

She was called Debbie, but he could not bring himself to use the name, which seemed too young and frivolous for the situation. 'He seems very serene. Ready to meet his maker in Heaven.' It was easier when they had a serene faith in the afterlife. Too many of his parishioners now were troubled and uncertain about what awaited them. Father John couldn't tell them that he shared many of their uncertainties, that in his darkest hours he hoped above all that there was no Hell.

'Did you hear his confession, Father?'

'I did, Mrs Fogarty. A few little things that I'm not sure the Good Lord would see as even venial sins. There was nothing big that he's been concealing from you for years, Debbie.' He smiled at her. He'd managed the name at last, probably when it was most needed. Everyone knew that you couldn't divulge the sins that a man had revealed in the secrecy of his Confession, but you were surely allowed this kindly negative. Spouses liked to be reassured that there were no dark and tremendous secrets that had been concealed from all until the hour of death.

Father Devoy went back into the November world outside, carrying his own dark and tremendous secret locked in his heart.

Frank and Rosemary Dunne held each other's hands tightly in the back of the police Rover as it drove into the small car park behind the mortuary, preparing themselves for a very different death from the one being handled with quiet dignity by Mrs Fogarty.

Brendan Murphy took them slowly through what must happen, as much to allow them a moment to compose themselves in this alien place as to explain the forms one of them must sign if this was indeed their daughter.

Frank Dunne said decisively, 'I'll do this. You stay here.' His wife looked for a moment as if she would argue. Then she sat down again, and remained silently with her hand in the young policewoman's, scarcely older than the daughter she had lost, as the attendant led her husband away through the double doors.

He had already slid out the drawer in the steel cabinet of death to allow him to extract the relevant corpse and move it into the room they used for identifications. At least this way the corpse gained a little individuality, instead of being one of many immersed in the anonymity of death. Now he asked the older man at his side if he was ready, received a nod of assent, and drew back the sheet cautiously from the young head.

They had sewn up the skull skilfully after the cuts of the post-mortem; with the hair combed forward over the white brow, the necessary indignities visited upon the head of the corpse were not very visible. He was careful to keep the sheet tight under the chin. There was no need for a stricken father to see the black marks of strangulation around the throat, let alone the huge incision from the chest to the pubis of the slender body to allow the removal of the vital organs for investigation by the pathologist.

He heard the sharp snatching of breath from the man beside him, watched him nodding vigorously, unable to trust himself with words. Then he drew the sheet swiftly back over the head as Brendan Murphy led the father away.

Frank Dunne signed the certificate of identification with a hand he had to force into the formation of the familiar letters. He stood still until his wife, face wet with tears, came to clutch his arm. Then they went out again to the police car and began the worst week of their lives.

Father Devoy found Tuesday nights the worst of all.

There were no confessions to hear in the booths of the high, gloomy Victorian church, built as a proud statement of freedom in the decades following the Catholic Emancipation

Acts of 1851. It was the junior night at the youth club, and he had stopped going there since the revelations about paedophilia among Catholic priests had set tongues wagging in the early years of the new century.

That was ironic. He had never been tempted by children of either sex. And he told himself that he was better than those priests who committed adultery, destroying families and bringing contumely upon the Church.

There were other people before him who had ventured out among the women of the night. There was Gladstone, for one: a man who had commanded a great following in Brunton in those far-off days. But Gladstone had been taking soup to the prostitutes, bringing them home and offering them spiritual comfort. The Lord Jesus Christ above, who saw everything in pitiless detail, would know that John Devoy wasn't offering either of those.

He was gratifying his own beastly instincts, those thrusting sexual urges he had promised to abandon when he became a priest.

But within his despair and self-loathing, a small voice put another argument. Were they really as helpless as they had been in Gladstone's day, these women who offered their bodies for hire upon the street? They didn't have to do it: there was a welfare state now, which would not let them starve, even the worst of them. They were putting temptation in people's way. Oh, he knew he was weak, was much worse than weak, but these women were contributing to his sins, to the sins which pierced the side of his Lord as surely as the Roman soldier's lance when he was upon the Cross.

They were irretrievable, these women, these creatures of the night. They deserved to suffer, even to die, if they persisted in the ways of Satan. It was even good that someone made that happen: it might prevent other weak women from following the same evil path.

Somewhere in the maelstrom of the priest's whirling emotions, the word Charity belatedly presented itself. With a capital letter: the greatest of the Christian virtues. He stood up unsteadily and walked over to the heavy oak-framed mirror on the wall of his room. The face he saw there was trembling so much that it took a few seconds for it to become clear. It was a grey face, with wild blue eyes set deep within it: it did not seem to belong to the man who ministered so ably to his flock during the day.

Sometimes John Devoy thought he was going mad.

Eight

The post-mortem report was on Peach's desk by nine o'clock on Wednesday morning, not much more than thirty-six hours after the body of Sarah Dunne had been discovered.

When it was put together with the results of the house-to-house enquiries which were being collated on the police computers, they were able to make a surprisingly accurate assessment of the time of death. The body found in the shed on Monday evening had been dead for at least two and a half days and not more than four. The stomach contents revealed a meal of fish and chips consumed some three to five hours before death: the fish was cooked in batter, which indicated that the food had almost certainly been purchased in a local fish and chip shop.

The latest sighting of Sarah Dunne so far established was at four thirty on that Friday evening, when she had purchased milk and bread at a small shop near to her rented accommodation. However, a girl answering her description was remembered by the proprietor of the Jolly Fryer fish and chip shop. This girl had bought fish and chips over the counter at around six o'clock on Friday evening.

Putting this together with the evidence of the stomach contents, it looked as if Sarah Dunne had died between nine and eleven on the evening of Friday, the fourteenth of November. But whom had she been with during the evening, after her purchase of her fish and chip meal at six o'clock?

The girl had been killed with her own scarf, tightened fiercely round her neck, almost certainly by someone standing behind her and twisting the ends of it. No great physical strength was necessarily involved: by twisting the scarf

59

around a stick, a woman or even a child could have killed Sarah Dunne. Peach's lips twisted sardonically as he read this; it was forensic's duty to set out the facts, but no one had a woman in the frame for this one, and still less a child.

Sarah Dunne had had sexual intercourse not long before her death. There were female sexual fluids on the inner side of her upper thighs and on her underclothing. A stocking had soaked up a semen spillage. There was no evidence that she had not been a willing party to sexual congress, no bruising around the genital area, no cuts or abrasions elsewhere on the body. There was no skin or other matter beneath the girl's nails which would give a clue to her attacker.

Peach said to Lucy Blake when she had read the PM report, 'It doesn't necessarily mean that she was a willing party to the sexual exchange, of course. Some rape victims are so terrified that they offer no resistance in the hope of escaping further violence.'

'But we know from the girl I interviewed, Karen Jones, that Sarah was trying her hand at prostitution. This could be a customer who went wrong, perhaps a man who simply didn't want to pay.'

Peach shook his head. 'Unlikely. She still had twenty-five quid in the pocket of her anorak when those kids found her. Even if he didn't pay her, someone like that would probably have rifled her pockets.'

'Unless he didn't really mean to kill her. Perhaps he panicked when she died and just wanted to get out quickly.'

'I don't think so. For one thing, the evidence indicates a quite deliberate and cold-blooded killing with that scarf. For another, he didn't kill her in the shed but saw her off somewhere else and dumped her there. So he didn't panic and run away as soon as he found himself with a corpse on his hands. We can't even be certain yet that the person who had sex with her was also her murderer: it's probable, but not by any means certain.'

'So who are we looking for?'

'Too early to say. We need to answer two questions. First, was this premeditated or was it a killing improvised on the spur of the moment? Secondly, was the murderer a stranger to Sarah Dunne, or someone known personally to her before last Friday night?'

David Strachan might have been interested in DCI Peach's thoughts on the death of Sarah Dunne. But for the moment he had other things on his mind.

Strachan was a computer salesman. Every industry needs computers nowadays, and because many people made hand-some profits in the early days of the trade, the public thinks selling such electronic wizardry is an easy path to affluence. David Strachan could have swiftly removed such delusions.

Selling computers and their associated software was as difficult as selling anything else; perhaps more difficult, indeed, as the competition among makers and distributors was now so intense. In the last years of the twentieth century, profit margins had been comfortable and there had been enough business for all, as firms realized they could not do without the newest technology and sales exploded. In the first decade of the twenty-first century, life had become much more difficult.

The people responsible for replacement machines were much better informed than the people who had bluffed their way through in the old days. David had often sold then to people who had no idea what questions they should ask. Now senior executives met him armed with a sheet of questions about what they needed and what his machines could do for them. And they had probably put the same questions to someone else earlier in the week.

On the afternoon of Wednesday, the nineteenth of November, David Strachan was going through what he regarded as the ultimate nightmare of the sales representative. He was having to behave as if he was nonchalant whilst trying to clinch an order which was crucially important to him.

He was forty-six now: old for a rep on the road. He had hoped to be a sales director by this stage of his career, planning policy in a comfortable office, setting targets for different areas, sending out his salesmen to achieve them. Instead of that, he was still a rep himself.

And he was having to sell nowadays to men much younger

than he was, who sometimes felt themselves better briefed about what he had to sell than he was himself. The man on the other side of the low table, where the coffee dregs had long gone cold in the cups, was such a man. Each time David made a point about what his system could do, the man smiled patronizingly, as if he had heard all this before and recognized it for the advertising copy it was.

When David now pointed out how swiftly and efficiently the wages for this large printing concern could be handled, the man said, 'Oh, of course – I would expect no less than that,' and nodded his squat, complacent face beneath the neatly coiffured brown hair. 'What kind of discount do you offer on an order of this size, which must be worth quite a lot to a small company like yours?'

David wanted to wipe the smug smile off that face which was ten years younger than his, to tell him that the margins had already been cut to the bone, that he wouldn't do better anywhere else. It was probably true, but he couldn't be absolutely certain of that, and this cocksure young puppy knew it. David gave him his 'we're men of the world together' smile to acknowledge how clever he was and massage his ego. 'You've already shown me how well-informed you are, Jason. So you must realize that we've already offered you a very good price.'

The man lifted a hand to that immaculate hair, as if to reassure himself that it was still in place. He was pleased with the compliment he had just been offered, despite himself. Flattery was still an Achilles heel for young go-getters like him. He steepled the fingers of his hands and leaned back contemplatively in his chair, as he had seen a director of the firm do in an interview with him on the previous day. 'I have a duty to get the very best price for my company, you know,' he said with a smile of complicity.

It was good to hear him say that. David knew that you were near to clinching a deal when they said things like that. He took a deep breath and made the sacrifice for the deal he must take away with him, taking two per cent off his already slender commission of five per cent. He forced a wide smile. 'I'm confident you won't do better than that anywhere, Jason.

You drive a hard bargain, but you know enough about this business to be aware that I'm speaking the truth.'

The younger man pursed his lips for the ritual three seconds, nodded as if he were digesting Strachan's statement and finding it convincing, and said, 'All right, it's a deal. I should probably be looking at other offers. But we're very busy and I prefer to rely on our relationship, David.'

He stood up and offered his hand with a wide, practised smile. David Strachan shook the hand firmly, struggling not to show the measure of his relief, hoping the wetness of his palm would not be apparent. He tried to look as if he secured orders of this size every day of the week

But both of them knew that he wouldn't still be on the road if he did.

'Have you rounded up the local perverts?' Superintendent Thomas Bulstrode Tucker was nothing if not conventional.

'Doubt if it's one of them, sir. Not their style,' said Peach glumly.

'And what *is* their style?' said Tucker with heavy scepticism.

'Flashing and groping. Not killing,' said Peach.

'You mark my words,' said his chief. 'Men who start off by flashing go on to rape and murder.'

As a generalization, it wasn't true. Peach remained silent, looking at the ceiling and nodding steadily.

'Well? What are you doing?'

Peach returned to a contemplation of his chief. 'I was marking your words, sir. Sorry, sir.'

'What are your thoughts, then, if you haven't yet made an arrest?' Tucker leaned forward over his desk, doing his impression of a keen-eyed man whom nothing escaped.

'Don't like it, sir. It's no ordinary murder, this. By which I mean that it doesn't have an obvious motive. I don't like those.'

'Surely this was someone in pursuit of sex or money? You're too subtle sometimes, you know, Peach.' Tucker had never thought he'd hear himself saying that to this man. He immediately wished he hadn't.

Percy beamed delightedly at him. 'Always been one of my faults, that, sir. That's what the lads and lasses at the crime face downstairs tell me. "You're much too subtle," they tell me. "You should learn to go for the vulgar and the obvious, if you want to reach the top in the CID." I think they may be right, sir. It's good to have it confirmed by you.'

Tucker glared at him, but the DCI's attention was on the wall behind his chief's head, his face fixed in that relaxed but inscrutable expression which he reserved for Tommy Bloody Tucker. The Superintendent said heavily, 'So have you any thoughts at all, then?'

'Don't think it's a local sex offender with previous convictions, sir. They're too lightweight, our local sex men. I've had the computers looking for similar crimes elsewhere. That's to say, killings without any obvious motive and using a similar modus operandi.' He produced the full Latin phrase instead of the usual police initials: it was always good to surprise Tommy B.T.

'And what has this profound research revealed to you?' Tucker tried to be heavily sarcastic, but sarcasm was always difficult when it produced no reaction in the victim.

'Three killings in the last year which look similar to this one. Prostitutes killed with a piece of rope or something similar, taken from behind and killed within seconds. Not conclusive. I'm getting further details from the investigating officers involved and keeping an open mind.'

Tucker sighed. He had thought of this as a sordid, straightforward crime and hoped for a swift arrest and a trumpeting on his part of a rediscovered efficiency. 'Any other thoughts?'

'Just one, sir. This one could be related to those other killings in a different way. It could be a local after all, wanting us to think this was done by someone who's killed previously in other parts of the country.'

'A copycat killing?'

'Precisely, sir. I knew you'd have the phrase for it.'

David Strachan enjoyed his modest meal at the Happy Eater, lingering over his mixed grill, reading the paper his nervousness had prevented him from studying earlier in the day.

He'd got the contract: that was the main thing. He was pretty sure that his Sales Director back in Birmingham hadn't thought he could get it. And if he hadn't, he'd have been out on his ear. No one had said so, but when you'd been in this game as long as he had, you could read the signs. He was safe for a year now, in all probability. Well, six months, at least.

He'd had to cut his commission precious hard to clinch the sale, but it was well worth it. And he'd make it up on other jobs, now that the pressure was off him. You couldn't sell well when you weren't relaxed: those pricks at head office should realize that. But you couldn't tell those people anything. Experience counted for nothing, these days.

He didn't want to move out of the bright warmth of the eating place into the cold and damp of the night outside. He treated himself to a custard tart, went and ordered a second coffee when he thought he caught the girl behind the counter looking at him impatiently. She had good breasts, tight behind her uniform, the way he liked them, and a cheeky smile that said she knew what he was thinking when he looked at them and almost touched them as he reached out for his change.

It was good to feel randy. He'd had too many anxious days lately to enjoy the pleasure of a little harmless lechery with his meals. Perhaps he should celebrate what he had done today. It would cost him, because he always seemed to have to pay for it these days; that old idea of the commercial traveller who put it about a bit was long out of date, as far as he could see.

But what he'd achieved against the odds in that printing company merited a reward. Some woman was going to be lucky tonight! David Strachan felt a stirring within his loins which deserved to be sated properly. He went into the gents and washed his hands and face. He slicked back the thinning hair and gave his teeth a quick scrub with the brush he kept always in the pocket of his car coat. No harm in offering a woman a little hygiene, even if you were paying her for her favours.

He'd been coming to Brunton for years, so he knew where to look for what he wanted. He drove his car slowly along the street below the park. But not too slowly: there was no point in risking being picked up for kerb-crawling. A girl had died near here less than a week ago, so the police would be vigilant.

He saw what he wanted quickly enough. Blonde and buxom. He liked them buxom, liked a good handful of what you were paying for. She gave him a nice smile and looked keen for his custom. That was good enough for him, even if she looked older than he'd taken her for when he'd first seen her.

It was a meeting of like minds: he was eager for a woman, and Sally Aspin was eager for a customer. She was out early, knowing that some of the girls were wary after that girl had been killed on the game last week. Sally knew she couldn't afford to be choosy, at her age, knew that she must bring in the punters or be banished from the streets by Joe Johnson.

'Give you a good time, love!' she assured David Strachan huskily as he looked over the goods.

'You bet you will! And *you* won't be disappointed either!' He looked up and down the street, then clapped her hand on his rampant weapon.

Sally gripped the familiar object as it thrust against the familiar zip. 'Let's get moving, big boy!' she hissed throatily into what seemed a pleasingly clean and odour-free ear. She wasn't going to fluff lines as easily learned as this one.

He didn't disappoint her. Not with the sex: Sally Aspin had long since learned to set her sights very low indeed on what happened under the sheets. But this man was a good customer, very nearly the ideal one. He paid her the money without argument before he started. He laid his clothes neatly across the chair she indicated to him, only prevented from folding them by the urgency of his desire. He didn't demand anything kinky, though she would have done whatever he wanted, within reason.

He grasped her hard, even passionately, but not roughly enough to leave any serious bruises. He murmured gratifying things about her bum and her breasts. And he came quickly and efficiently when she commanded him to with a couple of four-letter words, without needing any of the blandishments she had sometimes to employ to ensure orgasm and full delivery.

And when she said three minutes later that it was time for him to go unless he wanted to pay double for all night, he rose obediently and went to wash himself in the tiny bathroom.

It was only when he was getting dressed that he said something odd. 'One of you girls was killed last week, wasn't she?'

'Yes. Slip of a kid. Didn't know what she was about. Didn't recognize the danger signals, I expect.'

'Nasty business. Meet a lot of violence, do you, Sally?'

She'd given him her name in the hope of further custom. Now she began to wish that she hadn't. 'Not a lot. There are some vicious buggers about everywhere, though, aren't there, nowadays?'

'There are indeed.' He stroked her plump shoulder for a moment as she put on her bra, and she managed not to flinch away from the touch.

'At least your hands are warm!' she said and took his fingers between hers, passing her lips softly across them for a second. The punters were entitled to call the tune, but he'd had what he'd paid for now, and she was conscious that she wanted to change the subject of this conversation.

'Never been one for violence myself,' he said, his hand lingering for a moment on her wrist as he stood ridiculous with his trousers around his knees. 'But I suppose a little bit of brutality has a certain attraction, when it's combined with sex.' He looked at her in the big mirror she had fixed to the wall beside the bed for those with a taste for such things, trying to will her into assent.

'Want a bit of Miss Whiplash, do you, love?' she said mockingly, handing him his jacket. He hadn't given her his name, and you never asked for information: that was part of the code.

He grinned at her, but said nothing. He was at the door before he spoke again. Then he lifted his arms to her shoulders and said, 'You're a very desirable woman, Sally. And there's plenty of you. I like that. Perhaps I'll be back for a bit of Miss Whiplash. Might even bring Mr Whiplash along for the ride!'

He had vanished into the night before she could find any words of refusal.

Nine

Percy Peach for once did as Tucker suggested. He went and talked to one of the longest established flashers on his patch.

He didn't for a moment think that Billy Bedford had killed Sarah Dunne, but he wanted information. And Billy Bedford was a voyeur as well as a flasher. He was out on the meaner streets of Brunton on most nights, looking for a bit of cheap entertainment to light up his hopelessly shabby life.

Billy lived with his aged mother, a woman whom Percy had got to know over the years of her son's shame, a woman for whom he had affection as well as pity. 'He's in trouble again, Mrs Bedford!' said Percy, shaking his head sympathetically at the old lady in the rocking chair. He was conscious of Billy hovering with hands clasped at the edge of the room; it gratified Peach to see the anxiety which the man had exhibited from the moment he saw Peach in the doorway of the tiny terraced house stepped up another notch.

'I never set foot outside the 'ouse! Me mum'll tell you that!' The wheedling denial came automatically from the thin lips.

Percy swung to look at him. 'Too quick, Billy Bedford! I haven't said which night I was interested in yet. Makes me feel you already know which night it was, that you've got something very nasty to hide, that does.'

Mrs Bedford said, 'He's not a bad lad, really, Mr Peach. He's good to his old mum, in his own way, is Billy.' She looked at the Chief Inspector appealingly, with her head on one side and her small bright eyes fixed on him like those of a hungry sparrow. It was a long time since Percy had seen someone with her arms and shoulders invisible beneath a thick blanket of woollen shawl. He wondered how many of those shawls she had gone through since she had worn her first one and clattered in her clogs to the mill, during and after Hitler's war.

'I'm glad to hear he's good to his mum, Mrs Bedford. Because he's got precious few other virtues. Where were you last Friday night, Billy?' He rapped the question into the man's face with a sudden switch.

Billy Bedford was a pathetic rather than a dangerous creature. Peach realized that he had rarely if ever seen him before in natural light. It didn't improve the man. His cheap green shirt was grubby at the neck and had a button missing. The diamond patterns on his cardigan had long since faded and there were holes in the sleeves and food on the front of it. He ran a hand automatically through his thinning, greasy grey hair at every challenge which was offered to him.

But Bedford had endured many hours of police questioning, during dark nights on the streets and under the harsh artificial glare of police interview rooms. He forced the fear from his watery grey eyes, made them carefully blank, and said, 'Can't remember where I was last Friday, it's almost a week ago. But I ain't done nothing, Mr Peach, 'onest I ain't.'

Peach could have terrified him into submission, easily enough. But he didn't want a mother in her eighties to see her son at his most abject. He shook his head at Billy and turned back to the old lady. Without taking his eyes from her face he opened the briefcase at his side and drew forth a bottle of Guinness, producing with the action a delighted glint in those aged sparrow eyes. 'Glass please, Billy,' he said.

He poured the black stout with elaborate care into the dimpled tankard Billy brought from the scullery, tilting the glass expertly to avoid too frothy a head, setting it at length upon the table beside her. 'Where was he, Mrs Bedford?'

'He was out, I expect. He usually is, on a Friday, once he's watched *Coronation Street* with his old mum.' She took a long sip at the Guinness, without lowering the level very much; she was going to make it last, this black gold. Then, as if the magic draught had made her more acute, she wiped

69

her withered top lip, leaned forward and said, ''Ere, it wasn't Friday when that girl was killed, was it?'

'We think it might have been, Mrs Bedford. Though we haven't released the information to the press yet. So you're ahead of the *Evening Telegraph* this time, aren't you?'

She looked at the dishevelled copy of the evening paper beyond her tankard on the table and giggled delightedly. Then her eyes narrowed. 'But you're not saying my Billy had anything to do with that, are you?'

'My chief thinks he might have, I'm afraid.' He registered the son's alarm out of the corner of his eye with satisfaction. 'But between you and me, Mrs Bedford, I don't believe Billy has it in him to kill anybody. His best policy would be to come clean and give us all the help he can.'

She digested this for a moment. Then the sparrow's head nodded as abruptly and repeatedly as if it was attacking a worm. 'You 'ear what Mr Peach says, son. Better give 'im all the help you can, lad.'

'I always do, Mum. Always try to 'elp the police. More than they ever do for me, that is!'

Peach grinned at him. 'Very touching, Billy, I'm sure. Well, if you want to keep Chief Superintendent Tucker off your back, you'd better answer every question I ask you as honestly and completely as you can. I know that will be breaking the habit of a lifetime, but believe me and believe your mum, it will be much the best thing.'

Bedford looked from one to the other, the idea of telling the truth filling his eyes with apprehension; he looked like a rabbit caught in the glare of a headlight. The stench of his breath swept into Peach's face, but the DCI didn't flinch: his eyes bored into the frightened features as though they would be taken apart if he didn't get the truth. He repeated with soft menace, 'Much the best thing, Billy.'

'All right. I was out, like Mum says. But I didn't see anything, honest I didn't.'

'Looking for a quick flash, were you, Billy? Bit cold for that, in November.' Peach kept his eyes on the thin, wretched face, though he was aware of the old lady shaking her head sadly as she sipped her Guinness.

'No. I've given all that up, Mr Peach.' He took a big breath. Telling the truth to the police required a tremendous effort of his puny will. 'I was just walking around. Trying to enjoy what I saw.'

'And what did you see, Billy?'

The old lady looked at her son with distaste. 'He watches the tarts, don't he? Watches them flashing their legs to excite those who pay them. Always one for a free show, weren't you, Billy?'

Peach wondered what childhood excesses she was recalling to this disaster of a son. Had he peeped through the bedroom keyhole at the performance of his long-dead father? He said hastily, 'Watching the tarts on Friday, were you, Billy?'

'I might have been. All right, I did, for a bit. They show their suspenders, you know, Mr Peach! Sometimes you even get a flash of their pants, if you're in the right place and they have to lead the punters on a bit!'

He was trying to excite some deeply based male cama-raderie, some moment of mutual recognition of the delights he cherished and carried with him to the musty privacy of his damp bedroom above them. Peach said, 'On the edge of the park, were you, trying to get the best view you could?'

'Yes. It's locked up at night, but you can get underneath the big trees on the edge without being inside the park. The willows are best – they hang nearly down to the ground.'

'And how much did you see of this young girl who was killed?'

'Nothing, Mr Peach, honest! Nothing at all!' Bedford was pathetically anxious to convince. For a man who concealed the truth as a habit, it was a difficult and rather pathetic performance.

'Sure of that, Billy, are you? Now's the time to speak, if you saw anything at all that might be suspicious. Accessory after the fact, you could be, if you concealed information. Wouldn't like to see you in the dock for that, would we, Mrs Bedford?'

The old lady's sharp sparrow eyes peered hard into her son's fearful countenance. 'He don't know nothing, Mr

71

Peach. More's the pity. I want you to get the bugger who killed that girl, even if she was a tart.'

'We will, Mrs Bedford. And sooner rather than later, if we get the help from the public that we need. Listen, Billy, you hear a lot of what's going on around here. That's why I'm here, if you want to know. You must have heard something that might be of use to us.'

Bedford's thin lips set into a sullen, instinctive mask of non-cooperation. 'Ain't no grass!' he said automatically.

'Accessory after the fact,' Peach reminded him.

Bedford fought a small battle in his confused and sordid mind. 'I did 'ear something in the Coach and Horses last week. Might have nothing to do with this girl, though.'

'Let's have it, Billy.'

'It might be nothing.'

'Of course it might. And it might be important.'

'Well, I 'eard someone saying as one or two young tarts who were putting it about had been warned off. Told they sold it through the firm or not at all, as you might say.'

'One of the big pimps, was it?'

'The biggest round 'ere.' For a moment, Bedford was proud of the claim and the importance it gave him. Then fear submerged that tiny, unaccustomed pride. 'You won't tell him, will you, Mr Peach? Be more than my life's worth, if it got out I'd been talking to you.'

Peach reflected that this man's life wasn't worth very much, but he didn't say so in front of his old mother. 'No one will know what you said, Billy. Some pimp's gorillas were putting the word about, were they?'

'Yes, that's it.' Billy was glad to have the detail voiced by the filth; somehow it made his own treachery less heinous if someone else provided most of the words. Then a crafty look belatedly replaced the fear in his face. 'Anything in it for me, is there, if this information should be useful?'

Peach sat back a little from the foul breath and regarded his man with distaste. Then he said, 'Yes, there is, Billy. Payment in advance, before we've even tested your information. Another small reward for the only woman who loves you.' He reached down to his briefcase and produced the second bottle of Guinness he had kept for his departure. He placed it beside the empty one on the scarred table and said, 'With my compliments, Mrs Bedford.' The old lady raised her tankard towards him in a gesture of delighted acceptance.

Peach had never taken his eyes off the disappointed Bedford. He now said, 'And which pimp would this be, Billy?'

Bedford looked automatically to right and left, in a Pavlovian reaction which suggested that even here there might be listening ears. Then he said in a low voice, 'Joe Johnson, Mr Peach.'

The computers were ticking up a lot of information, a lot of cross-referenced files. There was a murder team of thirty-four working on the murder of Sarah Dunne in and around Brunton.

On the night of Thursday the twentieth of November, six days after Sarah had died, there was also another policeman in the area. This one was not only in plain clothes but very much off duty. He was not even stationed at Brunton. If he had been, he would have been seeking what he wanted many miles away from the old cotton town.

Inspector Boyd was from Blackpool, thirty miles to the west. All seaside towns are difficult to police, and Blackpool, as the largest holiday town in Britain, is the most difficult of all. The problem is a simple one of numbers, but the solution is not so simple. The winter population of Blackpool is under two hundred thousand. At the height of its summer season, the packed hotels and boarding houses of the town and its satellites house almost ten times that number.

A permanent police force to cope with that number would leave the town vastly and expensively over-policed during the winter months. Yet a winter-sized police service would invite anarchy in the summer. One of the solutions is to import police officers from the towns whence the visitors come, and this works very well with the big influxes, such as those who throng the town in what is known as the 'Glasgow weeks', when Scottish banknotes fill the tills of the shops and Scottish drunks fight the good fight outside the town's multitude of pubs.

Whatever logic is employed by the planners, one of the results of the situation is that the Blackpool police work a lot of overtime in the summer and are correspondingly much freer in the winter.

Tom Boyd knew by now that for him too much freedom was not always a good thing. He was forty-eight, divorced, and without many hobbies to occupy him when the winds howled over the deserted Blackpool promenade in winter. He was too old now for the football he had enjoyed in his youth; he regarded golf as a game for fops and posers; he was not yet old enough to immerse himself in indoor bowls. He wasn't a great reader, and he was so busy with his job in Traffic Control in the summer that he had lost the habit of watching television.

Inspector Boyd was divorced, with a daughter who lived in East Anglia whom he saw twice a year. He was lonely: he admitted that to himself now, though he had denied it for years. But only to himself: you didn't want to be classed as a sad loner when you went into a police station where most people seemed quite suddenly to be much younger than you.

It was all right in summer. You could work up to twelve hours a day, snatch a meal in the canteen, and enjoy a quick pint afterwards. If you wanted it, there was usually sex on your day off, if you weren't too choosy. Some of the women who visited the town in these enlightened days considered it part of their holiday to put it about a bit, and Tom knew where to go to pick them up.

He had enjoyed a threesome in his flat with a couple of married women from Yorkshire which had taught him quite a lot. They'd only been on a day trip on a coach, those two, but they'd made the most of their day! They'd only just caught their coach home and Inspector Boyd had been sore for a week afterwards.

But in the winter, it was different. Tom Boyd had accepted philosophically that he would have to pay to get what he wanted, if he wanted it regularly and with no strings attached. He didn't mind that. But you didn't go paying for it with the local toms in Blackpool. In the crude but universally accepted police parlance, you didn't shit upon your own doorstep.

The crude expression was quite good enough for Tom Boyd. He had some fairly crude sexual demands to make, and it was better to pay for them than to suffer the rejection which came your way from ordinary encounters.

He'd made the mistake at first of taking the youngest tarts he could get: they couldn't turn away your money, however ancient they thought you were. But they hadn't given him much satisfaction, the young ones. More like kids they were. You ended up frustrated, likely to do things you shouldn't think of doing. Treating them cruelly, the way you wouldn't do at all, in normal circumstances. Doing things you were ashamed of, that you certainly couldn't talk about to anyone else.

Tom Boyd had hesitated a little on that Thursday about whether to go into the Brunton area at all. It didn't take much of his police brain to work out that there would be heightened activity in the district in the week following a murder. But Tom was into bondage, and he had found a woman there last time who had suited his tastes exactly. It had cost a little more, but the woman had appeared to enjoy it. Perhaps she was just a good sexual actress – people said that was part of the equipment of the best tarts – but Inspector Boyd could have sworn she had actually shared his sexual tastes.

She was tall and statuesque, dark-haired and powerful, and she had strutted about most impressively. It was even more exciting to Tom that she had seemed to enjoy it when he had pranced about around the bed while she lay helpless upon it. He was sure he had glimpsed excitement in the glint of her dark eyes when he had laid his hands playfully and lightly upon her throat, letting the pressure of his fingers die softly into a caress.

It was all play-acting between the two of them, of course, nothing serious. But it made Tom Boyd more excited than he could remember feeling before.

That was why it was worth seeking this particular tart out, even if it involved a little danger. That was another thing he had admitted to himself in the last year: he enjoyed having a spice of danger in these encounters, found it added to the excitement. And you got precious little excitement in Traffic Policing. The better you were at your job, the less the excitement, as a rule.

He drove his Vauxhall Vectra unhurriedly along the M55 and skirted the plush suburbs on the north side of Preston. The roads were quiet and the Vectra was a good car for a mission like this: swift, reliable and, most important of all, anonymous. There were a lot of Vectras about and their styling was not particularly individual; Boyd knew from years of police experience that those were the two most important things if a car was not to excite too much notice.

He took the A59 for a stretch, then turned off it and went for a drink in a quiet pub in Mellor. Two men at the bar were talking about last week's murder in Brunton. He listened carefully whilst apparently immersed in the *West Lancs Evening Gazette* he had brought with him from Blackpool, but it was no more than desultory pub gossip: he already knew more about the crime and its investigation than these two had learned.

The DCI who was driving the investigation had been in touch with the station at Blackpool to see if they'd had any similar murders in the last two years, so Tom Boyd had every reason to be on his guard. He'd seen the e-mailed reply from Blackpool to Brunton. Blackpool CID had told this DCI Peach that they hadn't had any murders which remotely resembled the one in Brunton in the last five years. And the two prostitute killings they had experienced in the last five years had each been solved within a week: rival CID sections liked to get things like that in.

He couldn't see much evidence of police activity as he cruised around the nearly deserted streets of the district of Brunton where she operated. But that was what he would have expected: policemen were as human as the rest of the world, and the majority of even a large murder team wouldn't want to be walking the streets of a drab industrial town at ten o'clock on a cold November night. Besides, the overtime budget would be scrutinized, even when it was a murder case.

Some superintendent would be shaking his head over the extra payments.

On his first round of the familiar circuit, Tom Boyd thought that the woman he wanted wasn't about either. Then he saw her, walking tall and lithe, a little faster than those of her trade normally did, turning with practised provocation as she heard the car slowing behind her. She didn't know it was him at first: the Vectra proving itself again.

He pressed the button and lowered the window on the passenger side. 'Before you ask, Katie, I fancy a good time, yes. The mixture as before would do very nicely, thank you!'

Katie Clegg slid in beside him without hesitation. It was good to have a voice you recognized, after what had happened to that girl last week. And in a trade where people paid well to bonk you and be gone, she found she was disproportionately grateful when someone remembered her name. 'Nice and warm in here!' she said appreciatively, and gave his left arm a squeeze. Like any ordinary girlfriend appreciating a lift. She knew that it was safest to let them make the first move, but there couldn't be any harm in a little reassuring squeeze on the forearm. Not when you knew the punter.

'And I bet it's nice and warm in there!' he answered promptly, reaching across and stroking the inside of her thigh. She wished she had a pound for every time she'd heard that or something similar: the standard of wit among clients anxious to get their ends away was not high. But you mustn't set your sights too high; this man had caressed where many just grabbed, and his hand was warm. She inched herself forward in the seat, allowing his fingers to sweep up on to the lace of the knickers she wore for this job, easing her mound of Venus expertly back and forth between the quickening fingers. Then she whispered, 'All in good time, sweetheart,' and detached that left hand unhurriedly, pretending she was reluctant to let it go.

Tom was glad enough to drive on: he didn't want a stationary car exciting any attention in this situation. He remembered the turns to take and found her house without any guidance. She seemed impressed by that. He was a policeman, of course, but Katie didn't know that, didn't even know his name.

It was only ten pounds extra for what he wanted: a bargain if ever he saw one. And he saw quite a lot; Katie wasn't wearing much as she got out the fetters and fixed them to the top and base of the bed. The handcuffs were toys compared with the ones he had clapped on in many an arrest in the old days, but it wouldn't do to show professional knowledge, so he made no comment.

It was as good as he had anticipated. Better. As always, he found that the simulated cruelty excited him. By the time he reached orgasm, he could have ceased to pretend and committed some real aggression, done real damage to some human body. His head swam with the excitement of it all, sex and violence mingling in that now familiar compound which made his head swim and his body seem to belong to someone else, someone much wilder and less inhibited, less bound by the rules of a dull world.

It was a long time before he ceased to pant, and when his breathing slowed and his eyes opened, he found her looking at him curiously. It took him a moment to return fully to that room with the thick velvet curtains and the deep scarlet lampshade. She said, a little reluctantly, 'You can have a cup of tea before you go if you like. I shan't be going out into the cold again. It's a raw night out there.'

Katie made it a practice not to rush regular customers out of the place. You wanted to encourage them to patronize you again, and most men were foolish enough to believe that you might have a little affection for them, even after money had changed hands.

Yet this time she was glad when the man refused. There had been something very fierce about him at the end, some dangerous force she did not want to analyse too deeply.

Katie Clegg shuddered, wanting only to get back to her children and her other, normal life. She couldn't see any other way of earning the money she needed, but it worried her, sometimes, how much she now knew about men and the darker side of sexual life.

Tom Boyd smiled to himself as he went out into the

darkness and privacy of the night. It had been good, that. He had gone further than he'd gone before with that line of sex, and discovered how much the brutality of it excited him. He'd used a certain savagery before; he'd even been checked for it in his early days in the police, when he'd given young thugs more than the rules allowed. But he'd never combined violence with sex in this intoxicating way before.

Perhaps it was his exhilaration which made him careless. He didn't even look up and down the quiet road as he emerged from Katie's house, didn't see the men waiting in the shadows beneath the straggling shrubs at the end of the short front garden. He was opening the door of the Vectra when the hand fell upon his shoulder and the voice said, 'We'd like a few words with you, sir. At the station in Brunton, if you don't mind.'

Tom Boyd did mind. But as he saw the warrant card in the pale light of the street lamp, he knew there was no escape.

Ten

It was a huge modern house on a generous plot. It had six bedrooms, six bathrooms, garaging for five cars, and an indoor swimming pool with its own heating plant and changing rooms. Though the building had been completed only three years earlier, the gardens had an established air. Mature trees had been brought in with their huge root-balls intact and planted with special machines.

Money was never in short supply here. Some people called the development vulgar, but they were perhaps a little envious. The rawness of the bricks would merge happily into the setting after a few years. Brunton did not have many places of this quality, and this one would become one of the most desirable of all with the passing of time.

Almost the modern equivalent of the old manor house, where the occupant controlled most of what went on around him. But this was no manor house. This place was an architectural witness to the fact that crime paid. 'Hurst Leigh' was the name spelt out tastefully in the plaque on the tall gatepost. It was a name devised for something much more modest and rural than this ostentatious pile.

In so far as he loved anything, Joe Johnson loved every brick of this house.

Percy Peach, on the other hand, regarded the edifice with considerable distaste as he studied it through the elaborate wrought-iron security gates at the end of the drive. The place was a reminder to Peach that villains sometimes won, and he did not like that.

The electronic gates eased slowly back after he had rapped out his name into the microphone on the gatepost, and Lucy Blake drove the police Mondeo over the gravel and parked it neatly beneath the high northern elevation of the Johnson mansion. A maid opened the oak door and said, 'Mr Johnson is expecting you. He's in his study.' Ignoring Peach's snort at the word, she led them over plush carpets into a room with dimensions which most people would have welcomed in a sitting room.

Joe Johnson sat behind a big desk and watched their entry with a sardonic smile. It was a big desk, with a red leather top and an elaborate brass inkstand whose pens were never used. There was a leather Chesterfield on one wall, matching armchairs, where he indicated that his visitors should sit, a table of luxuriant house plants beneath the low Georgian window, prints of Alpine scenes on the walls. A copy of the previous weekend's *Sunday Times* lay on the table. The room's atmosphere of uncontroversial good taste might have been fashioned for a show house in a new development of luxury properties.

The only jarring note was struck by a cinema poster from the *Godfather* series, showing Don Corleone leering at his Mafia henchmen. Peach decided that this lurid and arresting image was the only thing in the room chosen by Johnson himself.

Joe Johnson sat back on his desk chair and looked down on the two he had positioned carefully below him in the armchairs. 'Thought I'd have our little discussion here at home,' he said with a smile which would have sat well on a shark. 'Don't like the filth coming into my working environment: it gives the workers a bad impression.'

Peach returned the smile with interest. 'We could always do this at the station, if you prefer it.'

'I don't think so. It's a long time since I was on a farm, but I distinctly recall that I didn't like the smell of pigs.'

Peach looked round the luxurious modern room. 'Didn't think you'd be a *Sunday Times* reader, Johnson: part of the image, is it?'

Johnson gave him an oily smile. 'It's not this week's edition. It's from January 2003. I keep it for the News Review section. There are two whole pages about the cock-ups the police made in the hunt for the Yorkshire Ripper. I enjoy reading accounts of police incompetence.'

Lucy Blake decided she'd had enough of hungry dogs circling each other. She said, 'I didn't tell you why we had made this appointment, Mr Johnson. We want to speak to you about the murder of Sarah Dunne.'

Johnson ignored her for a moment whilst he finished his eye contact with Peach. Then he swung his chair through thirty degrees to look her unhurriedly up and down, letting his gaze linger on the nyloned knees where they met the leather of the chair. It took Lucy a real effort of will not to pull at the hem of her skirt; she wished irrelevantly that she had worn trousers to come here. Against her wishes, she found herself saying, 'That's the girl who was killed last Friday.'

Johnson nodded. 'I thought I'd heard the name. She was murdered, wasn't she? And you haven't solved it yet, or you wouldn't be here looking for Joe Johnson's help! Isn't there some statistic which says that if you don't solve a murder mystery within the first week you don't solve it at all? Your week will be up tonight – and Miss Marple here obviously still hasn't a clue!' He turned back to the scowling Peach, then laughed at his witticism. The mirth did not extend to his cold grey eyes.

He reached into the top drawer of the desk, extracted a cigar, removed the band, and lit it carefully, in a long drawn-out charade of contempt. 'I'd offer you one, Peach, but I know you mustn't smoke on duty. And I'm sure this pretty lady isn't the kind of dyke who goes in for fat cigars.'

Peach tried not to show his physical tension. This odious man had defrauded the public of millions, had made more millions from vice, had almost certainly killed men, or had them killed. But in this context he was still officially a member of the public, helping the police with their enquiries. He was not under arrest, could refuse to answer their questions, could dismiss them from his house at whatever moment he chose. He said through clenched teeth, 'So where were you last Friday night between nine and eleven, Johnson?'

Johnson grinned, his grey eyes as expressionless as stone. 'You can do better than that, Peach. For the record, I expect I was in one of my clubs. I usually am, on a Friday night. But you don't for a moment think that I killed that stupid girl.'

'Your hard men might have killed her. Your enforcers.' He rolled his contempt round the last word.

'What a vivid imagination you have, Peach! It seems to have become more vivid, since your promotion.' He tapped the first grey disc of cigar ash into an ash tray, enjoying telling the man three yards away from him that he knew all about his elevation to DCI.

Lucy Blake said, 'You said the girl was "stupid", Mr Johnson. What reason have you to call her that, if you never knew her?'

For a moment, he was disconcerted. Joe Johnson was not used to being challenged these days. He was surrounded by yes-men; even the most violent people among his entourage were there to do his bidding, not to query his thinking. He said, 'Did I call her stupid? Well, perhaps that's because my experience has led me to think of all girls as stupid. Sorry about that, darling!'

She tried to mimic his insulting grin, to throw it back at him as a mirror would. 'You can do better than that, Mr Johnson, if you choose to. Even you.'

He looked at her for a moment, refusing to be offended, letting a leer creep over the flat features, trying hard to convey to her just what he would like to do to her in other circumstances. Then he said, 'All right. I'm sorry that poor girl was killed, but she was stupid to be roaming the streets of Brunton on her own at that time of night. It's a dangerous place after dark. The police don't seem able to keep order, you see!'

'It's not easy with your gorillas roaming free,' said Peach.

'Don't expect me to shed crocodile tears for that girl. Any girl who goes round trying to sell herself is asking for trouble.'

It was his first mistake: probably the result of over-confidence, of enjoying the discomfiture of the CID officers too much.

Peach said, 'How'd you know she was on the game, Johnson?'

'It was in the papers.'

'No. That information has not been released.'

A pause. Johnson puffed his cigar and smiled. 'I must have assumed that any young girl who was on the streets at that hour was trying her hand at tarting. And it seems I was right. Perhaps I should be in the CID!'

'She'd been warned off, hadn't she? Warned not to interfere in a prostitution racket controlled by Joe Johnson.'

'Don't know what you mean, I'm sure. Prostitution racket? I make my money legitimately, from my casinos and my clubs. And not just round here, either! I make more than a rozzer could ever dream of making, Piggy Peach!' Joe Johnson looked unhurriedly round the warm, spacious room and out at the grounds to emphasize his point. 'She was asking for trouble, being on Alexandra Street at that time of night.'

'Know where she was killed, do you, Joe? Well, we'd expect that, when it was one of your men who topped her.' Peach's black eyes stared triumphantly from beneath his bald pate.

'She was killed on the streets, up that way somewhere. I'm sure I read that. Or heard it on the television.'

'You didn't, because that information also has not been released. Sarah Dunne's body was found in a shed, on a mill site that had been cleared for rebuilding. The television pictures showed that scene, and the newspaper and radio reports implied that she died there, because we haven't told anyone any different. We don't know exactly where she died, or didn't until now. It's interesting that you should be able to enlighten us. But not unexpected. That's why we came to see you.'

'I don't know where she died.'

'Can't expect us to believe that now, Joe.' Peach was somehow making effective bricks out of tiny wisps of straw.

'If I happened to realize she'd been killed elsewhere and then dumped in the shed, it was just a lucky guess.'

'You're too modest, Johnson. Not lucky, and not a guess, I'd say. Just well-informed.'

'I know nothing about this girl's death. You can't pin it on me, Peach!

'Make a note of this conversation, will you, DS Blake? Put down that Mr Johnson knew that the girl was on the game and knew exactly where she died, when that information has not been given in any official press release.'

Lucy went through the elaborate ritual of producing her small gold-plated ball pen and making an entry in her notebook. Johnson affected a lack of interest, but his nerve broke as the silence stretched and DS Blake wrote diligently. 'You can't use any of this in a court. I haven't even been cautioned.'

'True, that. But a prosecuting counsel may ask us about the impressions we formed at this stage of the inquiry, you see. Make an additional note about Mr Johnson's attitude, will you, DS Blake? I leave the actual words to you.' He turned his attention back to the flat-featured man across the desk. 'She's very good with words, DS Blake. Not just a pretty face, you see.'

'You won't pin this on me, Peach.' The cloak of urbanity, which had never sat easily upon Joe Johnson, had dropped away completely now. The lips were thin with fury and the scars were showing more clearly on the forehead above the thin, sallow face.

Peach stood up. 'Not yet, maybe. But give us time. The only weapon the dead have is that they can afford to be patient, you see. One of our officers will be in to your office for a list of your staff: we shall need to question them – thoroughly, in the light of what you've revealed today.'

'I haven't revealed anything.'

'Really? Note that, DS Blake. Even the nastiest members of our society are vulnerable, when they do not have self-knowledge. You're making me into quite a philosopher, Joe. Don't leave the area without informing us of your movements, will you?'

Father Devoy said his prayers, but they didn't seem to work. His most frenzied supplications to the Lord seemed worthless, these days, whenever he prayed about himself.

It was Friday night again, a week since that poor girl had died, and Satan was taunting Father John again. He could

85

keep the Devil at bay when he had the work of his ministry to help him. He had put evil to one side whilst he heard Confessions for an hour, listening behind the screen of his airless cubicle to the petty sins of the parish, summoning his weightiest tones for the occasional adulterer or wife-beater. Sometimes, in the worst cases, the two came together, and Father John wondered which was the greater of the evils.

He warned the sinners sternly that they must be genuinely penitent for their sins, must genuinely regret the pain they had caused to God and the damage they had done to their immortal souls. For without real repentance there could be no forgiveness for them, no sloughing off of their sins.

Even as he pronounced the words of absolution, Father Devoy was acutely aware of his own damned soul. How could he pretend that he regretted what he did, yet still go out under the cloak of night and do it again? Here was the very basis of the sacrament of Penance, the thing non-Catholics did not understand. You didn't just confess and wipe the slate clean, you had to be genuinely sorry for what you had done, genuinely resolved not to do it again.

So when his parishioners had gone away and he had shut up the church for the night, Father John prayed in front of the high altar, by the single dim red light that was kept burning always before the Blessed Sacrament in the Tabernacle. Yet even as he prayed for the grace of repentance and the strength to resist temptation, he could not be certain that he wanted his prayers to be answered.

He put on grey slacks and a roll-necked sweater and combed his hair, studiously avoiding meeting his own eyes in the mirror. He went across to the youth club, played a vigorous game of table tennis with a boy who had been an altar boy with him for years, made his usual good-natured fool of himself when he was called to make up a game at the dartboard.

At least he never felt any stirrings of desire towards these boys, he thought. The Church would get no scandal from him there. Nothing queer about Devoy, as they used to say in the seminary. There'd been some odd buggers there, when he thought back on it. Most of them hadn't lasted the course, but some of them were priests now, and God alone knew what problems they would be causing.

Well, there would never be any sexual abuse of minors from Father John. Even the girls were safe from that. Father John took his filthy urges off elsewhere, didn't he? Took them where they could affect only those who were already strangers to God's grace.

There was dancing in the youth club now; it was time for Father John to go.

He went to the caretaker's room and picked up the dark blue anorak which someone had left behind in the club a year or more ago. It was a little too big for him. He was not even conscious of putting it on. But when he found its familiar looseness about his shoulders, he knew what he was going to do.

There were low clouds scudding across the sky. There was no moon and only the occasional, fleeting star. It seemed a good night to him; there wouldn't be many innocent people abroad tonight. Just Satan's priest and the women of the Devil.

Father John thrust his hands deep into the pockets of the anorak, pulled up the collar, sunk his head like a tortoise deeper into his shell.

'Looking for a bit of fun, love?'

He was startled by the words. He had been marching along with his eyes still on the ground, only dimly aware that he was entering the area where these women operated.

And Toyah Burgess was glad as she looked into the startled face to see a man who did not look like a killer. She was nervous despite herself, after what had happened to that girl last week. The rumour was that she'd been trying her hand at this game, without a pimp to give her his dubious protection.

The man responded in a voice that was absurdly polite, 'I wouldn't mind a bit of fun, no. So long as it isn't too expensive.'

You were supposed to be curt with the tightwads, to tell them that prices were not negotiable, that if they didn't want to pay for the goods that they could piss off and wank. But this one seemed nice. There was a gentleness about him that she didn't see in many of the men who paid for her services.

So Toyah said, 'You'll get value for money, love. That's what counts, isn't it?' She wrested his hand from his pocket and placed it against her breast, feeling it tremble violently as she held it there. Fear? Excitement? Christ, there weren't too many who were excited by the touch of a tit nowadays! Which was a pity, because it meant that girls like her had to work harder.

He looked into her face as she moved his hand up and down against her cleavage. 'You're beautiful!' he said. 'And so young.' He stooped and buried his face suddenly and without warning between her breasts.

It was curiously innocent. These were the same words Toyah got from lots of her clients, but spoken as if they were a surprise to the speaker, not practised and feeble chat-up phrases. Most men thought there was no need for chat-up with a whore, anyway. Toyah hadn't seen this kind of fearful and tremulous excitement since she had had her first boyfriend at fourteen.

And guilt. She met that often enough of course, when a frigid or hostile wife had been left at home. Perhaps this man had a wife like that. He was about the right age, older than she had thought at first, with an open face and desperate blue eyes. Quite attractive, really, in an arrested sort of way. Somehow she couldn't see a wife spurning this man.

She took a firm grip on his hand, lowered it to her side and kept hold of it as she moved him into a walk. He seemed grateful for that; it was as if he wished them to be seen as an ordinary pair of lovers. 'Do you have a car?' she said.

'No. I'm on foot. Does it matter?' It hadn't ever mattered before.

'No, of course it doesn't. If you've got the money, that is.'

He nodded, seeming suddenly afraid to speak.

'It's not far,' she said, and led him swiftly away into the side road and towards her bed-sit.

He kept glancing right and left as they moved over stone flags which glistened with moisture from the showers earlier in the evening. So he was scared of being spotted. Well, she was used enough to that in her clients. He said again, 'You're very young,' almost as though it were an accusation.

'I'm nineteen,' Toyah whispered into his ear. 'Quite old enough to give you a good time!' Usually she added a couple of years, but for some reason she wanted to be honest with this one. She wasn't much good at ages, but he must be over forty. Yet he seemed to her absurdly young in some respects. He made her feel that it was she who was in charge of the situation.

He had the money ready as soon as she had shut the door into the bed-sit. He brought it tumbling from his trouser pocket without being asked for it: one tenner and seven fives, with the last five in coins. He was like a child emptying his money box, tremulous with excitement for something for which he had been saving for a long time.

He turned his back whilst she stripped. That made her feel quite odd. Most men took the stripping as part of what they had paid for. She took his hand and ran the back of it against her naked side, then took his fingers round to the curves of her firm buttocks. Toyah was proud of her bottom, though no one had called it that since her mother many years ago. Somehow this man reminded her of those years, which she had not thought about in many months.

His hand shuddered when it touched her naked flesh. He said again, 'You're very young!' in a breathy, uneven voice, and she feared suddenly that she might have to lead him on, that he might even be impotent.

She eased her body against his, and they fell on the bed together with giggles of release. He seemed still reluctant to move, so she eased himself on top of him. 'Stroke my arse for me!' she said into his ear. Most men liked to call it that, and when the word and the command came from her it usually excited them.

He certainly wasn't impotent. He was rough once he started. Straightforward, but rough, carried forward by his passionate urge as his inhibitions dropped away. It was swift, concentrated, violent. It left both of them panting for breath.

He didn't move afterwards but remained clinging to her, his face buried in the softness of her breasts. It was not until she eased herself gently away that she was even sure that he was awake. Sometimes men dozed off afterwards, when they had spent themselves inside you, and not all of them took it well when you had to wake them and send them out into the winter night.

He didn't ask whether it had been good for her, thank goodness. Some of the less experienced men did that, as if it had been a normal, voluntary coupling. And this one, for all that he was in his forties and should have known more about life than her at nineteen, seemed curiously inexperienced, so that Toyah expected naïve questions from him. She would be kind if he asked them: he had been a good if rather disturbing customer.

But he didn't ask her anything. Indeed, once it was over, he never looked at her again. He dressed quickly, with his eyes on the ground, zipping his anorak to the neck and pulling its collar high about his face, even in a room now made oppressively warm by the gas fire. Toyah Burgess repeated the light-hearted formula she gave to all satisfactory clients: 'Glad to see you again whenever you fancy it, sir. Come up and see me some time!'

She usually struck her Mae West pose against the corner of the bed on that line, jutting her hip appreciatively towards the customer. But it would have been useless with this one. He didn't acknowledge that she had spoken, didn't even look at her. His eyes remained steadily on the fraying carpet as he dressed. He did not even look into the mirror to take away an oblique remembrance of her.

She saw him to the door of the house, muttered a ritual 'Take care, then!' But he disappeared without a backward glance into the darkness. A queer fish, that one, for all his boyish ways. A strange mixture of tenderness and something very like danger. Toyah Burgess shivered a little as she shut the door upon the night.

Her customer did not check his stride nor lift his eyes from the glistening flagstones until he was back in the presbytery behind the church. He went straight to his room and sat on the edge of the bed with his face in his hands. He was safely back in the place where he was Father John Devoy, respected priest and counsellor.

But he felt like Jekyll and Hyde.

Jekyll wanted to go out and save the sinner. And Hyde wanted to go out and punish the girl who was beyond redemption. Hyde wanted to get rid of that Jezebel before she led further men astray.

Hyde wanted to kill the woman who had sold herself to him.

Eleven

Percy Peach wasn't used to seeing Superintendent Tucker on a Saturday morning. But you had to prepare yourself for anything in the modern police service. Even the most unpleasant surprises had to be taken in your stride.

'Thought it would help to keep the team up to the mark if they saw me slaving away over the weekend,' said Tucker cheerfully.

Peach didn't think Tommy Bloody Tucker had ever slaved away over a weekend. Not at work, certainly: he couldn't be sure about what lengths Brünnhilde Barbara Tucker had driven him to in bedroom and kitchen. He said enigmatically, 'I'm sure the officers working ten-hour days will be impressed, sir.'

'Of course, I won't be here tomorrow. I've been selected for an important match at my golf club, actually. We're taking on the North Lancs. But we're playing at home, so I've every hope of success.'

So that was why he was here. To boast about his golf. Ill-advised, that, when you were as bad at the game as Tommy Tucker. Percy said, 'Congratulations, sir. The first team, is it?'

'Oh no, nothing like that. It's the social team – the C team, I think they call it. We play off handicaps. I don't approve of all this cut-throat competitive stuff. I play the game for enjoyment.'

Which is shorthand for saying you're a bloody awful golfer who would never even be considered for any serious golf team, thought Percy. 'I see, sir. What handicap would you be playing off, nowadays?'

'Oh, I think I'm around twenty. I haven't played in

many serious competitions whilst you were away.' Having introduced the subject of golf to allow himself a modest bit of boasting, Tucker now wished he could get away from the game. But invention deserted him and he said lamely, 'Still playing at the North Lancs, are you, Percy?'

'When I can get the time I am, yes, sir.' The North Lancashire Golf Club had the best course in the area and was the one most golfers wanted to join. It was a source of great satisfaction to Peach and of intense irritation to Tucker that Percy had been accepted for membership there when he had only been playing for a couple of years, whereas Tucker's reputation as a golfing hacker meant that he had been repeatedly turned down.

Tucker sought desperately for something insulting to say. The best he could come up with was, 'Got an official handicap, have you? It's a tough course, the North Lancs.'

'Yes, sir. I'm still nine there. Hope to get it down next season, if the crime figures allow it.'

Tucker knew that he would never get down to a nine handicap, even if he were able to practise all day and every day. He said fretfully, 'Speaking of which, you still don't seem to be anywhere near an arrest in this Sarah Dunne case.'

'That's right, sir. A masterly summing-up, if I might say so. Shows your usual grasp of the whole picture, your usual understanding of the difficulties of a particular case.'

'Well, it's not good enough, is it? I expected better than this when I promoted you to DCI, you know.'

So he was claiming the promotion was all his own work now. Peach wondered how best to send Tucker away disturbed for the rest of his weekend. He said mysteriously, 'We do have certain leads, sir.'

'Ah! At last! This is more like it.'

'One of them's a copper, sir.' Peach dropped his bombshell with an expertise bred from much practice.

'A policeman?' Tucker's jaw dropped most appealingly. 'One of our men's going around the town killing whores?'

The word sounded curiously old-fashioned, coming from Tucker. 'He's not a local, sir. One of the boys in blue from

Blackpool, sir. Inspector, as a matter of fact. Forty-eight years old. Probably hoping to make Superintendent, before he retires. I haven't been able to check whether he's a Mason or not, yet.'

Tucker elected to ignore the Masonic slur, deciding that as this year's Master of his local lodge he should be above such petty snipings. 'We've enough on our plate, without a senior policeman killing whores.' The Superintendent looked at Peach as if he suspected him of arranging this situation especially to upset him. 'Have you arrested him?'

'No, sir. He's just one suspect among several. We're checking on commercial travellers and the like as well, to see if there's a possible connection with killings in the Midlands. And there are one or two local possibilities who need following up. But I shall be seeing Inspector Boyd myself this afternoon. We shall see what he has to say for himself.'

Tucker looked very anxious. 'Go easy, Peach. You're treading on the toes of another force, here.'

'I'll be my normal diplomatic self, sir,' Peach smiled.

The assurance did not fill Tucker with confidence.

Peach went back to his office and made a swift phone call to the Secretary of the North Lancashire Golf Club. 'Good morning, David. The C team match against Brunton Golf Club tomorrow. I suppose you have a full team of players?'

'We had,' said the Secretary gloomily. 'But Joe Briggs has just rung in to say he's got flu. And Brunton's not the most popular of the courses we play. You don't know of anyone who might—'

'Look no further, David. I'll be delighted to play myself!'

A man was entitled to a little innocent pleasure, even in the midst of a murder inquiry.

Tom Boyd was doing the autumn tidy-up in his garden when they arrived.

He lived in Poulton-le-Fylde, a few miles inland from Blackpool and the coast, where the land was protected from the worst of the coast's salt-laden gales. Poulton was the nearest place to the coast where trees would grow properly, the locals said, and Boyd, like many policemen, enjoyed his gardening.

He was stacking the dead top growth of phlox and peonies into his wheelbarrow, when a voice over the low wall of his garden said, 'Burn well, that will, when you get the bonfire going.' He recognized Peach as a copper immediately, as much by his bearing as his appearance. He was less sure about the pretty young woman with the red-brown hair at his side, until she was introduced to him as Detective Sergeant Blake.

Boyd thought of saying that things had looked up since his days as a young constable, but decided that even compliments might be interpreted as sexist: you couldn't be too careful, these days. So he merely said heavily, 'I was expecting a visit from CID. You'd better come into the house.'

He was ten years older than Peach, twenty years older than the watchful young woman beside him, but he knew that the age differential would afford him no privileges in this situation. He had the kettle ready and the biscuit tin beside it, but they refused tea. They sat in his neat, rather sterile lounge, which had so much less of him in it than the garden outside. He looked not at them but out through the window, at the greenhouse he had just filled with chrysanthemums in bud, as he said, 'I'm embarrassed by this, but no more than that. I've been foolish, but I haven't done anything criminal.'

'Remains to be seen, Inspector Boyd.' Peach dismissed the sympathy he felt for a lonely fellow-officer and summoned his normal acerbic tone: this man was a policeman, but he might also be a murderer. Guilty until proved innocent was the watchword here. 'Kerb-crawling in search of sex. That's an offence to start with. Before you've started, as you might say.'

Boyd looked at him sharply. 'I'm from the firm, Peach. Surely that should count for something!'

'Already has done. You know better than most that we could have held you in Brunton nick for twenty-four hours. Thirty-six, with a superintendent's say-so. We could have grilled you there, yesterday. Instead of which, we've driven thirty miles on a Saturday afternoon to see you in your own house.'

'All I was doing was paying for my sexual pleasures. I was quite frank about that. Surely my honesty and my rank in the service should mean something.'

'Could do, perhaps, with lesser crimes. But not when someone's committed murder. Was it you, Inspector Boyd?'

'No, of course it wasn't.'

'Then convince us of that, and we'll go away and leave you in peace.'

Tom Boyd glanced automatically at the young woman beside Peach. He had long since learned to accept women in the police service, working beside him, sometimes even giving him instructions. Yet his acceptance had not run as deep as he thought it had: in this crisis, he did not relish saying the things he would have to say in front of DS Blake.

He was powerful and broad-shouldered, with hair slicked back on either side of a parting which was nearly central: he looked like a footballer on one of the cigarette cards of the nineteen thirties. He said to Lucy, 'You're the same age as my daughter, love. It's not easy for me to talk about this.'

'You don't have a choice, Inspector Boyd.' Peach's words cut like a whiplash across the man's plea.

Boyd looked at him with a face full of fury, so that they glimpsed for a moment a man with the possibility of murder within him. Then his square face resumed its mask and he said, 'All right. I live on my own. I'm divorced. It's par for the course, in the police. You should know that.'

'I'm divorced myself,' said Peach quietly.

'Well then. I'm forty-eight, not seventy-eight. I still have urges. Still need to satisfy them.' He gave an instinctive nervous look at Lucy Blake's face, but her blue-green eyes were on her notebook, her face studiously impassive.

'So you come and indulge them in Brunton.' Peach's black eyes had never left his subject.

'Where I'm off my own patch. Where I'm not shitting on my own doorstep.'

'Where a girl was murdered a week earlier. Where as a copper you should have known you'd be asking for trouble.'

Boyd's lips set in a thin line beneath the broad nose. 'I didn't kill anyone.'

'Convince us of that, and we're on our way. We've got better things to do on a Saturday afternoon, like you.'

Tom Boyd allowed himself a thin smile. 'I've nothing really to add to what I said last night in Brunton. My first inclination was to get well away from Blackpool. Preston was too near. The first place where I felt comfortable was Brunton. I drove out there, had a drink in a pub to bolster my nerve – I'm not as used to picking up tarts as you might think.'

'Where?'

'Mellor. The Miller's Arms.'

'Time?'

'I wasn't checking that. It must have been nearly half past nine by the time I got there. I didn't stay long in the pub. There were two blokes at the bar talking about the murder of that call-girl the week before. They might or might not remember me: I didn't speak to them.'

'It's not important at this stage. What time did you start cruising?'

Boyd noticed the use of the offensive word, but did not pick up on it. He knew that if you lost your rag it made you more vulnerable. 'I told you, I wasn't checking the time, it wasn't important to me. I picked a girl up in Brunton at about ten, I should think.'

'Why Brunton?'

'I told you, it was the nearest place where—'

'Come off it, Inspector Boyd. You're a copper, a man who knows his way around well enough to have made Inspector. You know the ropes well enough not to go whoring in a town where a pro's been murdered seven days earlier!'

'Why shouldn't I?'

'Because there was a very good chance of landing yourself in the situation you're in now. A very good chance of being caught with your trousers down and dragged into a murder inquiry.'

'I – I suppose I should have been more careful, yes. I just didn't think this would happen. I took a chance and—'

'No, Inspector Boyd! You're not a chance-taker, are you?

Your whole career, your progress to date, is evidence of that.'

'All right, Peach! We're not all the kind of chancers who make DCI in the CID. Some of us play life a bit more carefully.'

He had allowed himself to be angered after all, and it wasn't doing his case any good. Peach looked at him steadily, without the animosity the man had shown to him. 'You weren't just picking up a tart and paying for it, as you've said so far. You were looking for a particular girl, weren't you?'

Tom Boyd looked for a moment as if he would deny it. Then he said sullenly, 'So what if I was? If you find a girl you like and go back to her, it makes it a bit more personal, doesn't it?' He glanced into Lucy Blake's unlined face and said bitterly, 'A bit more like the real thing, see?'

'So you admit that when you were kerb-crawling, you were looking for a particular girl? That the reason you took the risk of going back to Brunton was to seek out a particular hooker?'

'All right, yes! Since you seem to know so bloody much about it, yes! I'd seen the girl before. Paid her for sex. Liked what I got. Thought it would be nice to repeat the experience. That's all.'

Peach regarded him steadily as his breathing came in uneven gasps. Tom Boyd had conducted plenty of interviews, even though he was not CID. But he could not remember when he had last been interviewed himself, and he felt unexpectedly helpless in the situation.

Peach looked at him as if he was a fish floundering on a river bank, studying his increasing discomfort with a disconcerting objectivity. Then he said quietly, 'She gave special services, this particular girl, didn't she, Tom? That's why you were so anxious to find her.'

Boyd was still trying to steady his breathing, feeling that if he could get that back to normal, his brain would work better. He knew he must be careful. For all he knew, these people had already talked to the girl, had received a full account of everything they had done last night. He said, 'You don't know what it's like being on your own. When you get a girl you like, you go back, even though you're paying for it. You feel better in yourself about going to one you know than going to anyone who will take your money, working your way through a whole succession of girls.'

He looked pathetically at Lucy Blake, as if he might get more sympathy from her, as if she might understand that this was a little less dishonourable, that even among prostitutes you could be less promiscuous if you chose to be.

She smiled at him. She wanted to use his first name, to use her softness to draw from him things which he might deny to Peach's harsh approach. But the training of rank was hard to dismiss: even here she could not bring herself to address an inspector by his first name. She said, 'What was it that Katie Clegg offered that made you go back to her, Inspector Boyd?'

They knew the girl's name then. Ten to one they'd had her in and got every detail of what they'd done last night out of her. Bloody CID! They wouldn't pull any punches when they saw a uniformed officer from another force in trouble. He muttered, 'I didn't even know her name. She did a few extras, that's all.'

Peach, sensing that his resistance was ended, spoke quietly now. 'What sort of extras, Tom?'

'Nothing much. Nothing very unusual, for these days. An extra ten quids' worth, a bit of fun for me and a nice little bonus for her.'

'So tell us what you paid the extra for.'

Boyd made a last desperate plea. 'Look, there's no need to humiliate me like this, is there? What do you want, Peach? A cheap thrill in front of a pretty sergeant, is it? Is that what you get off on, the fantasies some poor old bugger has to pay to indulge? Is that—'

'Inspector Boyd, this is a murder inquiry! Until we learn something different, you are a suspect in that inquiry. You know the score as well as anyone. Now, answer the question please, or we shall have to record the fact that you refused.'

Boyd looked at Peach's round face, at his unsmiling mouth and the relentless dark eyes which would not leave him. Then his big shoulders gave a hopeless shrug and he said in an even voice, 'It was no great deal. Not nowadays. I find I enjoy a bit of bondage as I get older, that's all. She got out the fetters and the handcuffs: I can't be the only one, can I, or she wouldn't have them so handy?'

'And you enjoyed a bit of violence to go with it.' Peach made it a statement, not a question, this time.

'God, you want your pound of flesh, don't you? Well, believe it or not, I can't recall it very clearly. I got my rocks off, which is what I'd gone there for, and the preliminaries got me pretty excited. We got a bit aggressive with each other as I came towards orgasm, even knocked each other about a bit, I suppose. Is that what she told you?'

Peach smiled. 'You know the system too well to expect an answer to that, Inspector Boyd. You also know that in the light of the murder of a prostitute a week earlier, we are going to have special interest in anyone who admits getting off on violent sex with a lady of the streets.'

Boyd nodded slowly. 'All the same, you're barking up the wrong tree here. I'm not your man.'

'Where were you on the night of Friday the fourteenth of November?'

The tough, squat-featured man glanced from one to the other with something like panic in his eyes. 'I was at home. I didn't go out on that night.'

They noted that the answer had been ready, that he hadn't needed to think much about it. Lucy Blake, making a note of his reply, said softly, without looking up, 'And were you alone?'

'Yes. I finished duty at the Blackpool nick, had a pint with another officer in the pub near the station, and went home. I was at home from six thirty onwards.'

Peach and Boyd eyed each other steadily whilst the implications of this hung heavily between them. Then Peach said, 'Is there anyone who could vouch for your whereabouts on that night?'

'No.' The reply came almost too promptly.

'You didn't make or receive any phone calls during the evening?'

'I'd have told you if I had done. There's no one who can vouch for the fact that I was sitting quietly in my own house on the night when that girl was killed. And unlike most criminals, I don't have a wife who will conveniently swear to anything her man requires.'

They were policemen together for a moment as he said that, smiling sourly at the petty thief's traditional alibi. But this was not petty thieving.

Boyd took them to the door of the clean, characterless house whose garden said so much more about the occupant than the interior. He made a last attempt to reassure himself as they left. 'We both know I didn't kill that girl on the fourteenth, Inspector Peach.'

Peach turned to look into the square face beneath the straight, slicked-back hair. 'We both *hope* you didn't: you more than me. But we haven't got anyone lined up for this, so you know the score as well as I do. You remain in the frame, Inspector Boyd. If you think of anything which might take you out of it, ring Brunton CID immediately and ask for me.'

Twelve

Saturday night was quiet in the murder room. The week's information had been logged on to the computers, cross-referenced in accordance with the latest practices. Local prostitutes had been interviewed about their clients. The clients themselves were varied but anonymous, but were in many cases being quizzed about their activities. Tom Boyd wasn't the only man to be asked to account for his movements on the night of the fourteenth of November.

But the few officers who were working on the night of Saturday the twenty-second of November were out on the streets of Brunton. Apart from DC Gordon Pickering, who was alone in the murder room, manning the phones and trying hard to feel like the man in temporary charge of things.

It was ten thirty when the significant phone call came in. Gordon was listening to the sound of the first aggressive drunks of the night being cautioned and put in the cells. It was curious how sound penetrated quite thick walls when all else was quiet in the building.

The voice on the phone sounded a little slurred, as if it too might have been drinking. It said, 'You haven't caught the man who killed Sarah Dunne yet.'

It was a statement, not a question, and it banished abruptly the yawn which DC Pickering had just embarked upon. He put his hand over the mouthpiece and pressed the buzzer which would tell the switchboard that this call should be traced. He felt a tingle in the short hairs at the back of his head: for the first time in his life he might be talking on the phone to a murderer. As calmly as he could, Gordon said, 'Who's speaking, please?'

A laugh at the other end of the line. Probably not near to

the mouthpiece: it sounded distant, almost as if it came from another room. 'That would be telling, wouldn't it? Who am I addressing?'

'This is DC Pickering. What is it you have to report, please?'

'Nothing to report. Just checking on what *you* have to report, actually. Which seems to be practically nothing.'

'Give me your name, please.'

Again that distant, sardonic laugh. 'Is Superintendent Tucker there?'

'No. I'm the only CID officer in the station at present. What is it you have to tell me?' Pickering was trying desperately to place the accent. He'd thought at first that it might be Liverpool, but this was no Scouser. Gordon wasn't good at accents; it had never mattered until now.

'I wanted to speak to the organ grinder, not the monkey. Well, never mind. Just you tell your Superintendent Tucker that he won't catch this murderer.'

Pickering had the accent now. It was Birmingham, or Black Country: he didn't know enough to distinguish between the two; wasn't even sure in fact that there was a distinction.

He found himself striving to keep his voice steady as the hairs crept anew on the back of his neck. He'd never met this situation before, never even envisaged meeting it. The secret was to keep the voice talking on the phone until the call could be traced, until you could send a squad car screaming to the scene. Or preferably not screaming: such advance notice of arrival should be confined to television series. 'I'm in charge here tonight. I'm empowered to record whatever it is you have to tell us. It will be passed on to Superintendent Tucker and everyone else involved in the case. Please start with your name.'

'In your dreams, lad. Tell your boss I just wanted to make sure the filth were as baffled by this one as by my previous two in this neck of the woods. Good night, son.'

'Please keep talking, sir. I may be able to—'

To what? Gordon Pickering wondered. But it didn't matter now, for the phone was dead. He was still staring at the receiver in his hand when the switchboard came through

103

with the information that the call had come from a public phone booth in the centre of Birmingham.

Percy Peach was strictly off duty at the moment when Gordon Pickering was taking his call from Birmingham. Even his mobile phone was off duty; it lay on the chest of drawers with its battery switched off.

Lucy Blake looked into the full-length mirror in the wardrobe and saw the lubricious look she had feared lighting up the round features which had terrified so many villains. She said, 'I think you're a secret knicker fetishist.'

'Wrong!' said Percy Peach cheerfully. 'I've never made a secret of it.'

Lucy measured the distance to the bed with her eye, making sure that she was just out of his reach. He might be reclining on one elbow in his bed like a Roman emperor, but she knew from experience that those powerful arms of his were unexpectedly long, when lust drove them on. Almost telescopic, at times.

The emerald green pants and bra had seemed a good idea, in the bright fluorescent lights of the shop. 'Always buy something which would shock your mum!' the shopgirl had advised, and they had enjoyed a giggle together about the thought. But here in Percy Peach's bedroom the colour seemed to deepen and grow richer; that was all right of itself, but when applied to these garments perhaps it was tarty. The low moan from behind her as she stepped out of her slip did nothing to reassure her.

'I've told you before, you make me self-conscious, ogling me like that,' she complained.

'You should be conscious, not self-conscious,' said Percy happily. 'I've always thought women should be fully conscious of the pleasure they're giving. It is better to give than to receive, they tell me. Never quite fathomed that idea myself, but I feel that I should report that you're giving me a great deal of pleasure at the moment. Very civilized pleasure, of course!' He allowed himself another moan, elongating it further than she would have thought possible without drawing a breath.

'You're no expert on civilization, Percy Peach!'

104

'Much overrated, civilization is. Gandhi said he thought Western civilization would be rather a good idea!'

'Not a good man for you to quote, Mahatma Gandhi. He believed in controlling his animal instincts where young women were concerned. And I seem to remember that he gave up sex at thirty-six.'

'More fool Mahatma! It just shows that even great men can have daft ideas for some of the time. Hurry up into bed, will you, or my animal instincts may get the better of me!'

Lucy whipped her bra off and deposited it over the back of the chair above the rest of her clothes, provoking a roar of delight from the bed and a shout of 'Come and test my Bristol Rovers!'

She paused for a moment in front of the mirror, studying her breasts, keeping her rounded derrière carefully just out of the range of those dangerous arms, enjoying the rare feeling of being in control of DCI Peach. 'There's no knowing where you could go, Percy Peach, if you concentrated on everything in life as intensely as you concentrate on knickers.'

'Knickers are easy for concentration. They're small, you see, and that helps. And of course their contents are totally delicious. Focus the mind beautifully, your drawers do, Lucy Blake!'

Deciding that attack was the best and perhaps the only form of defence, she turned and leapt suddenly upon him in the bed.

The tactic was successful, up to a point. He wasn't as good at removing knickers as at fantasizing about them. At least the attempt stopped him talking for a while, thought Lucy: she eventually had to provide him with assistance, to prevent her expensive lingerie being damaged by his incompetence.

Percy's telescopic arm eventually emerged from beneath the sheets to turn off the light at the bedside switch. 'It's my Catholic breeding,' he explained. 'Even rude thoughts were only allowed in the dark.'

He disappeared comprehensively beneath the bedclothes and a muffled 'Bloody 'ell, Norah!' was his only verbal outburst during the next few minutes.

After a period of frenzied activity in which she lost all

sense of time, Lucy said in tones of exhausted admiration, 'It takes a lot to shut you up, Percy Peach!'

'And a lot is what you've got, Lucy Blake.' The reply came promptly through the warm darkness. And then, in drowsy but delighted recollection, 'I never knew that something so rounded and soft could become so muscular when the occasion demanded it.'

Lucy frowned a little, then decided not to ask him to be more specific. After all, Percy had probably intended it as a compliment.

Thirteen

D avid Strachan made a desultory attempt at Sunday morning sex with his wife. There was no answering caress when he rolled against the sinewy back and put his arm round her, so he desisted quickly. Sod her! She needn't think that what she had to offer was so bloody marvellous. Unresponsive cow!

He didn't say any of these things, of course. Instead, he rolled on his back, stared at the grubby woodchip paper on the ceiling, and remembered the woman he had enjoyed in Brunton. He now thought of her as Miss Whiplash, and her ample curves represented a new excitement in his drab life. Miss Whiplash wouldn't turn him down on a Sunday morning! Miss Whiplash understood what a man needed after a week in a taxing and demeaning job.

He heard the heavy crash of the Sunday papers on the mat downstairs and eased himself out of bed. 'I'll bring you a cup of tea up, Eileen,' he said, his animosity already subsumed in his dreams of the blonde woman in Brunton. That was how mature women should look! There was no reason why a few extra years should necessarily diminish a woman's attractions. Eileen! He should have known what to expect of a woman with a name like that: the name had already been a generation out of date when he had met her in the supposedly permissive seventies.

He put the kettle on and scanned quickly through the pages of the *News of the World* and the *People*. There didn't seem to be anything very new about the murder of the girl in Brunton nine days ago. They said it was now clear that the girl had been a prostitute, but that had been obvious long ago. There couldn't be any fresh news: they liked what they termed 'call-girl killings', these papers, and they'd certainly have fastened on any new details of the hunt.

He knew he shouldn't really go back to Brunton, not yet. But Miss Whiplash was awfully tempting; in the hothouse of his imagination, Sally Aspin's curves grew more ample, her strutting more stately and arrogant, and her dominance more satisfying. And his own retributory violence became more extreme.

And he knew he was due to make a call at a textiles warehouse in Preston on Tuesday. And Preston was only ten miles from Brunton . . .

He heard the toilet flush upstairs as he poured the tea. Eileen was waiting expectantly in bed when he took the tray into the bedroom, lean, frumpish, her hair straggling untidily across her head, the sheets drawn up tight over her non-existent bosom. He forced himself to say cheerfully, 'I brought the papers up for you, Eileen. If you want to have a bit of a lie-in, I'll make some toast and you can have your breakfast in bed.'

She looked at him steadily from watery eyes that were the colour of slate. Her mouth continued to droop disapprovingly at the corners. 'Up to something, are you, David?' she said. Then she turned her attention to the papers, not expecting any reply from him.

Sometimes David thought he hated all women. The young ones were the worst: you caught them sniggering behind your back sometimes, in the office. And he was pretty sure that on occasions he glimpsed the same contempt among the receptionists and the secretaries at the firms he had to visit. He couldn't see anything funny in the work he did, the things he had to say when he was trying to get orders. But they did.

And always the young ones, the ones with smooth skins and bright eyes and curvy, supple figures seemed to be the worst. Sometimes David Strachan longed to show them who was really the boss.

He made the toast and another pot of tea, moving very deliberately, because his thoughts were elsewhere. He ate his first piece of toast very slowly, his jaws masticating regularly as his mind dealt with other things.

By the time he had drunk his tea, David Strachan's mind was made up. He listened for a moment to his wife moving about in the bedroom above his head. He went out and looked at the grey sky above the drab grey lawn behind the house, sniffing the damp cold of late November. There was still no one about at this early Sunday hour.

He went out to the garage and put the piece of rope into the boot of his car.

Superintendent Thomas Bulstrode Tucker was partnering the Captain of his golf club. The Captain was a pleasant chap, who thought it was part of his duties in his year as Captain to play with as wide a cross-section of his members as possible. Such altruism should be rewarded.

Perhaps it is, in heaven. But on the afternoon of Sunday, the twenty-third of November, the Captain was very much on this earth. And his charity was to be very much unrewarded.

On a mild afternoon beneath a pale yellow sun, Tucker's first and greatest shock came as he walked around the side of the clubhouse to the first tee. Two figures detached themselves from the crowd on the practice putting green and came over to greet them by the side of the first tee: obviously the men who were to be their opponents in this four-ball match. The first of these was a lithe young man whose practice swings as he waited to tee off looked ominously smooth.

The second was Percy Peach. He wore smart new maroon golfing trousers, a cap to cover his bald dome, and a smile which seemed to stretch from ear to ear across his round face. 'Good afternoon, sir. It was nice for me to get into our team as a late reserve. Now it's even nicer to find that the luck of the draw has paired me with my respected chief.'

Tucker was quite certain that there was no luck of the draw in this situation, that Peach had engineered the pairings so that he should play against him. The Chief Superintendent licked his lips, introduced the Captain to Percy and his companion, and said, as affably as he could through clenched teeth, 'You must call me Thomas on the golf course, just as I shall call you Percy.'

'Excellent, Thomas. And may the best team win!' Percy was all easy bonhomie, even as Tucker felt his muscles tensing up.

It emerged that Percy's fit young partner played off six handicap, whilst the Captain and Percy were both nine. Tucker had to admit to a handicap of twenty-four. He stared hard at the sky when he had done so, knowing that he had told Peach that he was 'about twenty', not willing to look into that face, which he knew would be so full of childish delight.

The Captain said to Tucker, 'You'll be getting shots on fourteen holes, Tom, and on your own course as well!'

'Looks as if the match will hinge on those shots,' said Peach, shaking his head sadly. 'I can't see us being able to compete, but we'll do our very best to give you some sort of game.'

The blood pounded already in Tucker's temples as he went to the first tee.

It is not kind to dwell upon human suffering. Thomas Bulstrode Tucker spent an afternoon stretched upon the golfing rack, which is better not described in detail. Had the Captain not played valiantly, the match would have been all over after eleven or twelve holes.

'I haven't been as bad as this for ages,' said Tucker desperately as he sliced the ball into the woods for the fifth time.

So the bugger has played before, thought the Captain. He summoned a wan smile and said, 'Don't worry about it, Tom. Everyone has bad days.'

Meanwhile Percy and his taciturn young companion played briskly and competently, and went further and further ahead in the match. Peach had selected the most affable of his many smiles; it broadened each time he addressed Tucker, his sympathy ever more patronizing, his careful enunciation of the name Thomas becoming a caricature of urbane politeness.

Matters came to a head on the fourteenth, when Tucker, aiming a savage and desperate mow at his ball on the tee, scythed it high and right. 'Where did that one go?' he said hopelessly.

'It's all right, Thomas, I've got it marked. It's on very nearly the same line as my ball, I think.'

The Captain and Peach's partner had each hit their balls down the left, so Peach bustled cheerfully towards his ball on the other side of the fairway. Tucker, plodding hopelessly after him with his electric trolley, arrived to find his tormentor gazing glumly at a ball which was only just visible. 'Do you think it might be plugged?' he said.

Tucker's spirits rose. Here was a chance to get some of his own back, especially with the other two players well away to their left and out of earshot. In the rules of golf, if not in the playing of the game, he was an expert. He affected to study the ball. 'It's just lying well down in the grass, Percy. It's certainly not plugged,' he said truculently.

'No.' Percy looked at the ball and shook his head in sad agreement. 'But under the winter rules, one is allowed to move it six inches on the fairway, surely?'

For the first time in two and a half hours, Tucker began to enjoy himself. He stood behind the ball and looked towards the green, pretending to study the line left by the greenkeeper's mowers. 'I'm afraid this ball isn't on the fairway, Percy. Look, you can see the line of the cut grass. This ball is a good foot off the shortly mown area.' He tried hard to look sad, but that proved beyond him.

Percy nodded his acceptance. Then his face brightened for the third and last time as he stooped nearer to the ball. 'But look, aren't these rabbit droppings around it, Thomas? No wonder the ball's lying so badly – it's in a rabbit scrape. This must be a hole made by a burrowing animal, which would allow a free drop.'

Tucker crouched low over the ball. He knew what he was going to say, but he wanted it to make maximum impact. This loathsome little bouncing ball of golfing exuberance could be put in his place, at last. 'I'm sorry, but this isn't a rabbit scrape, Percy. A few droppings aren't enough: I've studied the ball closely and there is no evidence that this indentation was made by a burrowing animal. I'm afraid there is no relief available.'

Peach studied the ball sadly for a last few seconds. 'I have to agree with you, I'm afraid, Thomas.'

He stood sadly and silently three yards from the troublesome ball, making no attempt at movement. The other two players in this little drama were watching the pantomime of debate from the other side of the fairway, unable to hear a word but growing increasingly impatient.

'Well, what are you waiting for?' said Tucker petulantly. 'The ball may be in an impossible position, but the sooner you make some attempt to play it, the sooner we can all get on with the game.'

'Oh, I can't possibly play it, Thomas,' said Percy happily.

Tucker said heavily, 'Then for God's sake pick it up, and let's get on with the game.'

'I can't do that either, Thomas. It's not my ball, you see. Mine's forty yards on, down there. This one's yours.'

Tucker spluttered. Peach found it a most appealing sound. Eventually, his chief hacked at the ball and moved it about two feet, amidst a hail of flying soil. Tucker was not normally a man given to invective, but he now hurled a horrible oath at the inoffensive ball and the gods of golf.

'Bad luck, Thomas!' said the voice of his tormentor behind him. When they eventually rejoined the other members of the match, Peach explained to the Captain, 'It was an impossible lie. I thought your partner was entitled to relief without penalty, but he sportingly refused to take it.'

The Captain muttered an unprintable phrase about his partner and stalked on to the green. A moment later, the partnership had lost five and four.

Thomas Bulstrode Tucker's discomfort was made complete in the speeches after the meal which followed the match. To a company grown jovial with ale and whisky, the Captain recounted in detail the incident of the ball on the fourteenth. Tucker had to force a sickly smile and keep it fixed upon his countenance for fully four minutes, right through the howls of laughter which greeted the denouement of the story.

Percy Peach's smile and hilarity were much more genuine.

*   *   *

There was no danger of frost. But it was now a dismal evening; a thin mist hung over the town and the long street glistened with moisture as far as she could see it. The mist made the girl nervous, conjuring up pictures of hansom cabs and Sherlock Holmes, and then, much worse, of Jack the Ripper.

Not much chance of that sort of thing in twenty-first century Brunton, she told herself, wishing she had not made herself so familiar with the details of the Ripper's crimes and the things he had practised upon the bodies of those long-dead women. Then a more relevant horror began to gnaw at her mind; she could not dismiss the thought that a girl not much younger than her had died a few streets from here nine days earlier.

A girl who, it now seemed, had been trying to do just what she was doing now. She'd read that in the paper today.

It wasn't her first time, but Jenny Pitt wasn't yet experienced enough to know the best times to sell her body. Sunday was a quiet night for tarts in Brunton, much quieter than Friday or Saturday. And she was out on the wet pavements too early: the typical patron needed to be primed with drink before he mustered the urge to spend his money on a woman of the streets.

Jenny hadn't realized it would be as cold as this. You couldn't walk briskly, when you were looking for this sort of trade; the last thing you wanted was to look as if you were actually going somewhere. Saunter like Mae West or Marilyn, the old hands had told her, it still works. Wiggle your bottom in a tight skirt – it might be obvious, but it still gets the men reaching for their money.

She'd seen pictures of Monroe, blonde and pouting, threatening a wiggle with every movement, but Mae West was just a name to this nineteen-year-old. She wondered as she strove to suppress her shivers whether either of these vamps had ever operated on a cold wet street in November, in a town tight with its money and drawing its curtains against the onset of winter.

She checked to make sure that the street was still deserted, then flapped her arms vigorously across her chest, trying to beat some warmth back into her slim young frame. You couldn't wear a proper winter coat, and these leather skirts, tight round your bum and slit well up the thigh, might be all right when you were indoors with central heating, but they were bloody cold when you were out on the bleak and deserted streets of industrial Lancashire.

Jenny Pitt was beginning to despair when she heard the car turn the corner behind her. Its powerful engine made very little noise; had she not been listening hard, she would scarcely have registered it. But it did not accelerate once it was on the straight stretch behind her, as she would have anticipated. Its engine note was no more than a tiny, persistent hum, moving slowly closer to her.

She resisted the temptation to look round. Not yet, she told herself. You must be like a fisherman luring trout; any sudden movement might scare your prey away. For the first time, with the fear of the unknown creeping cold and uninvited into her brain, she began to wonder who was the victim and who was the predator in this strange exchange.

Jenny moved to the very edge of the pavement, hitching her short coat a little beneath her elbows to reveal the full rounded contours of her bottom beneath the tightly stretched leather, taking a slightly longer stride to let the slit in her skirt ride higher still up her shapely thigh. Wiggle your bum now, girl, give it all you've got: there might not be another desperate lecher driving around tonight.

She forced herself not to look round until the car was almost beside her, until she sensed the near wing of the Jaguar opposite her waist. Then she turned and stopped, throwing her right hip out to the edge of the pavement, hitching the skirt almost to her crotch, looking half over her shoulder at the driver, giving him the wide, excited smile she had practised in front of the mirror, licking the full lips in anticipation of pleasures to come.

The electric window buzzed down beside her, within two feet of the hip she was proffering. A male voice from the darkness on the other side of the car said tersely, 'Get in!'

She hesitated, despite the number of times she had told herself that the successful temptress must never falter: if you showed any uncertainty, nervous clients would catch on to it and back off. She didn't like the sound of that voice; didn't like venturing into the warm cave of the car. Because this was someone else's cave, not hers. You should keep control, whenever you could.

Whenever you could: the phrase acknowledged that you weren't always in a position to dictate what happened, that this was, whatever precautions you chose to take, an uncertain and dangerous business. She slid into the passenger seat beside the voice, finding the leather of her skirt moved easily over the answering leather of the seat, finding that the warm cave smelt of cigars and of that strange, indefinable scent of a man in pursuit of sexual pleasure.

Was it testosterone? Could you smell that, or did you just sense that you could? Jenny Pitt took a breath and muttered what now sounded in her ears like a ritual phrase, 'Fancy a good fuck, do you, my love?'

She had practised that phrase too, in front of her mirror. All the experienced girls said the punters liked the good old four-letter words, that a 'fuck' or a 'quim' or a 'cunt' got them going, was a promise of high sexual jinks to come. And she'd put that 'my love' in herself, to make it more personal, trying to convince her clients that they weren't just paying for any girl, but getting personal service.

The voice beside her said, 'You're going to get yourself into trouble. Serious fucking trouble. Do you realize that, my girl?'

She hadn't looked directly at him: they didn't always like the challenge of a full-frontal inspection. Now she regretted that: his anonymity made him more fearsome. The car had lit up briefly when she'd opened the door to get in, and she could have taken advantage of that sudden brief illumination. She said nervously, 'I give good value. Blow jobs, bondage, all the usual stuff. Anything you want, within reason. And my prices are competitive.'

She wondered if her voice gave away how nervous she felt. She wanted to fling open the wide door of the Jaguar and flee for her life along those damp flagstones she had a minute ago been so glad to leave. But she had a sudden knowledge that she would never even get out of the low seat of the car, that a restraining arm would be flung across her the moment she attempted her first move.

As if he read her thoughts, the driver eased the car softly forward, and the glistening pavement slid away beside her. 'Competitive are they, your prices? Well, we know why that is, don't we?'

'Why?' She repeated the word stupidly, as if she were a wooden dummy, with the man beside her operating her jaws.

'No overheads, that's why.'

'Overheads?' He might have had his hand up to the back of her neck: the word came out as if she had not spoken it herself.

'Overheads. You must accept certain overheads, when you go on the game, my pet.'

She tried not to cringe at the word. 'If you mean—'

'I'll tell you exactly what I mean, shall I!' The voice came like machine-gun fire out of the darkness. 'If you're not to be in danger on the streets, you need certain protection.'

'Protection?'

'You need it, and it doesn't come cheap. But it's well worth having. I'd go so far as to say that you can't operate in this town, even in this part of Lancashire, without it.'

'I don't know—'

'You need to operate under an umbrella, to have the protection of a guardian angel, as you might say. It costs, but it makes life easier. Cuts down the opposition, you see.'

'How much?'

'Technically, you see, I'd have to see you as opposition, at the moment. And you wouldn't like what happens to opposition. But I won't go into that, I'll let you use your imagination.'

'But you can't stop me! You can't prevent people from sleeping with whomever they want to!' Jenny wanted to laugh at herself for getting her grammar right: in that moment, she realized how close she was to hysteria. 'If they want to charge money for it, that's their choice!'

A hand gloved in black leather took her wrist in a grip of steel. 'Don't be silly, pet! I took you for more intelligent than that. If you want to sell it in this town, you sell it under my umbrella. Anyone who doesn't gets what's coming to them. And believe me, it isn't nice.'

'I believe you. You mean what happened to that girl last week. That girl who was throttled. Sarah Dunne.' The name came leaping to her lips, when she hadn't even thought she knew it.

'I couldn't possibly comment, pet. But thank goodness you've got the message. I'd hate to see that pretty young face get damaged.'

'How much does it cost, this protection?'

'Fifty per cent, to start with. Maybe a little less than that, if you're a good girl and increase your turnover. If you'll pardon the expression!' A coarse laugh burst from the darkness into her right ear. 'On your way, and think about it. We'll be in contact: we know where you live. And don't let me find you flashing it around here again, until you've joined our happy band.'

Jenny Pitt wanted to argue, but she knew no words were going to come. And she wanted more than anything else to be away from this car, away from the streets, back in the close and claustrophobic warmth of her own small room. She caught a glimpse of squat, cruel features as she tumbled from the car and half-ran, half-stumbled away from it on her pathetic, ridiculous high heels.

The driver watched her disappear with the slowly broadening smile of a sadist. Shapely little arse, he thought, in the right hands. And the right hands would be his, before the year was out. He could have got somebody else to warn the girl off, but there were advantages in this hands-on management!

Joe Johnson pressed his foot softly on the accelerator and felt the power of the Jaguar thrust the seat against his back as he drove away.

Fourteen

T he man certainly looked like a murderer, thought Lucy Blake. Then she pulled herself up short. Murderers came in all shapes and sizes, and often in the most unlikely guises. It was unprofessional to decide that anyone 'looked like a murderer'; CID sergeants shouldn't even think like that.

Well then, he looked guilty. That was surely fair enough. He was in his late twenties, with a growth of black stubble around his chin and his cheeks which was undoubtably not due to fashion. He had straight black hair, lank because it needed a wash. His eyes were rimmed with red, as though he had not slept well for many nights. He might have been good-looking in better times, but he looked as if those times were a long way behind him.

His clothes had been of good quality when new, but they were shabby with age and neglect now. His shirt had a button missing at its frayed neck. His black leather jacket was scarred, with one of the pockets half torn away.

And at ten thirty on this Monday morning, in the airless confines of the interview room, on the other side of the small square of table beneath the pitiless overhead light, he smelt. The man had that stale, unwashed, defeated odour which is familiar to all policemen.

He was nervous. He did not know what to do with his hands. He put them on the edge of the table in front of him, then down by his sides, then on to his thighs under the table. If they'd given him a chair with arms, he would have gripped them and kept his hands still that way. Now he was trying to avoid rubbing them together, to avoid giving these people that outward sign of his inner anxiety. He glanced sharply at the faces of Peach and Blake as they came into the small

118

room with its scratched green walls, then dropped his gaze to the floor and kept it there.

Peach studied him with distaste for a moment before he said, 'You are Nigel Rogan?'

The man nodded, glanced briefly up into the Chief Inspector's dark eyes, and dropped his gaze again. 'You don't look like a Nigel to me,' said Peach inconsequentially. 'More a Fred or a Bert, I'd have said. Someone with dirty fingernails and a taste for the squalid. Still, perhaps you were more charming as a child.' He looked as if that didn't seem to him a very likely thing. 'Do you want a brief?'

'No. I don't need one. I shouldn't be here.' The defiance of the words was undermined by the dull hopelessness of the delivery.

Peach reached over and set the cassette turning in the recorder, announced the names of the principals in this little drama, and allowed himself a theatrical sigh. 'Mr Rogan, you are here to answer questions concerning the murder of Sarah Dunne on the night of Friday the fourteenth of November last.'

'Don't know why. I didn't even know the girl.' With his eyes on the floor and his automatic, unthinking denial, he looked like a scruffy schoolboy brought before the headmaster after a prank gone wrong, hopelessly denying what he and everyone else knew was true.

'You knew her, Mr Rogan. In every sense of the word, including the biblical one.'

The red-rimmed eyes lifted up again at that, and for a brief moment fear flashed into the grey pupils. 'I didn't know that girl. Didn't kill her. That's the truth, so I'll go on repeating it.' He glanced automatically at the silently turning wheels of the recorder.

'You may well do just that, Mr Rogan. You may repeat it in court, for all we care. If the evidence against you is strong enough, it won't matter a jot.' Peach smiled his satisfaction at that thought. He'd never been quite sure what a jot was, but it usually seemed to impress villains.

It was the mention of court which seemed to stir Rogan from the apathy of despair. He looked hard at Peach, apprehension stirring him into life. 'You haven't got any evidence against me.'

Peach studied him, as hard and unashamedly as if he were a slide under a microscope. 'You'll have to do a lot better than this, Mr Rogan. We have the dead girl's clothing. Forensic can learn a lot from that, you know. We also have the DNA sample you were kind enough to volunteer to us last night.'

'I didn't even know the girl.'

Peach shook his head sadly. Lucy Blake said, 'Where were you on the night of Friday the fourteenth of November, Mr Rogan?'

'I don't know. Not just like that. It's a long time ago.'

'Nine days. Not so very long, is it?'

He seemed to come to a decision. 'All right. I was in Brunton. But I didn't murder anyone.'

'What were you doing on that night, Nigel?'

He looked into the DS's green-blue eyes, so much brighter than his own lustreless ones, and seemed to come to a decision. 'I picked up a girl that night. It's nothing to be proud of, is it? That's why I didn't want to talk about it.'

'Can you give us her name?'

'No. It – it wasn't that kind of pick-up. I – well, I made an arrangement with her.'

'You made an arrangement to pay her for sex, didn't you?'

'Yes.' He glanced at Peach. 'She was only young. She made the first move – offered herself, like. She was the first one to speak. I think she said I didn't come from round here.'

Peach took up the questioning again, more quietly than he had spoken originally. 'Where did this sparkling exchange take place?'

'In the Fox and Pheasant.'

It was one of the town's seedier pubs, in one of the districts where the rows of small terraced houses had lived on long after the mills they had been built to serve had closed down. It could hardly have had a less appropriate name, being as far from green fields as any of the town's hostelries. It was the kind of place where women of the streets often went looking for trade.

It was also within three hundred yards of the spot where Sarah Dunne's body had been found.

Peach said, 'They'd remember you, would they, in the Fox and Pheasant? Be able to confirm this part of your story at least?'

'They might. I think I only had one drink. The girl was anxious to get on with it, you see.'

Peach leaned back, as if to get a fuller view of a man he might want to remember. 'Describe her to us, Mr Rogan.'

Panic flashed into the watery-grey, red-rimmed eyes. 'I can't remember much about her.'

'Try. In your own interests, as well as ours.'

'She was young. Slim. Wearing a short skirt.'

'Brilliant. That's really going to help us to identify her!'

'I'm sorry. I didn't think I'd be questioned about it like this, did I? When you're paying for it, you want to get on with it, you don't—'

'Colour of eyes?'

'I – I don't remember. Blue, I think, but I'm not certain.'

'Colour of hair?'

The thin, sharp features contorted into a frown. 'Not blonde. But not a brunette either.'

Lucy Blake leaned forward. 'Like mine, was it, Nigel?'

He looked at her rich chestnut hair as if there must be some hidden trap in the invitation. 'Not – not quite like that. Not as long as yours. And not as shiny. And without that reddish tinge. Light brown, I'd have said, this girl's hair was. And straight and shortish, I think. That's as near as I can get.'

'Anything else?'

'She had some kind of short coat or jacket above her skirt, I think. And – and I don't think she'd done much of it before.'

'Much of what, Nigel?'

'Prostitution. Whoring. Whatever you like to call it.'

'And what was it that made you think that?'

Again that intense concentration. If the man was acting, he was very good at it, and the rest of his bearing and appearance didn't suggest he had the resources for acting. 'I don't quite know. She was very young, as I say, but it was more than that. It was something in the way she went about it. For a start, after she'd spoken, she sort of waited for me to make the next move, instead of making the running. And she seemed almost grateful when I asked her to name her price – they're usually only too anxious to tell you what it will cost, to set out the terms of the transaction.'

They caught a flash of searing self-contempt in the last phrase, a little of the world he had left to become the parody of the man he used to be. He seemed for a moment to be immersed in his own thoughts, so that Lucy Blake had to prompt him with, 'And was there anything else to make you think this girl was new to the game, Nigel?'

He shrugged hopelessly. 'Her conduct generally, I suppose. She didn't – well, didn't control things the way these women usually do. She seemed almost as though she was going to back off when we left the pub. I had to take her hand and lead her along.' He struggled with himself for a moment, then said quickly, 'We were going to her place, but when I suggested a quicky in my car at half price, she accepted immediately – seemed almost relieved.'

'And how much was half price?'

'Twenty-five. She'd asked for fifty. That shows she was new to it, doesn't it, accepting half like that?' He was pathetically anxious to convince them now, pathetically anxious to put his head into the trap he had set up for himself. 'They don't usually cut their prices in half, once they've agreed a fee, do they?'

'No, they don't, Nigel, that's right. So you went to your car. And sex took place there, did it?'

'Yes.' Perhaps this was the moment when he realized for the first time the implications of convincing them of his story. 'I gave her the twenty-five pounds and sex took place.' He repeated the phrase woodenly, as if it had some mystical power of its own.

'On the back seat of your car?'

'Yes. Do the details matter?'

'They may do, Nigel. We shall probably need to examine your car, in due course.'

The fear was back in the face which a moment ago had

122

been anxious only to convince them of the authenticity of his story. 'Why would you want to do that? I told you, I didn't kill anyone on that night.'

Peach took over again, his voice harsh and hostile after Blake's softer tones. 'So you did, Mr Rogan. But we may need a lot of convincing about that. Where did this exchange take place?'

'I don't know the name of the street where I was parked. It was only about two hundred yards from the pub, I should think.' He brightened a little as a thought occurred to him. 'There were some lock-up garages, away from any houses. I'd parked in the shadows beside them.'

'So tell me again how much you paid this girl.'

'Twenty-five pounds. I told you, she'd asked for fifty at first, but that was taking me back to her room. We were on our way there when I suggested a quicky in the back of my car for twenty-five.'

'And she accepted? Just like that?'

'Yes. She didn't argue. I was a bit surprised at that. I told you, that's what made me think that she was quite new to—'

'How did you pay her? Can you remember the denominations of the notes you gave to her?'

Rogan thought hard, as if he could win himself some credit for accuracy here. 'A twenty and a five, I think. Yes, I'm sure it was, because I remember taking new notes out of my—'

'And what happened after you'd had your bit of fun on the back seat of your car?'

'I – I was anxious to get away, as far as I can remember. I told her I had to be off. She didn't argue; she just snatched up her pants from the floor and left and I drove away. But before she went, she leant across and kissed me on the forehead.' His hand rose to his forehead at the sudden memory of it. 'That was another thing that made me think she must be new to the game.'

There was a pause of several seconds whilst they contemplated each other. Nigel Rogan's eyes flashed from Peach's implacable face to the softer features of Lucy Blake, trying unsuccessfully to read what was going on in the minds behind the eyes which studied him so relentlessly. He had forgotten all about hiding his hands now; they twisted and untwisted on the edge of the square table in front of him.

Peach said slowly, 'You're a cocaine addict, Mr Rogan. That's what brought you to our attention last night.'

'I'm not an addict. I like my crack, like it a bit too much perhaps, but I'm in control. I'm going to give it up.'

The protestation of addicts the world over, whether it be gambling, alcohol or hard drugs. Peach smiled sourly. 'If the amount of crack cocaine you had in your possession was for sale, we'll have you for dealing. If it was all for your own use, I'd say you were an addict. You've lost a wife and two children, and I should think you're well on the way to losing your job.'

Rogan stared down at his twitching fingers. 'You know how to kick a man when he's down. I'm going to give it up. Being brought in here like this, spending a night in your cells, has brought me to my senses.'

He meant it, thought Peach. Really believed he could do it. At this moment he believed it, but the resolution wouldn't last. It never did: that was part of being an addict. He said, 'You'll need help. Don't make the mistake of thinking you can do it on your own. But we aren't concerned with your habit. Not here. We're concerned with the death of Sarah Dunne on the night of the fourteenth of November.'

'That was nothing to do with me. I've told you, I—'

'You still don't get it, do you, Rogan? Your brain's so addled with crack that you can't see where all this has been leading.'

'I've told you what I did on that night. I may not be proud of it, but—'

'What time did this episode take place, Mr Rogan?'

He shook his head several times, not in denial, but apparently in an attempt to clear it. 'I'm not sure. Around ten o'clock, I should think.'

'The report on the post-mortem examination tells us that Sarah Dunne was killed between nine and eleven on that night.'

'Not by me, she wasn't.'

'The description of the girl you picked up in that pub. The one you took to your car. The one you gave your money to.'

'It's not complete. It's the best I can do.'

'Maybe. It's also a description of the girl who was murdered on that night. A description of Sarah Dunne. It may not be complete, but every detail you've given us tallies.'

'But – But I didn't—'

'The girl who was in your car on that night was Sarah Dunne, Mr Rogan.'

The name he had never known was being thrown at him now like a series of stones. He licked his pale lips, felt the sharp stubble against his dry tongue, said desperately, 'You can't be sure of that. If you take me round the town, show me some of the young girls on the game, I'll try to pick out the one who—'

'You won't. It would be a pointless exercise. Sarah Dunne had twenty-five pounds in her pocket when she was eventually found. In the form of a twenty pound note and a five pound note.'

The hands gripped the edge of the table convulsively. 'That's still not conclusive. In a court of law they'd say—'

'The DNA sample you gave us last night. It's been tested this morning. It matches the semen samples taken from the body of Sarah Dunne.'

Rogan's eyes glazed with defeat, his breath suddenly the loudest sound in that small, stifling room. After a few seconds, he said hoarsely, 'I didn't kill her.' Neither of the CID officers helped him out with a comment, and eventually he added inconsequentially, 'I'm sorry she's dead. She seemed like a good kid, to me.'

Tom Boyd knew that this must be done, but he wasn't enjoying it.

The Inspector had only spoken to his Chief Constable once before, and that had been at a social function, when they were bidding farewell to a retiring Superintendent. He found that the top man was at any rate a good listener. He heard Tom out with only a couple of terse questions. And he gave the impression that he had heard much worse than this, that nothing would shock him.

The CC thought for a few seconds when the sordid little tale was complete, or as complete as Tom was prepared to make it. Those seconds seemed like minutes to Tom. He could not know that this experienced senior policeman was evaluating what he had heard, wondering just what had been held back, conjecturing whether this grizzled officer who stood shame-faced in front of him could indeed be a murderer, and what the repercussions might be if he was. The CC said eventually, 'What is your marital status, Inspector Boyd?'

'I'm divorced, sir. I have one child, sir, a grown-up daughter, who's married and lives in Norfolk. I see her only about twice a year.'

'And you don't have a regular partner?'

'No, sir.'

The CC had come across many men like this in his time. Divorce was an occupational hazard of police work. Men remained sexually active, but without an obvious outlet. And Boyd certainly wasn't handsome; he might have made a reliable husband, but at pushing fifty, stolid and flat-faced, with the haircut and the bearing of an earlier generation, he wasn't going to have too many offers.

The CC felt a sudden, disturbing spurt of sympathy for the man who stood embarrassed before him. 'And where were you on the night of the fourteenth of November, when this girl was killed?'

'I was at home, sir. Alone, unfortunately.'

'I know that's what you told this DCI and his side-kick from Brunton. I'm asking you now whether it's the truth.'

'It is, sir, yes.'

'Right. You did right to come to see me. Let me know if there are any more developments. We'll do whatever we can for you if there are enquiries from Brunton. That is to say, we'll say you've given impeccable service here, and been of good character. It may not be much, but bear in mind that they won't have many suspects for this who'll have that kind of support.'

'No, sir. Thank you, sir. And I'm sorry for bringing this embarrassment upon the service.'

'These things happen, Inspector Boyd. It won't count against you here. Providing you didn't commit this murder, of course.'

He had meant it as a little joke to conclude the interview, but neither of them felt much like laughing.

Thirty miles away, in another police station at Brunton, Thomas Bulstrode Tucker had prepared the words he proposed to deliver to his Chief Inspector. He tried not to issue them through clenched teeth as he said, 'I enjoyed our golf yesterday, Peach. I can't remember when I last played so badly, but it was an enjoyable afternoon.'

He can't even lie convincingly, thought Percy Peach. Not to me, anyway: he must have been able to lie persuasively to someone, to have got to where he is. 'Glad to hear it, sir. Your Captain seemed to enjoy it, too, judging by his speech at the dinner. Very pleasant chap, I thought.'

'Yes, well, this is all very nice, but back to business, eh?' Tucker spoke as if Peach and not he had introduced the diversion of golf. 'How near are we to clearing up this prostitute's murder? The media are pressurizing me to hold an update briefing, but if you've nothing to deliver, I'll need to hold them off.'

'There's been progress, sir. We interviewed the copper in the case on Saturday afternoon. It didn't seem appropriate to report our findings to you in a social situation at the golf club yesterday.'

'Quite right.' Tucker reflected that he had suffered quite enough without having a policeman thrown into the conversation as a murder suspect.

'An Inspector Tom Boyd, sir. From the Blackpool force. Traffic section.'

'At least he's not one of ours.' Tucker's relief was so great that he voiced it aloud.

'No, sir. Playing away from home, he was. He got that bit

127

right, at least. But he'd have been better to go further afield. He's admitted to conducting aggressive sex with a Brunton tom last Thursday night.'

'Aggressive sex?'

Tucker looked nonplussed, and Peach had a sudden glorious vision of Brünnhilde Barbara pursuing Tommy Bloody Tucker round the house in her underwear, uttering whoops of sexual excitement. Bloody hell!

He kept his face commendably straight as he said, 'Boyd gave us certain details, sir, but I think we shall find out more if we can interview the tom in question. We hope to find her some time today.'

'Has this Inspector Boyd given any indication that he might have killed Sarah Dunne?'

'No, sir. He vigorously denies it. But he has no alibi for the night of her murder.'

The Chief Superintendent shook his well-groomed head doubtfully. 'I can't see it being a policeman, you know.' Tucker had apparently wiped from his memory the fact that a member of his own CID team, a man dubbed by the press as the 'Lancashire Leopard', had proved to be responsible for a series of four killings less than two years ago. He sighed heavily, like a patient man who has much to bear. 'Have you any more likely suspects?'

'We've got a man down in the cells who looks as guilty as hell, sir.' Peach, remembering the hopeless droop of Nigel Rogan's shoulders as he had been led from the interview room, decided that this was a fair description.

Tucker brightened. He moved into his elder statesman mode and leant forward, placing his elbows on the surface of his large, empty desk, steepling his fingers and nodding sagely. 'Have we got enough to charge him, Peach?'

Peach pursed his lips, then nodded slowly. 'I think we have, if we choose to. He's admitted picking up Sarah Dunne on that night, admitted to paying for her sexual favours, admitted to giving her one on the back seat of his car. A cut-price one, as a matter of interest, sir. He admits to giving her a twenty pound note and a five pound note in payment.'

'And?' said Tucker.

The bugger obviously doesn't read the details I submit to him in memos, thought Percy. I don't know why I bother – except that I have to, because Tommy Bloody Tucker demands that I keep him briefed in writing. 'The notes we found in the pocket of the girl's jacket were a twenty and a five, sir.'

'Ah!' A great and welcome light illuminated the features beneath the distinguished silver hair. 'It begins to look as if we have our man.'

'The man is a crack cocaine addict, sir. In my view, that is: I don't suppose for a minute that he's registered as an addict. He works a night shift in a printing works. My impression is that he won't keep the job much longer with his crack habit, but that's by the way.'

'It will be if I can charge him with murder!'

Peach let the switch to the singular pass without comment. 'Perhaps partly because he was off his head on crack when he was brought in last night, Rogan volunteered a sample of his hair for DNA analysis. It has been matched this morning with that of the semen samples taken from the body of Sarah Dunne.'

'Right! Let's charge the bugger. I'll call a media conference for this afternoon and announce that we've got our man!' Tucker jutted his jaw forward in a rare image: the steely man of action.

It was tempting, but Percy decided he could not let this run. 'I've questioned him this morning with DS Blake, sir. I'm not satisfied that he is our man.'

'But you said yourself he'd paid her for sex in the back of his car. We have the banknotes he passed to her. And if the semen sample tallies with his DNA, how much more do we need?'

'No more, sir. We've got an excellent case. And he admits all the things I've told you. But he denies murdering the girl.'

'And you believe him?' Tucker was suddenly full of contempt for the naivety of his DCI.

'I think I probably do, sir, yes. Of course, if you'd like to speak to him yourself, he's still in custody. Be very useful to have the opinion of the man in charge of the CID section on this.'

Tucker was tempted. It would be splendid to produce a confession from the man who had hoodwinked Peach. But he did not want to break the habit of the last ten years and get involved with the gritty reality of an investigation. Moreover, there lurked at the back of his mind a respect he dare not express for the methods and opinions of the egregious Peach. If the DCI thought the man was innocent, if Percy Peach hadn't wrung a confession from him, then it was unlikely anyone else was going to succeed.

The Chief Superintendent said reluctantly, 'Let's presume you're right and this Rogan man's not guilty, for the moment. Have you anything else of interest to report on this case?'

'Yes, sir. Phone call to CID at 22.17 hours on Saturday night, sir. By a man purporting to be the murderer of Sarah Dunne. Asking for you, sir. But taken by DC Pickering, who was alone in the murder room at the time.'

'Phone call saying what, Peach?'

'Call purporting to be from the murderer, sir. Made from a public phone booth in Birmingham. By a man with a Brummie accent. Brummie or Black Country, sir. We've got the recording of the call, so we can submit it to a voice expert at Forensic.'

'You think our killer is from the Midlands?'

'Difficult to say, sir. This could be a hoax call. Chummy didn't use any information he couldn't have got from the press. But he referred to the two similar killings of toms in the Birmingham area and claimed responsibility for those as well as for Sarah Dunne. I have the tape here, sir.'

'Right. Leave it with me. I'll pass it on to Forensic.'

'Yes, sir. Bear in mind that it may be a hoax, though. There are—'

'I'll be the judge of that, Peach. It's part of being in charge of an investigation, to make judgements on things like this.'

'Yes, sir. Rather you than me, sir.'

'That's all right. You get about your business and stop wasting valuable time.'

130

Tucker's lethargic imagination had been stirred into vigorous life. He picked up the internal phone and began immediate arrangements for a media briefing at three o'clock. With a man under arrest and a DNA semen match, plus a phone call from a man claiming responsibility for this and two other murders, there was much to report. He'd show the critics that Chief Superintendent Thomas Tucker was a man to be reckoned with, a man who got things done.

It hadn't yet occurred to him that these two new items of information were in fact contradictory.

Fifteen

Father Devoy liked going into the primary school behind the church. Until the last few months, he had always found it easy to lose himself in his conversations with the children, to forget that other side of his life which was beginning to tear his very soul apart.

He liked the classes for the First Communion best, where you were surrounded by excited innocence and preparing the children for a family celebration. He sometimes thought that if he could have had a family himself, all might still have been well with him.

But the First Confession and First Communion classes were usually in the spring, with the children enjoying the great day of their First Communion on the feast of Corpus Christi in June. At various times during the last few days, John Devoy had wondered whether he would ever see another spring, whether the demons within him would destroy him before then.

He was all right as long as he had the children in front of him. Those round, unlined, credulous faces compelled his attention, made him concentrate on them and them alone. At least, they always had until now. The children told him the old, old things. The things which should have reassured him in his vocation as a priest. The things he had learned when he was a boy, the things his father and his grandfather had parroted off in school until they knew them by heart.

The children didn't sit in desks any more. But a little girl told him from beside her table that God had made her; had made her in His own image and likeness.

She looked very pleased with herself when she had told him that, knowing that she had got it right, that the teacher would

132

be relieved because she had got it right in front of Father Devoy. Teachers were as human, as insecure, as anyone else, and John Devoy knew that the woman who stood out of sight behind his right shoulder would be absurdly pleased that her small charges were not letting her down when the priest came in from the big, high stone church behind the small modern school.

Father Devoy wanted to ask the smiling little girl what she meant by 'in his own image and likeness', to see what this cocksure eight-year-old would make of the picture of God transformed into a toothy girl in a pretty dress and the green school sweater, but he knew that it would not be fair. Not fair to the smug little child who had given the right answer; not fair to the 23-year-old teacher smiling her approval behind him.

Not fair even to himself, for it might expose Father Devoy as the thinking man he was; the man who questioned what his religion fed to children; the man who had doubts about his calling to the priesthood; the man who knew the way he was living his life was wrong, and yet could do nothing about it.

The man who preached from the pulpit about the dangers of lust and fornication, yet who dared not turn and smile at the young woman behind him, in case her full lips and soft curves made him reveal his lechery in his face. The man who thrust his hands deep into the vents at the side of his cassock lest they too might somehow give him away, as his arms cut through the empty air.

The man who was living a lie and could not go on doing so for much longer.

Joe Johnson enjoyed being in control.

He had never been one for democracy. He realized that as his empire grew he must delegate, so he had brought managers into his clubs and casinos. He was even willing to listen to their views, on occasions: the occasions when he had asked for them. His underlings soon learned not to venture a thought about policy unless they had been asked for it.

Things worked perfectly well, so long as everyone understood that they were working for an autocrat.

The man in front of Johnson on this Monday morning would never have dreamed of offering an opinion. He was a big man, with a powerful torso and massive forearms, but he stood in front of the desk in the boss's office as an abject parody of subjection. He was a man whose trade was physical violence, but at this moment he might have been a puny child.

Johnson looked at the man as if he was something he had just scraped off his shoe. He knew what he was going to do, but he enjoyed watching fear ooze like sweat from the hulk standing waiting upon his judgement. He took a cigar from the box in front of him, studied its band unhurriedly, smelt the Havana tobacco appreciatively whilst his shambling employee suffered. Then he sneered, 'Enjoy your holiday, did you?'

'It – it was good, yes. Not that there's a lot to do at the seaside at this time of year. I went—'

'Well, that's good, then. Got you well away from me, too. Which was a good thing, because I wasn't pleased with you. Not pleased at all.'

'No. I'm sorry, I didn't think that—'

'Exactly. You didn't think. Not really a defence though, that, is it?'

'No. I—'

'I suppose you'd say I don't pay you to think. Your talents, such as they are, lie in other directions. Well, you must be expecting to collect your cards today.' He paused, waiting for a reaction from the mountain of muscle, but the man merely shifted his weight absurdly from foot to foot, like a small boy unable to stand still before a fearsome superior.

Johnson curled his lip and went on, 'Well, I've got good news for you. I've still got a job you can do, in one of my clubs.'

The big face, battered as a pugilist's but simple as a child's, cracked from apprehension into a crooked smile. 'Bouncer, is it, boss? I can do that. I've done it before. No one will get away with anything with me on the door.

I can handle any of the roughs we get round here. No one gets past—'

'Shut it, will you?' Johnson was suddenly sick of the sight of this dullard with danger in his fists. The dolt seemed to take him back to his earliest days, when violence had been the only tool he employed to make his way, before the days of the clubs and the casinos and the upper-class brothels and the capital he now controlled and directed towards the extension of his empire. He'd rather have dispensed with a thug like this, but it was better to have him under his eye, still within the organization, rather than shooting his mouth off elsewhere about the things he'd seen and done.

Johnson did not trouble to disguise the disgust he felt as he said, 'It's a last chance, this. Don't be under any illusion about that. You go too far once more, and I won't protect you again. Understood?'

'Understood, boss.'

Johnson looked at the blank surface of the door the man had shut behind him as he left. He thought of how far he had come, of how much more he now had at his disposal than men like that. But you couldn't do without force: it was violence which instilled the fear which was still so necessary to most of his enterprises. He pressed a button on his desk and spoke into the intercom. 'Send Shepherd in here, will you?'

The man who slipped in and took the chair when it was indicated that he should sit was at first sight very unlike the ponderous bruiser who had just left. He was thin, for a start, and not much over average height. But there was a sinewy power about him, a steel which was more stealthy but just as uncompromising as that of the dull heavyweight who had been here before him. There was also a coldness about his slightly narrowed, watchful eyes which meant that you would not want him as an enemy.

'Little job for you,' said Johnson. 'Won't take you long, and you could do it in your sleep, but it's one you might enjoy.' He smiled at the thought.

'What is it, Mr Johnson?'

'A girl needs a little – well, a little discipline, shall we call it, Shepherd?'

The thin lips gave him a mirthless smile, a sadist responding eagerly to the sadism in his chief. 'I'll enjoy that, Mr Johnson. Been stepping out of line, has she, this girl?'

Johnson smiled back. This man was much more on his wavelength than the one he had just seen, though still subservient, of course. He liked that. 'Young girl who's been flashing her fanny about. Trying to make the most of her arsets, as you might say.' He strung out the word and smiled at his simple joke, showing his staff that Joe Johnson liked a bit of humour, in the right context.

The thin lips opposite him twisted into a soundless, sycophantic chuckle.

A chuckle that never made it into sound would have disconcerted some people, but not Joe Johnson. He said, 'I've no objection to women putting tasty quims on the market, as you know, but it has to be under our umbrella. This silly tart's trying to work just for herself.'

'Not a wise thing to do, that, Mr Johnson. Not in this neck of the woods.'

'Not wise at all, as you say. She's only nineteen, and she needs to be protected from herself. I had a word with her myself last night: explained the necessity for her to have protection. I think that message needs reinforcing. I told her we'd be in touch. She needs looking after, so I thought I'd send out the good Shepherd to have a word with her. To invite her to join our flock.'

It was a joke he had made before, but Shepherd laughed dutifully again at his inappropriate name. 'I'll see she gets the message, Mr Johnson,' he said.

The birthday tea was a tradition. In the midst of a murder investigation, Lucy Blake had thought it would need to be abandoned or postponed. It was Percy Peach who insisted that tradition should be honoured.

'Your mum will be looking forward to it. We must fit it in, even if we only spend a couple of hours with her,' he said decisively. 'And besides all that, she makes the best scones I've ever tasted!'

The lights in the little stone cottage looked unnaturally

bright in the early winter darkness as they drove into the quiet lane with its row of cottages in the lee of the fell. Far away from any street lights here, they could appreciate the grandeur of a sapphire sky and myriad stars. To the west, there were no major rises in the land as it stretched away over the plush northern suburbs of Preston to the invisible coast at Blackpool; to the north was the long, low mound of Longridge Fell; to the east a slim bright crescent of a new moon illuminated the great mound of Pendle Hill.

It seemed a long way from the narrow streets and sordid murder they had left behind them.

There was a coal fire burning cheerfully in the low-ceilinged sitting room and Percy warmed his hands at it as he said, 'Getting pretty parky out there, Mrs Blake. Be a frost before morning.'

'Not before time,' said Agnes Blake. 'The geraniums and the dahlias have been flowering on, but tonight will see the last of them.' She spoke without regret. You lived with the rhythms of the seasons in the country: it was time for winter to bite and make itself felt.

Percy tucked into his scones and Agnes watched him admiringly. She was one of the last representatives of a generation of Lancashire women who liked to see men eat and loved it when they appreciated their food. She was sixty-nine today, a child born into the nineteen thirties depression, who seemed to have had some of the lessons of that hard era bred into her bones. She behaved as if the man of the house was still the only breadwinner, the centre of the family who had to be kept healthy and vigorous if the ship was not to founder. She knew she was out of date, was even prepared to laugh at herself. But kept up the pretence before her working daughter as a kind of rebuke to her career aspirations.

Agnes was disgusted with some petty local vandalism, and Percy retailed the details of how years ago he and a fellow DC had trapped some young hooligan graffiti artists in Brunton by posing as bill-posters.

'You'd make a lovely parent, Percy Peach,' Agnes decided through her laughter. 'You'd give your kids some discipline

– that's what they need. It's the parents we should be fining for all this damage.'

Percy read the warning signs, but he had just taken in the last mouthful of his scone. When he nodded and reached a tentative hand towards the sponge cake, Agnes followed up smartly with, 'Ever thought of having children, Percy? I expect you must have.'

Percy ignored Lucy's warning look. 'Can't say I have, Mrs Blake. Never thought I'd make a very good dad.' He shook his head without resentment.

'Oh, but you would! An extremely good dad. I've some experience, you know, and I can spot a good dad when I see one.' She glanced at the photograph of her dead husband which stood beside that of Percy on the mantelpiece. 'And you'd be able to teach the lad cricket. You'd enjoy that, Percy.'

He stifled a smile. 'No knowing it would be a lad, is there, Mrs Blake?'

'That's true. And you'd want lads, I know. Wouldn't wish girls on anyone. Wilful creatures, girls are.' She sniffed her derision, falling into her now familiar humorous partnership with Peach.

'Really? Well it's interesting you find it so, with all your experience, Mrs Blake. I certainly find women difficult to work with. You never know quite where you are with them. Unpredictable, at the best of times, they are.'

'That's modern women for you, Percy. It was different in my time. Women knew their place, then.'

Lucy decided it was time to intervene. She knew from experience that the pair could go on in this vein indefinitely. She said desperately, 'He probably wouldn't make a good dad at all, Mother. You should see your precious Percy with some of the young people we have to deal with. Nearly bites their heads off, he does. Frightens them to death.'

Agnes Blake smiled with satisfaction. 'That's what I mean, our Lucy. Discipline! I expect it's just what they need. If Percy puts them back on the straight and narrow, they'll be grateful to him in the years ahead.'

Percy Peach beamed with satisfaction at the thought of

the tattooed yobbos who would be saved by his firmness. 'Social worker in disguise, I am, Mrs B. Cruel only to be kind, that's me. I only wish I had people around me who were as intelligent as you, able to take the long-term view and see that I'm really a bright angel in heavy disguise!'

Even the smiling Mrs Blake was taken aback for a moment by this unlikely image, and Lucy took advantage of this to say contemptuously, 'Some angel! More like a Japanese warlord he is, the way he lays into them. You haven't seen him at work, Mum! Reduces burly young thugs to tears, he does. Well, nearly to tears, anyway.'

The two faces on the other side of the table beamed at her in delighted unison at this evidence of huge talent, and she sensed that she was never going to win this argument. Percy winked at her and bit into her mother's fruit cake. There was a moment of contented silence from the duo before Agnes Blake switched effortlessly into the minor key and said plaintively, 'Anyway, we'll never know how good a father he'd make if he's never given the chance, will we, Percy?'

Lucy thought that the question would shatter his air of content, but he said with scarcely a pause, 'That's quite right, Mrs B. You hit the nail on the head with your usual precision. If a man's never been tested, it's not fair to judge him, is it? At the moment, I have to do the best I can to be an unofficial father to the shattered young humanity that passes through my world.' He cast his eyes contentedly at the ceiling and assumed the most seraphic of his many smiles.

Lucy couldn't help herself. She burst out laughing at the absurdity of the thought and said, 'Bloody hell, Percy!'

'Language, our Lucy!' said Agnes Blake primly.

Two of the people in the room were enjoying her birthday tea very much indeed.

Only a single, shadeless, sixty-watt bulb lit up the deserted caretaker's room at the end of the church youth club. Father Devoy pulled on the dark-blue anorak he always wore for these nocturnal expeditions.

He pulled the hood up over his head as he went out into

139

the night. Though it was the coldest night of the winter so far, this was for concealment, not warmth. The sky was clearer than he would have wished, much clearer. The stars seemed to give almost as much light as the dim street lighting in the narrow side streets of the town, and the sliver of moon seemed unnaturally bright. There was not a cloud to be seen; he had never prowled the streets before on a night as clear as this.

A prowler: that is what he was now. Or what this other side of the priest who operated by day was. He tried to hurt himself with that word 'prowler', to lacerate the man who took over when he went out on to the streets of Brunton like this. But it was too late for that now: there was no hurt from the word: it was merely an accurate description. John Devoy moved forward with no more than a grim tightening of the mouth.

He was not sure what he was going to do, why he had ventured out so soon after his last night of sin. Impulse had driven him, an impulse that was so strong that he had scarcely attempted to resist it. Was it going to be always like this now, then? Had he lost the will to fight the Devil? Would he have no control over his actions as this lust moved into the very blood of his body, coursing obscenely through his veins, preparing to tighten like a vice-like grip upon his very soul?

John Devoy stood for a moment in the darkness of the doorway of a closed corner shop, hearing the faint sound of Asian music from the back of the building, wondering for a moment how his life might have differed if he had been born into that other and very different culture. But then the blood pounded anew in his temples, driving out that speculation, pounding away all rational thought, until his only release was in physical movement.

His steps took him to where he felt he had always been heading. There was an inevitability about this, a feeling that something outside himself had brought him here, was leading him onwards, would release him only when he had finished what he must do tonight. He was becoming calmer with his movement. It was a cold calm, which seemed to make his body more than naturally strong.

140

And then he sighted the girl.

She was exactly where he had thought she would be. His sense of fulfilling a destiny, of acting at the behest of some agency outside himself, grew as he glimpsed her. He had always known she would be there, despite the coldness of the night. Evil did not yield to climate.

He was in no hurry, now that he was here. His limbs felt suddenly light, as if he was floating on water, letting the current buoy him up and take him where it would. One of the street lamps was broken, and he stood in the shadows beneath its standard for a moment, watching the girl move uncertainly along the kerb, seventy yards ahead of him. Uncertainly. Was there hope still, even for a whore, if she was uncertain in what she did, if the Devil did not have her yet securely in his goatish grasp?

John Devoy moved smoothly forward, as if on wheels powered by some unseen force.

He was almost upon her before she turned, flashing her thigh through the slit in her skirt. 'Looking for a bit of fun, love?'

The same words she had used to him on Friday. Was that only three tortured nights ago? She reached for his hand, tried to draw it beneath her skirt, to press it throbbing against the warmth of her hidden, private, exotically scented parts.

And for a moment he almost let her. Then he snatched his hand back before she could control it, as if her touch had been red-hot. 'I haven't the money. Not tonight!' he gasped hoarsely.

Toyah Burgess was disturbed at the desperate note in his voice. She thought she might have seen him before, but she couldn't be certain of that; he had the light behind him, and the hood of his anorak over his head. She could see nothing of his face, and that made him infinitely more sinister. She said uncertainly, 'You'll get value for money, love. That's what counts, isn't it?'

The same words again! Exactly the same! How many other men had heard those words in the last three nights as the whore practised her trade? The words she had used for him, the words he had thought at the time were individual. He said, 'You shouldn't be doing this. I've come to save you from yourself.'

Toyah Burgess was suddenly afraid. They still hadn't caught the man who'd killed that girl ten days ago, not half a mile from here. She said, 'Look, mister, I'm a working girl. If you haven't got the money for it, get on your way and leave me to earn a living.'

'You don't understand. I'm here to save your immortal soul. To save the souls of the deluded men who go with you.'

A religious nutter. That was all she needed, with the cold biting into her bones and a murderer lurking in the town. Toyah said, 'Look, mate, not everyone shares your beliefs, do they? Some men want a good time, and I'm one of the girls who can give them a good time. Simple as that, you see. You're wasting valuable working time for me, so if you don't want the goods, will you please piss off!'

So young, and so far gone in sin! John Devoy flicked the hood of the anorak back, saw her shy away for an instant as if he had struck her, and was riven with pity for the sinner. He spoke urgently. 'You must listen to me! There is still time for you. The Lord is merciful, but you must heed His message.'

Toyah Burgess was suddenly annoyed with him. 'I'm not doing anyone any harm. I'm bringing pleasure to people. Helping lonely men to get their ends away is a social service. You can't see it, mate, but it's probably preventing rape and violence, if you only knew it.'

'The wages of sin is death. I'm here to give you that message. To prevent you spending the glories of your body where they should not be spent. To prevent you from spreading your corruption among others.'

She backed away from him as his voice rose, and he moved forward after her, so that the light of the street lamp fell harsh and full upon his face. Toyah knew the man now. He had been with her on Friday night, had spent himself within her, violently, urgently, with a desperate release.

She saw the grey hairs at his temples, silver in the white light of the lamp. Yet his face in its vehemence still looked youthful, almost boyish. She was unnerved by this strange mixture of the biblical and the juvenile, wanted to look up and down the street to see if any relieving presence might be at hand. Yet something prevented her from taking her eyes from this man's face. She was aware how feeble her own voice sounded against his ringing conviction as she said, 'Look, let's just agree to differ, shall we? You go your way, and I'll—'

'No! We can't agree to differ, this is far too important. You must see that your immortal soul is in danger. You are acting as an instrument of the Devil, and taking fallible men with you into perdition.' His eyes were wild, and he lifted his hands suddenly towards her head.

Too suddenly, for before she could move, he had his hands on the thin chiffon scarf she had donned as her only concession to the cold. She felt his fingers touch her cheeks, then run up and down her throat. They were surprisingly warm, when she had expected them to be icy. 'Please leave me alone!' she said, her voice breathy with the fear she could no longer control.

'I cannot do that! You must see that I cannot do that. You are not only a sinner, but the occasion of sin in others. We men are but weak vessels at the best of times. We need protection from the wiles of Satan. The temptation must be removed from our paths if we are to survive.'

His eyes glittered with conviction in the harsh white light of the street lamp. He was looking not at her but past her, as if he saw some demon that must be exorcized. Toyah Burgess felt his hands fastening upon the thin stuff of her chiffon scarf, felt it tightening about her throat, strove in vain to discover words which would bring him back to her.

A car turned into the street, perhaps a hundred and fifty yards away from the pair who stood frozen as statues beneath the street light. Toyah did not dare turn to watch it: its lights seemed to her to be advancing towards them with a dreadful slowness. She tore herself from beneath those awful hands, turned her back upon her challenger, moved as quickly as she dared away from him.

Something told her not to try to run. In her tight skirt

and high heels, she could never outdistance a pursuer. And somehow she knew that if she ran, she would be pursued. Her heart thumped in her chest, in her temples, in her ears, so that she could hear nothing else as she marched as quickly as her dress allowed down the street.

But he was not following her. She was at the corner of the street before she risked looking back. He was still beneath the street light, motionless, staring down at his hands as if they belonged to someone else.

Sixteen

Peach rang Tucker on the internal telephone. 'The forensic audiologist is here, sir. Shall I bring him up?'

'Er—'

'He's a busy man, sir. Has to be away in quarter of an hour. But you said you wanted to see him.'

'Did I? I'd really rather you dealt with—'

'The voice expert, sir.' Peach took pity on Tucker and himself. There was no time to be wasted this morning, even on making a fool of Tommy Bloody Tucker. 'The man who's going to give us an opinion on how genuine that Birmingham phone call was.'

'Ah!' With that single syllable of understanding, Peach could almost see the relief on his chief's face from two storeys below him. 'The man who's analysed the tape of that phone call on Saturday night. Well, don't keep him waiting there, bring him straight up here. And you'd better wait and hear what he has to say yourself, DCI Peach.'

Silly sod's switched into his assertive mode, thought Peach without rancour. He took his bearded visitor up the stairs and ushered him into the Chief Superintendent's room.

Tucker announced himself as the man in charge of 'this most interesting case' and outlined what he thought had happened so far in the investigation. Even with some notable omissions, this took some time, and the man with the beard and the expert knowledge eventually glanced at his watch. 'I have to be at the University by ten o'clock,' he explained apologetically.

'Well, what is it you have to tell us?' asked a ruffled Tucker.

'Not a lot. In my opinion, the caller was a genuine

145

Midlander. Almost certainly a man brought up in Birmingham or within ten miles of the city.'

'Ah! You realize that this may mean that we have a serial killer on our hands? There have been two similar murders in the last year in the Birmingham area.'

He spoke so aggressively that the bearded expert said, 'I can only tell you that this voice was not a hoax, in the sense that the man was not in my view assuming an accent. What you make of that information is a police matter.'

Tucker nodded sagely and stroked his chin, almost as if he wished for a moment that he too had a beard to give him extra gravitas. Then he stood up and donned the cloak of diplomacy he reserved for important members of the general public. 'It is most gratifying when citizens recognize it as their duty to come forward to offer their expertise like this,' he said unctuously.

'I didn't. Chief Inspector Peach asked me for an expert opinion. I've been paid for my services. The voice on the tape is that of a man who's spent most or all of his life in Birmingham; he's probably between twenty and forty-five, though I couldn't be positive about that if I was under oath in court. And now, unless you've any further questions, I must be on my way.'

The forensic audiologist had already formed an accurate opinion of Tommy Bloody Tucker's talents. Peach smiled at him appreciatively as he showed him out. When he returned, Tucker was drumming his fingers on his desk. 'I'll get in touch with our colleagues in the Birmingham CID. Tell them the man they haven't caught there is spreading his net wider. Ask them to check carefully on all the lorry drivers and commercial travellers they've interviewed in connection with those two murders down there.' His nose was lifted higher than usual, as if he had caught the scent of the quarry and the hunt was on.

Peach had already taken all this information from the national computer system in the CID section. 'The MO is similar, sir, but not exactly the same. And this one is a long way from those other killings. I wouldn't at this stage be sure—'

'When you've been in this business as long as I have, you'll have developed a nose for these things.' Tucker lifted the angle of his own proboscis five degrees higher, so that it pointed at the corner of the ceiling. He pressed the button on the intercom and spoke to the station's Press Officer. 'The press briefing you were organizing for two o'clock. Make it a full media conference, will you? And I'll take it myself.' He permitted himself a slow smile, then looked at Peach with sharp distaste, as if he was surprised to find him still in the room. 'Was there anything else, Peach. Because as you can see—'

'Pants, sir.'

'Pants?'

'Yes, sir. Knickers, if you prefer it.'

'Look, Peach, if you're trying to be gratuitously—'

'We haven't found them, sir.'

Tucker came reluctantly back to earth, his nose making a cautious return to the horizontal plane. He said heavily, 'Are you bothering me with the theft of underwear when we have much weightier matters to deal with?'

'Sarah Dunne's knickers, sir. They weren't found with the body. And they weren't in Nigel Rogan's car.'

'Nigel Rogan?'

'The man who picked her up in the Fox and Pheasant on the night she died, sir. The man who paid her to have sex with him, in the back of his car. The man whose twenty-five pounds was found in the pocket of her coat. The man you wanted to charge with the murder of Sarah Dunne yesterday.'

'Ah, *that* Rogan.' Tucker spoke as if he saw hundreds of Rogans stretching away into the distance, like the vision of future kings afforded to Macbeth by the witches. He sighed with infinite patience and said vacantly, 'So the girl's knickers weren't in his car.'

'No, sir. He said she snatched them up as she left him, if you remember.'

Tucker looked puzzled. 'And now you tell me the garments are not in his car. I can't really see how this makes him guilty.'

147

It's like leading a five-year-old along, thought Peach. 'It doesn't, sir. In so far as it does anything, it supports his story. But the girl's pants haven't turned up. It's possible they were taken away by some person who killed her after she'd left Nigel Rogan. Taken away as a trophy, perhaps. Or dropped in the street and removed by some other person totally unconnected with the crime, of course.' His doleful face suggested that this was the most likely and least helpful possibility; the policeman's lot was not a happy one.

Tucker moved back into masterful mode. He said incisively, 'Has this Rogan got a Birmingham accent?'

'No, sir.'

'Then I think we can rule him out. You were a little hasty in jumping to the conclusion that he was our man.'

'I don't think that I—'

'We have a real clue at last, Peach. Our killer is clearly not a local one, so you needn't waste my time with any more details of Lancashire suspects.'

'I see, sir. Personally, I have to say that I'm not convinced that our murder is definitely linked with the Midland stranglings. I'd need more—'

'Leave the overview to me, Peach, there's a good fellow. You get on with the day-to-day work and let me handle the strategy.'

Peach got out before his chief could move into his Field Marshal Montgomery mode. He'd be talking about hitting the criminal fraternity for six if he got any encouragement.

Tommy Bloody Tucker was in danger of going off at half-cock again, his DCI reckoned. Which in his case, strangely enough, usually produced an awful lot of cock.

You don't expect danger at eleven o'clock in the morning. When you are nineteen, you think chains on doors are for old ladies and people who are scared by all the stuff in the papers about the increase in violent crime.

It wasn't that she was unconscious of the danger. When Joe Johnson had made her get into his car and threatened her on Sunday night, Jenny Pitt had been thoroughly unnerved. Subsequent enquiries among her acquaintances had only confirmed that Johnson's threats were not to be taken lightly. She had locked her doors at night and made sure she was not alone on the streets or in the pubs and clubs of Brunton.

Yet when you were enjoying a late breakfast on a bright Tuesday morning, with the sun streaming in through the windows as if it were spring, not late autumn, you were somehow unprepared for violence.

She did not open the front door of the small terraced house very wide, and she kept her small foot against the back of it as she said, 'Yes?'

But the gap was wide enough. The man threw his shoulder against the door without responding to her question and was inside the house.

He was a slim man, but surprisingly powerful, and with a steely strength in his arms. Some absurd rhyme of her father's came back to her, which said that people who were strong in the arm were weak in the head. It was not a helpful thought to her at that moment. And this man's thin, wolfish features looked not unintelligent but cruel.

Jenny Pitt was suddenly very frightened indeed.

She tried to put all the outrage she felt into her voice as she said, 'You've no right to burst in here like this!' But the high, strained note of her voice sounded in her ears like the feeble bleating of a helpless lamb.

The man smiled unpleasantly at her. His teeth were uneven, with the front ones large and pointed. In another context, they might have made him look comic. But there was nothing remotely comic about this alien presence in the small, low-ceilinged living room. The teeth merely made the malevolent face look more wolfish and sinister. He said, 'I hear you've been a naughty girl, Jenny Pitt.'

He knew her name. She'd never seen him before, she was sure of that, but he knew her name. She said, 'I don't want you in my house. Leave now, please, or I'll call the police.'

He gave her that evil, lopsided grin again. 'I don't think you'll do that, Jenny. It would be most unwise.'

He was enjoying her fear and her vulnerability, and that made both of them worse. His sallow skin was pitted with small indentations all over his narrow face, and he had not shaved this morning.

She said, 'I can't think why you should have come here. I've no idea why you've forced your way into my house, or how you know my name, but—'

'Lot of things you don't know, young Jenny Pitt. And quite a lot of things I do. Know you're on the game, for a start. Or trying to be. Without taking the necessary precautions.'

'Precautions?' She had an absurd vision of condoms.

'Precautions, my dear. Lucrative game, prostitution, but dangerous. You need protection, young Jenny Pitt. You need people like me on your side, if you're not to come to serious harm.'

'If you're trying to—'

'Very serious harm. Look what happened to that silly Sarah Dunne girl week before last. She was trying to put it about without the necessary protection, and some bugger topped her. She was a very silly girl.'

'You're saying you killed her? Just because—'

'Saying nothing of the sort, Jenny Pitt. Get yourself into serious trouble, if you go about saying things like that. We don't know who killed her. Neither do the police, who you seem to think might be interested in a foolish little tart like you. But in my opinion, if she'd had protection, Sarah Dunne would be alive today.' He swept her with that confident ogre's grin again, enjoying her fear, fancying now that he could smell the terror upon her.

'You work for that man who took me into his Jaguar the other night, don't you?' She tried to sound contemptuous, but she could feel her palms cold and clammy in the warm room.

Ray Shepherd grinned down at her. 'That would be telling, my dear, wouldn't it?' He looked round the featureless living room, with its conventional prints on the wall and yesterday's newspapers still on the sofa. 'Pity for you that your friends are out and you're in the house alone. But that gave us the chance for a private talk, see, Jenny Pitt. A chance to make sure there are no misunderstandings between us. A chance for you to see sense.' His voice hissed on the sibilants, scattering her shirt with tiny globules of spit. His tone hardened into an unmistakable threat on the last phrase.

Suddenly, Jenny was full of a fierce rage: the rage of a nineteen-year-old who has never been seriously threatened before in her young life. 'Go to hell, whoever you are! And get out of my house, or—'

'Or what, Jenny Pitt? Just what will you do to me?' Shepherd stood between her and the phone, less than three feet from her face, tall and threatening, laughing outright at her helplessness.

'I'll go to the police. You'll have to leave here some time, and I'll tell them just what you've—'

It was the back of his hand which hit her, on the top of her cheek, just below her left eye. It was so swift, so utterly without warning, that she had a moment of incomprehension before the white flash of pain went through her face and into her brain. She found herself on the floor at his feet, tasting the salt blood in her mouth, wondering if her cheekbone was broken, feeling the eye already beginning to close. She drew her knees up instinctively against her breast in a foetal folding, wondering where he might hit her next, how far this beating which had burst upon her from nowhere was going to go.

The voice from above her said harshly, 'You won't be on the streets for a few nights now, Jenny Pitt. Which will mean that you've already lost in earnings what would have bought you weeks of protection. Silly girl, aren't you?' He put his foot against the trousered thigh and rolled it over, savouring the whimper of terror as the girl threw her hands across her already damaged face. He kicked each of the trousered thighs with great deliberation, feeling the spurt of sadistic pleasure within him as if it had been a drug.'When you do try putting it about again, you'll make sure you have protection, won't you, Jenny Pitt?'

She muttered, 'Go away! Get out of my house!'

She was blubbering now, and Shepherd enjoyed the squelch of blood and snot and tears behind her small fingers, so inadequate to protect what had a moment ago been such an attractive young face. 'Do you know what, Jenny Pitt?

151

I'm going to do just that, now. Go away, and leave you to think things over. Because I think you've learned your lesson. Learned that you need protection before you try to sell your arse upon the streets! One of our representatives will be back later in the week to discuss terms. Might even be me, if you're lucky!'

Shepherd allowed himself a last chuckle, gave a departing kick to the rounded backside, and slammed the front door behind him as he left.

Chief Superintendent Tucker felt a welcome buzz of excitement as he came into the crowded room. He nodded confidently at the audience whilst he projected urbanity, polish, security.

The girl from Granada Television began by asking him if there was anything to report on the Sarah Dunne killing. Tucker gave her his slight, man-in-control smile, the one that combined a becoming modesty with easy competence. He said, 'You know me pretty well by now, I think. I wouldn't have brought you here if there was nothing to report. I don't believe in wasting your time and mine in just going through the motions of public relations.'

'You've made an arrest then, Mr Tucker?' The question came from the back of the room, where Alf Houldsworth, the one-eyed veteran reporter from the local evening paper had stretched out his legs and lit a hand-rolled cigarette.

'Well, no, we haven't done that, Mr Houldsworth. Miracles take a little longer.' Tucker chuckled at the cliché. He got one or two dutiful sniggers from the rows of faces in front of him, but his attempt at humour fell rather flat.

The reporter from the *Sun* said with his pen poised over his notebook, 'Do we take it that you consider the possibility of an arrest in a murder case so rare as to constitute a miracle?' and got many more appreciative sniggers than Thomas Bulstrode Tucker had drawn.

Tucker said quickly, 'That wasn't what I meant at all. It was – well, it was a figure of speech, that's all.'

The *Sun* man mouthed 'figure of speech' as he wrote the words down laboriously in longhand. Tucker watched his pen with an awful fascination. He was aware that he must offer the meeting something quickly or lose the sympathy of the assembled journos. He said, 'We have made considerable progress. I am about to brief you on that, if you will allow me the chance to do so.' He looked accusingly from Alf Houldsworth to the *Sun* man, but journalists develop hard shells early in life, and he made no impression.

It was the young woman from Granada who eventually fed him the question he wanted. 'What sort of progress, Chief Superintendent Tucker?'

'We have narrowed the field, Sally. Eliminated some fifty or sixty suspects from the original field of our inquiry.' That sounded quite impressive, and they surely couldn't check it out.

'Have you anyone in custody at the moment?'

'No one has yet been charged with the murder of Sarah Dunne. A man has been helping us with our enquiries. A man who was with the young lady on the night she died.' He tried to look like a man who could tell them a lot more, if only the system had allowed him to do so. He knew that Peach felt that Nigel Rogan hadn't killed the girl, but he himself was not so convinced.

Houldsworth looked at the smoking end of his cigarette as he said, 'But he hasn't been charged, so he didn't do it.'

Tucker refused to be ruffled by the old reprobate. He smiled patronizingly. 'If only CID work was as straightforward as you seem to think, Mr Houldsworth. I am happy to say that in this country we still need evidence before we throw a man into jail and charge him with murder. Whatever we think about a man's guilt, we have to provide the Crown Prosecution Service with the proper evidence, acquired in the proper manner, before they will take on a case.'

'You think you've got your man, though, do you? It's simply a matter of tying up the evidence before he's charged?' This was a large, overweight man from *The Times*, heavy with experience and expense-account lunches.

Tucker recognized him and smiled a sophisticated smile. 'You're too old a hand to expect to catch me that way, George. If the evidence is watertight, he'll be charged. Meanwhile, every lead is being followed. We don't believe in closing our minds, at Brunton CID.'

'What sort of leads, Chief Superintendent Tucker?'

It was good to hear his full title rolling off the tongue of an experienced man like this. Perhaps that thought made Tucker a little incautious. He said, 'As a matter of fact, we now have reason to believe that Sarah Dunne's death may be one of a chain of murders, which began in the Midlands. The modus operandi is almost exactly the same as that practised on two women murdered in the Birmingham area in the last year.'

He had them now. There was nothing they liked more than a serial killer, especially if he spread his crimes across a wide geographical area. Headlines and pictures of the scenes of the crimes, together with their sexual connotation, could send a collective frisson of fear through the nation. Always good for circulation, fear and sex.

He felt a little trepidation at the interest he had aroused, but there was too much of the ham in him not to exploit it. He told them about the phone call, purporting to be from the murderer, which had come into the station on Saturday night. There were the inevitable suggestions that it might be a hoax call.

Tucker leaned forward to add sincerity to his manner. 'All I am prepared to tell you – indeed, all that I *can* reveal at this stage – is that our forensic audiologist has listened to the tape of this conversation and reported his findings to me this morning.' He paused theatrically, revelling in the expectant, upturned faces below the platform where he sat. 'The expert was convinced that the voice was perfectly genuine, that the strong Birmingham accent was not being assumed to deceive us.'

There was no mistaking the buzz of interest in the room now. Two people tried to raise the idea that the voice might be a perfectly genuine Birmingham accent, and the speaker still a hoaxer, but Tucker retreated into a gnomic impassivity, folding his arms and smiling the smile which said he could tell them so much more if only protocol allowed it. His audience was not interested in pursuing him further, since the serial killer was much the most attractive journalistic possibility.

Tucker came away satisfied with the impression he had made. It was only half an hour later, when the adrenaline was leaking away, that he wondered what kind of hare he might have set running.

Toyah Burgess was very nervous outside Brunton Police Station. She walked up and down for several minutes in front of the brash new modern building, pretending to look at the displays in shop windows, telling herself that this was the thing she had to do, that she should not turn away now, when she had brought herself to the brink of revelation.

It was Lucy Blake who decided things for her. Detective Sergeant Blake noticed and recognized the young prostitute as she was turning her car into the police station car park. Something about the girl's demeanour convinced her that she was trying to pluck up the courage to enter the station, and Lucy went quietly back into the street when she had parked her car.

Toyah Burgess was staring unseeingly at hi-fi stacks and DVD players when the voice behind her said, 'Can't expect much trade outside the police station at three o'clock on a Tuesday afternoon, surely?'

She started as if struck, then said, 'It's once a tom always a tom, isn't it, with you pigs? A girl can't even walk round the town on a sunny afternoon without you thinking she's on the game!'

But there was no real venom in her words. Lucy Blake had taken her in to the nick in the past – a fair cop – and she had paid the usual fine before going back out on to the streets to sell herself again. But there had been no real malice in either the arrest or the subsequent charge. They had been two women on opposite sides of a barrier they both understood, divided by the law but in a curious way united by their jobs and their gender.

Each of them knew that Toyah was breaking the law by soliciting, and that the law had occasionally to be upheld by an arrest and a fine, but each of them behaved as if she was merely observing the rules of an elaborate game. Lucy had a secret, unspoken sympathy for girls like Toyah, and Toyah had a grudging respect for DS Blake and the way she did her job.

She was glad that Lucy Blake had spoken to her here. In her own mind, it had resolved her doubts and taken away the need for courage. She would now be dragged along in the wake of the older woman's energy.

Lucy said, 'You were thinking of coming in to see us, weren't you, Toyah? Trying to pluck up the courage to set foot in a police station.'

Toyah Burgess smiled ruefully. She was only nineteen, and Lucy thought how pretty the young-old face was when the strain left it. 'I've never gone into a nick before of my own accord. I've always been slung in the back of a cop car and driven in under arrest.'

'So now let's see you make use of your rights as a citizen.' Lucy took her firmly by the elbow and guided her steadily through the big doors and into the station. 'This lady's with me,' she said to the station sergeant at the front desk, forestalling any disparaging remarks to the girl at her side.

Lucy Blake hesitated before the door of an interview room, then took her charge into the less formal confines of the CID section. 'What is it you want to speak to us about, Toyah?' she asked.

'How'd you know I'd anything to say to you?' said Toyah, in genuine puzzlement. 'Just because you found me on the road outside—'

'Just a hunch. I played a hunch, kid!' Lucy did her version of a thick Chicago accent and won a reluctant smile from the girl standing next to her. 'What's it about, anyway?'

'Probably nothing, really.' Toyah Burgess found her confidence draining away in these surroundings, despite her friendly companion. 'It's just – well, I thought I should tell someone about it. I felt at the time that it might just have some connection with the killing of that girl, but now I think it's probably nothing at all.'

It was part of the unwritten contract between prostitute and clients that you preserved their anonymity, kept quiet about any odd sexual demands. Toyah was finding it difficult to break that taboo, and both the women understood it. Lucy said quietly, 'None of this need go any further, if it isn't connected with the Sarah Dunne murder. If it is, we need to hear everything you can tell us. You might be the next one, Toyah, if we don't.'

Before the girl could argue, she took her again by the elbow and propelled her through the open door of DCI Peach's office. 'Ms Toyah Burgess, sir, with some information she thinks might be relevant to the Dunne inquiry.'

Peach looked the new arrival quickly up and down, recognized her as one of the newer tarts on his patch, but took his cue from his DS and decided that this was not a time for bullying. 'Sit down, please, I won't be a moment,' he said, and shut the door of the room behind him as he left. He came back a minute later with three mugs of tea on a tray. 'Just get you some sugar. Me and DS Blake are sweet enough,' he said, and disappeared again.

'They told me he was a bugger,' said Toyah Burgess in wonderment.

Lucy Blake grinned. 'He can be. But he has other sides to him.'

'Like a many-faceted jewel,' said Toyah, who had read a lot of romantic fiction for one of her tender years.

Lucy thought it was the first time she had heard anyone from the other side of the law describe Percy as a jewel. Just as well her mother wasn't around to hear it. She was glad to talk about anything but the reason why the girl was here, for the moment. If Toyah could become just a little more at ease in this strange environment, she would find it easier to talk.

Peach came back in and shut the door. He sipped his tea meditatively for a moment, abandoning his normal briskness. Then he said, 'Bet it wasn't easy for you to come in here. But you did the right thing.'

'DS Blake found me outside and brought me in. I don't know whether I'd have plucked up the courage to come in here on my own.' Toyah spoke it as if it were an excuse, and Peach understood perfectly the feeling she had that she was betraying her caste by coming in here of her own accord.

He said quietly, 'Murder changes the rules, Miss Burgess. No one should hold back information when there's a murder investigation in progress. Do you think you're in danger, despite the dubious protection you enjoy from Joe Johnson and his heavies?'

He knew about that, then. Knew about Johnson and the way he controlled the drugs and prostitution in the town. She found that curiously reassuring: perhaps the town was not as securely in the hands of criminals as she had thought. And she had liked the way he called her 'Miss Burgess', as if she had never been pulled in for selling it on the streets. But young as she was, she knew better than to say anything Joe Johnson might trace back to her. 'It's probably nothing. I expect you'll think when you hear it that I'm just a silly girl, panicking over nothing.'

'If I had ten pounds for every time I've heard that phrase, "It's probably nothing", I'd be a rich man. Sometimes it's been true. More often than you'd think, it's been the prelude to some valuable piece of evidence.'

'It's nothing to do with Mr Johnson.'

'I thought it wouldn't be,' said Peach dryly.

'It's just – well, one of my clients behaved rather oddly. And with a girl even younger than me having been strangled, I wondered . . .'

'Wondered if you'd be the next. And didn't fancy it. A sensible enough thought. And you were even more sensible to bring it here.'

'I don't want anything to be done if it proves that I'm just overreacting. It doesn't – well, it—'

'It doesn't do for a tom to take the money and then make revelations about the way a customer behaved. No, I understand that, love. But the customers must also understand that when there's been a murder, they are going to be of interest to us. Business been poor in the last ten days, has it?

It was the first use of the sudden switch which was one of his ploys, and it disconcerted Toyah Burgess. 'It has, yes. Clients were very thin upon the ground last week. I tried to tell—' She stopped suddenly, realizing she had almost said more than she should.

'Tried to tell Mr Johnson about it, did you? I've no doubt he didn't take kindly to a drop in his takings. I expect he treated it as a feeble excuse, even when he knew it must be true. He's that kind of man, Joe Johnson.'

It was so accurate a summary that he might have been there. Toyah said nervously, 'I just thought you should know about one of my clients, that's all.' She took a long pull at her sweet tea, as if it could bolster her in this unaccustomed frankness with the police.

Lucy Blake mirrored the movement with an unhurried drinking of her own tea, as if the sisterhood could tackle this together. She said, 'When did this man visit you, Toyah?'

'Last Friday night. That was the first time.'

'And what was unusual about him?'

'He was just – well, odd. You learn not to take much notice of that: lots of the people who pay us for sex are oddballs. So long as they pay their money and don't damage you, you learn not to be shocked and not to complain.'

'But this man was odd in a different, more disturbing, way, or you wouldn't be here now, would you?'

Toyah shook her head. She still couldn't believe that she was here, sitting in a DCI's office, talking to him and a DS about what she did. 'There was a gentleness about this man – almost an innocence, when we first spoke to each other on the street. He – he reminded me of my first real boyfriend, when I was only fourteen.' She looked up quickly to see if they were laughing at her, a tom talking like this, but their faces were grave and attentive. 'I took him back to my room. He turned his back on me whilst I undressed. Not many of them do that. They regard the stripping as part of what they pay for, and it often gets them really turned on.'

Lucy nodded, anxious to keep the girl talking now that she had begun. 'Diffident, was he? But not impotent?'

'No! He certainly wasn't that. He was quite rough, once we got started.'

'Too rough? Is that what frightened you?'

'No. Nothing like that. He went at it pretty hard, once he'd got started, like as if he hadn't had it for a long time. But that didn't frighten me, not on Friday. He was just – well, odd, like I said. He was sort of – boyish, I suppose you'd call it.'

'But he wasn't a young man?'

'No. I'm not much good at ages.'

'Not many people of nineteen are. Would you say he was older than me? Older than DCI Peach?'

'Older than you, certainly. I'm not sure about Mr Peach.' She scarcely dared to look at him.

Lucy grinned at her; Peach was thirty-eight. 'Everyone thinks bald people are older than they are. We'd like you to tell us anything you can recall about this man. He was white, I presume?'

'Yes. And I'd say he was over forty. He had quite a young face, but he had a few grey hairs around his temples. He had a good head of hair, though, dark brown I think. And blue eyes.'

'Height?'

She shrugged helplessly. 'He was just a little taller than I am, and I'm five foot six. About average, I suppose.'

'Clothes?'

'He had a navy-blue anorak. I can't remember anything else about his clothing.'

'But he stood out because he behaved oddly.'

'Yes. When we'd finished, he scarcely looked at me again. I made a few jokey remarks, but he might not even have heard them, for all the notice he took. He went off into the darkness without looking back or saying goodbye. It was odd and abrupt. He was quite tender with me at the start, but by the time we parted I felt there was something dangerous about him.'

'Anything else?'

'Well, there was the way he paid.' She felt more treacherous about saying this than about revealing sexual details of a man's conduct, but she pressed on. 'I'd told him on the street it was fifty quid, and he brought it out of his trouser pocket as soon as we got into my room. A ten, seven fives, and the last five in one pound coins. It was almost as if he'd been saving up for it.'

There was a pause whilst the three of them wondered about the implications of this. Then Peach said, 'You said this was the first time you'd seen the man. You've seen him again since then?'

'Yes. Last night. That's really what brought me in here today. I wouldn't have come over what happened on Friday night.' She spoke as though she were still trying to mitigate the sin of speaking to the fuzz.

'So tell us what happened last night. For a start, did he pay you in the same way again?'

'He didn't offer to pay me at all. I don't think he had the money. He said he hadn't, and I believed him.'

'So did you send him packing?'

'No. I didn't realize he was the same man at first. He had the hood of his anorak up and his back to the light. I couldn't see his face. I suppose that made him more frightening, but it was his manner, really. He was sort of desperate.'

'And what did he say?'

'He said I shouldn't be living like this, that he'd come to save me from myself.'

'A religious nutter?'

She smiled, in spite of her nervousness. The very phrase she'd thought of herself, and coming from a policeman! 'That's what I thought. He said he'd come to save my soul. I told him to piss off and let me get on with earning my living!'

'And did he go?'

'No. He got more excited. Told me that the wages of sin is death and things like that. I said we'd have to agree to differ, but he wouldn't take that.'

'What did he do?'

He told me that I was acting as an instrument of the Devil. Said I was luring men with me to Hell and that he couldn't allow that.'

'Did he threaten you?'

'He did more than that. He put his hands on my neck, ran them up and down my face.' She shuddered suddenly at the remembrance of it. Her brow furrowed as she strove to dredge up the actual phrases that odd man had used. 'He said men needed protecting from the wiles of Satan. They were only weak vessels and temptation must be removed from their paths.'

Peach was working hard to keep calm, fearing that if

he betrayed his own excitement, the girl would become even more nervous and clam up. 'Did he offer you any violence?'

'Not exactly. But I felt that if I didn't get away from him he was going to. I had a chiffon scarf round my neck. He had his hands on it and I felt it tightening.'

'But you got away.'

'Yes. A car appeared at the corner, so I tore myself away from him and hurried off down the street'

'Didn't you run?'

She smiled for the first time since she had come into the room. 'You don't run very fast, in a tight skirt and the kind of heels you use for our job.'

He grinned back at her. 'Of course you don't. Did he follow you?'

'No. I was expecting him to, but he didn't. Maybe the car put him off. It was moving down the street towards him. I looked back when I got to the corner. The man was still beneath the lamp where I had left him. He was staring down at his hands.'

'Right. We'll have as full a description as you can give us, before you go. And we'd like you to look at some mugshots of men who have a record of violence.

Toyah Burgess nodded, resigned now to giving them all the help she could. She downed the rest of her tea, trying to control the violent shivering which was suddenly shaking her slim frame.

Like the other two people in the room, she was wondering if the man who had killed Sarah Dunne had laid his fingers upon her throat last night.

Seventeen

D avid Strachan looked out of the window at the spire of
the Catholic church. It stood tall and thin against the
blue sky of the late autumn afternoon, seeming to soar even
higher in the crispness of the cold, clear day. They said this
Preston church had the second highest in the country, with
only Salisbury Cathedral reaching higher towards heaven.
The sun was setting over the Fylde coast, ten miles to the
west, making the blue of the sky even deeper for the last
hour of the day. Soon it would be dark, and Strachan could
hardly wait for that to happen.

The manager of the textile warehouse was exceptionally
long-winded, in David's view. He was going to renew the
contract for the computers and their servicing. That had been
fairly clear from the outset, but this plump, middle-aged man
with the glasses on the end of his nose and the fringe of grey
hair around his balding pate was not going to be rushed. He
had ordered tea to be brought up for his meeting with David.
It was a courtesy the sales representative would normally have
appreciated, but today he just wanted to have the business side
of his day completed and be away to anticipate the wilder
pleasures of the night.

Miss Whiplash had grown in erotic stature through his
anticipation of the last few days, her allure more that of
a voluptuous femme fatale than that of a buxom prostitute
running a little to seed, which was the reality. He had gone
over and over in his mind the things they would do together,
the way he would threaten her, the way she would respond,
imprisoning his limbs, watching him break the bonds and
menace her anew in turn. They would lead each other on
to wilder and wilder things. At this moment, it was very

difficult for him to concentrate on the more mundane business of earning a living.

'So when will the new models actually be available? And when do you propose to deliver and install our new system?' The manager munched his digestive biscuit contentedly and looked at David Strachan over the top of his glasses.

'The new PLCs will be on the market from the first of January. And we'll have your new system up and running by the end of the month at the latest.'

'If we decide that we need the refurbishment, of course.' The manager smiled, applying the little turn of the screw that it was traditional for salesmen to suffer.

'Of course. But I think you'd be foolish not to modernize, Mr Woolley. Especially at the rates we are now offering you.'

Surely the old bugger wasn't going to back out now? Surely he was just going through the motions, trying ineffectively to make the representative suffer? David visualized this old buffer with Miss Whiplash. He'd be frightened to death! It gave him confidence to think of the man like that. David tried not to let his contempt come out in his tone as he said, 'We've agreed on the savings that an efficient system is going to afford you.'

'You've produced certain figures, I agree. Shown how we *could* make savings. Theoretically, that is. I always suspect figures. Lies, damn lies and statistics, you know.' The manager smiled patronizingly.

Strachan hadn't really the patience to begin to sell him the system all over again. He said, 'You can take it from me, Mr Woolley, that what we are offering will make you a more effective unit. And you won't beat us on price, either. I'm quite confident of that.'

'More tea, Mr – er, Strachan, isn't it?' He filled up David's cup without waiting for a reply. 'Well, I'll be perfectly honest, it seems to make sense to me. But I think I ought just to put it to our accountancy department, before we confirm the contract. Some smart young lads in there.'

That's what you were supposed to be doing between our last meeting and this one, thought David. Checking it out with your accountancy boys and coming back to me with any questions they raised. He forced a smile and said, 'I can assure you that they won't find any flaws in the scenario I've put to you, Mr Woolley. The computations we worked out and which I discussed with you a fortnight ago were based on your latest sales figures.' He wondered if he dare risk a threat. He drank a large mouthful of his unwanted, lukewarm tea and took the plunge. 'I wouldn't like to see you go backwards in the queue for our new models. Not after the relationship we've built up and the esteem in which I now hold your business.'

'I wasn't really questioning the deal we'd worked out. I was only trying to give the young Turks in the accountancy department their say, but I wouldn't like to jeopardize the relationship we've built up between us over the years.' David heard the welcome sound of an executive back-tracking. Woolley stood up and proffered his hand. 'You can take it as read that what we've agreed between us will go ahead. Let's shake on that now.'

In another ten minutes, David Strachan was out of the high Edwardian brick building and back in his car, scarcely feeling the cold of the November twilight. The sun had gone now, though the sky still showed red in the west. It was almost five o'clock. A few hours to kill yet before the excitements of the evening.

With an order under his belt, he would award himself a leisurely meal in a decent place, with three courses and an unhurried perusal of the morning paper he had been too preoccupied to read earlier. He turned the Vectra towards the coast and an excellent restaurant he knew in Lytham St Annes, moving deliberately in the opposite direction from Brunton, a man postponing a treat to make it all the sweeter when it came.

He would enjoy anticipating the drama, then relish even more the event itself. And the piece of rope lay clean and ready beneath his seat.

DCI Peach looked at Detective Constable Pickering with practised repugnance. 'I don't suppose it's anything to do with the case, but it's got to be checked out, so get your arse over to Bolton, lad, and do the checking.'

'Yes, sir. Could you just tell me what the background is, please? Let me know exactly what it is I'm supposed to be checking?'

Peach regarded the fresh-faced eagerness above the gangling frame with distaste. Pickering was so much his physical opposite, so much the counter to his own stocky, muscled frame, the DC's innocent features such a contrast to his own aggressive, experienced round face, that he felt bound to resent him. And at twenty-two, Pickering was a good sixteen years his junior: quite enough to warrant resentment in any man. Peach's irritation was triggered on a bad day by the fact that Gordon Pickering looked both naïve and gullible. The fact that the man within the lanky frame was neither gauche nor easily deceived was what had made Percy Peach select him for CID work. But there was no reason to remind him of that.

Peach looked at the note in front of him. 'Some bright spark over in Bolton has been on to us about what looks like a straightforward domestic. Apparently a nineteen-year-old girl's been badly knocked about by some bloke. But this keen young constable has spotted that it happened here in Brunton. And being as the girl's not very different in age from our murder victim, he thought there might just be a connection. Especially as the girl's keeping shtum about who did it, despite her mother's best efforts to make her talk.'

'Needs checking out, sir, as you say. Can I take DC McNair with me?'

'No you cannot, lad. You need to keep your mind on the job, not on your trousers.' DC Alison McNair was the latest addition to Brunton CID, a nubile blonde with a soft Scottish accent.

'Worth a try, sir.' Pickering was shrewd enough to have divined by now that Peach's bark was much worse than his bite, when he was dealing with colleagues rather than villains.

*   *   *

166

Thirty miles away on the Fylde coast, Detective Inspector Boyd was more straightforward with his orders than Percy Peach. Perhaps in the Traffic Section of policing, routine was what was needed.

A Tuesday night at the end of November in Blackpool was not going to cause many traffic problems, with the Illuminations over for the year and the landladies shutting down the guest houses and flying to Tenerife and Lanzarote. Tom Boyd left his instructions for the night, had a solitary drink in the pub near the station, and was microwaving a solitary meal at home by six thirty.

The devil finds work for idle hands, they say. Perhaps it was some small, very personal devil working within Boyd which made idleness such a danger for him. He tried to watch television, but he could find nothing that engaged his attention. Almost before he knew what he was doing, he found himself outside again, sitting behind the wheel of his car. He sat there for quite some time before he made the inevitable move and started the engine.

The Chief Constable had been a lot more sympathetic than Tom Boyd had expected. He'd said he'd give his Inspector every support with character references, if he was contacted by the CID at Brunton. Well, he deserved that: he'd kept his nose clean and done his job impeccably for twenty years and more: he wouldn't have made Inspector if he hadn't, would he? Nevertheless, he found that the CC's assurance of support had cheered him up.

He cruised past the road works on the A583, which he had been out to see earlier in the day, driving deliberately slowly, avoiding the M55 motorway, which would have whisked him eastwards, past Preston and towards danger. The east must be avoided. Inspector Boyd turned north, towards Lancaster and away from temptation. The Chief Constable certainly wouldn't expect him to venture near Brunton again, after the warnings he'd had.

And he wouldn't. Even from his own selfish point of view, he would be committing professional suicide if he was caught looking for women in that area again. And he had too much bitter experience of rebuttals to believe that he could pick up sex without paying for it. He'd have a quiet drink in a country pub, maybe exchange gossip with the locals if they were friendly, and then go back to his empty, soulless house and his solitary bed.

He found just the place when he turned off the main road and into the large village of Garstang. It was a friendly pub, with real ale, plenty of action around the dartboard, and locals ready to exchange conversation with him. He could spend a pleasant hour or two here, and then drive back to Blackpool as sedately as he had driven here.

But the images which he had put aside thrust themselves back into his mind. Katie Clegg, tall and lithe, dark-haired and sultry, waving the handcuffs in front of his eyes with that challenging, provocative smile, seemed to beckon to him like some modern siren. She was the right age for him, Katie, young enough to be highly desirable, old enough to offer him the experience he wanted.

He couldn't think now why he'd ever bothered with the very young ones, who weren't much more than kids. Katie Clegg was the one for him. He could almost feel her slim throat beneath his fingers, almost see the fear seeping into the wide brown eyes above the professional smile.

Tom Boyd's personal devil was active within him, fighting hard against the common sense and decorum which prevailed in the rest of his life, playing the trump card of lust at the key moment of the game. He forgot all about real ale and the conviviality of this pleasant place.

Tom Boyd turned the Vectra towards Brunton and quickened his speed.

Detective Constable Pickering was finding Mrs Pitt very difficult to deal with.

She was around fifty and she treated him as if he was a callow youth in need of her counsel. 'This should never have happened to her, you know. She's obviously got in with a bad crowd since she's left home.' Her brow darkened as she glanced again at her daughter's face. 'I'd just like to have five minutes on my own with the so-called boyfriend who did this, I can tell you!'

Gordon Pickering wondered how he could stem the tide and talk to the girl herself. Jenny Pitt didn't help him much. She cast occasional helpless glances at her mother in full flow, then returned her gaze to the carpet, without even looking at the fresh-faced young DC.

She certainly looked in need of care and attention. Her left eye was completely closed, and the swollen flesh around it was green and yellow, darkening into purple on the eyelid. In another day or so, this whole area of her face would be blue-black – a 'shiner' in the terms of the pub brawlers who often ended up in police hands, but something which seemed much worse in the shocked white face of an inexperienced young woman.

Pickering wondered quite how inexperienced the girl was. She had obviously been anxious to get away from this over-protective home in semi-detached suburbia. But she had not just rented a room or a shared flat in her home town, as many girls anxious to break the domestic ties did. She had gone to another town altogether, and perhaps taken on a completely different way of life.

As if she read these thoughts, Mrs Pitt said, 'She'd a job lined up for her at her father's firm, but would she take it? Too proud for that. Wanted to stand on her own two feet, she said. Wanted to make her own way in the world. The real world. Well, this is what the real world is like, Jenny. This is what happens to girls who don't heed the warnings they were given!'

She spoke harshly, unable to resist the triumphant vindication of her argument. Then her eyes came back to the distress in front of her and she put her arm round the shoulders of her unresisting daughter and drew her tightly against her. Jenny spoke for the first time since Pickering had arrived at the house. 'I can't talk with you here, Mum!'

'Now come on, Jenny, you know we've never—'

'It really would be better if I could speak to your daughter on her own, Mrs Pitt.' Pickering looked into the concerned maternal face and tried hard to make use of his youthful appeal. 'Not many of us find it easy to speak frankly in front of a close relative, you see. Not even when it's someone so obviously concerned to be helpful as you.'

'But I can't just leave her to struggle through on her own.'

'You can and you should, Mrs Pitt. Jenny's an adult. She's no need to have her mother present when we talk to her. And in any case, this isn't a formal interview. No one's suggesting Jenny's done anything wrong. All we want to do is to get to the bottom of who's done this to her. When we've done that, we can set about putting the person who harmed her behind bars.'

The older woman had been waiting to protest all through his speech, but the last words brought her up short. If he was trying to put the man her daughter wanted to protect into prison, this likeable young man was on her wavelength all right. She said, 'All right. I'll go and make us all a cup of tea, shall I?'

Thank God for the English addiction, thought Gordon Pickering. 'That would be very helpful, Mrs Pitt. I'm sure we'd all welcome a cup of tea.' Always give a parent something to do, or they'll listen at the door: that was one of Percy Peach's maxims.

The girl gave him a glance from her one good eye as soon as the door shut behind her mother. 'I can't talk. I can't tell you who did this. I don't know who did it and I couldn't tell you if I did.' The words came in a rush from the mouth which had remained closed for so long.

Gordon Pickering was three years older than this stricken girl, but he felt suddenly that the age-gap was much wider. He said gently, 'Let's just work it through, Jenny. You tell me what you know and I'll fit it into whatever knowledge we already have. We know more than you'd think about what goes on in Brunton.'

She looked at him sharply, her fingers stealing up to the bruised cheek beneath the closed eye, her face wincing as she touched it. 'The cheekbone isn't broken, you know. I thought it was, at first. I'll heal up OK, in a few days.'

'Boyfriend, was it?'

'No!' She looked shocked at the thought.

Her vulnerability made Pickering more determined to get to the bottom of this. And beneath his compassion, the nerve

170

which made him a CID man had begun to tingle. He was certain now that this was not a domestic, that it was linked to some more serious crime. There was even the faint possibility that it might have some tenuous connection with the Sarah Dunne murder, that he might not be here on a wild goose chase after all. He said, 'We can be very discreet when discretion is needed, Jenny. No one in Brunton except my boss is even aware that I'm here talking to you. So let's have the facts about this.'

She looked as if she wanted to speak, then shook her head hopelessly and glanced at the door. 'I can't speak to you. I really don't know who it was who did this. And my mother and dad would kill me, if they knew what I'd been doing in Brunton.'

Perhaps she didn't realize it, but her words were almost an invitation to press her further about that secret life. He heard the distant clatter of crockery in the kitchen at the back of the big old house and said quietly, 'We need to know about that, Miss Pitt. This is a criminal assault.'

The phrase and the more formal mode of address seemed to convince her that she had no choice in the matter. Or perhaps it was that she really wanted to talk and it was only her fear which was preventing her from doing so. She said in a voice which he could scarcely hear, 'I got out of my depth. It was my own fault, really. I brought this upon myself.'

It was a beginning, an invitation towards further questioning. Pickering said, 'And how exactly did you get out of your depth? Your mother will be back very shortly, you know.'

'You won't tell her?'

'Not if you don't want me to. You're an adult at nineteen, entitled by law to a certain privacy.'

She glanced again at the door, listened to the reassuring sounds of kitchen activity. They seemed unnaturally loud in the quiet house: perhaps Mrs Pitt was assuring them that she was no eavesdropper. Jenny said with the ghost of a smile, 'I was planning to break the law myself. That shocks you, doesn't it?'

'Not at all. You must remember that we spend our time

171

talking to people who break the law. They come from all sorts of backgrounds. You learn never to be surprised.'

'I was on the game, you know. Well, planning to be. I'd made a start.'

Pickering tried to keep the excitement from leaping into his voice, to speak as if he had known it all along, as he said, 'And it was in connection with this that you were attacked?'

She nodded, the memory of the man who had forced his way into her flat and hit her suddenly setting the blood pulsing in her temples and freezing her tongue.

Pickering saw her distress and prompted her. 'You were told you needed protection if you were going on the streets. That you'd need to pay for that protection.'

'Yes. A man warned me that prostitution in Brunton was controlled by him. That if I knew what was good for me, I'd pay a percentage of my earnings for his protection.'

Johnson! But could they pin it on him, at the end of all this? Gordon Pickering kept calm and said as formally as he could, 'Could you describe the circumstances of this warning?'

Another glance at the solid, firmly closed door. Then she spoke urgently, as if she appreciated that time might be limited. 'He pulled up beside me in a maroon car. A Jaguar, I think. Yes, I'm certain it was. Invited me to get in beside him. I thought – well, I thought—'

'Thought he wanted to pay you for sex. It's all right, Jenny. You've already told me that's what you were about.'

'Yes. Well, it turned out he didn't want to buy. He was warning me that I needed to come into his organization, that I'd suffer if I tried to go it alone.'

She described the man to him in answer to his simple urgent questioning. She remembered the build, the mouth, the small scars on his forehead and temple. It was Joe Johnson all right, though Pickering doubted whether they could make anything stick in the light of his inevitable denials and the absence of other witnesses. He made a note of where and when the warning had occurred, then said quietly, 'But it wasn't the man in the Jaguar who did this to you, was it?'

She shook her head. 'The man who did this came round to

the flat this morning, when the two girls I share with were out. I thought at first it was just another warning. I lost my temper and told him to get out of the house. That was when he hit me. With the back of his hand. He didn't give me any warning. The shock of it was almost worse than the pain.' She began to weep quietly at the memory, like a road accident victim with delayed shock.

One of Johnson's heavies, sent round to back up his master's message with a physical warning. Gordon had no idea which one, but he would dearly like to see justice done here. He said, 'You say he did this with the back of his hand. With a single blow, was it?'

'Yes. He kicked me a few times when I was on the floor, but I think he only hit me once with his hand.'

'Could you stand up for a moment? Show me exactly how it happened?'

She shuffled uncertainly to her feet, stood opposite the gangling young DC, cringed instinctively as he lifted his arm, even in slow motion. He raised the back of his hand to her cheek, touched it minimally, then stood reflectively for a moment, picturing the scene in the flat he had never seen.

They were frozen in this bizarre tableau when the door opened and Mrs Pitt pushed in a serving wagon with plates of biscuits and cakes and a pot of tea. 'Just trying to get a picture of the assault on your daughter,' Pickering explained, blushing furiously as he dropped his loose-jointed arms back to his side.

He acceded to the invitation to tea and a home-made scone, though it was now after seven in the evening. His mind was working furiously on what might be made of this when Peach and the rest of the team got busy upon it. He stood up as soon as he could. 'Thank you for your hospitality. A female officer will be round in the morning to take photographs of your face and any bruising on your legs, Miss Pitt.' He turned to the mother. 'It will be best if your daughter remains here with you for a while, Mrs Pitt. We'll let you know the outcome of our enquiries.'

He left mother and daughter with their arms round each

other's waists on the doorstep of the solid semi-detached house.

David Strachan felt good with a leisurely meal and half a bottle of wine inside him. He drove slowly through the streets, not at all worried when at first he could not find the woman he wanted. He was quite sure that he would find her sooner or later. He felt destiny hanging about his shoulders tonight.

Sure enough, he spotted Sally Aspin when he circled the block for the second time. She was wearing a cheap imitation fur coat, short enough to show the slit in her skirt, walking securely on the high heels with skill practised over many years, waggling her ample curves appealingly as she heard the car cruising behind her.

He drew up beside her and threw the car door open in invitation. 'It's me again, Sally! Mr Whiplash!' He laughed uproariously, surprising himself with the loudness of his own voice in his excitement.

She hesitated for a moment, then slid her bottom on to the seat beside him and put her hand on his arm, as if she could control his exuberance with her touch. 'Nice to see you again, big boy!' she said automatically. She didn't know how often she had used the phrase in her thirty-eight years, but it seemed to work as well as ever.

He said, 'Your place or mine, sweetheart?' and laughed loudly again. 'It had better be yours, I think!'

'Mine it is,' she said, as cheerfully as she could. She was finding this more difficult than she had thought it would be, now that it was upon her. She couldn't think she'd ever betrayed a customer before.

He drove the car to the house where she operated, needing only minimal instructions, since he remembered most of the way from his last visit. When he had switched off the engine, he turned to her, kissed her, caressed her neck, squeezed her arms, stroked a thigh, fondled a bountiful breast. In other circumstances, she might have welcomed it, from a regular customer. Sally didn't get much in the way of foreplay these days. It was wham, bang and thank you ma'am, most of the time, and they often forgot the thanks. But you couldn't grumble, so long as you got their money.

'We'll get a little more violent later, sweetheart,' he murmured into her ear.

She took that as the end of the preliminaries and slid her knees away from him and out of the car. 'You lock the car up,' she said. 'I'll go ahead and open the door.' She did not look back, in case he had any other ideas.

That meant that she did not see him get the short length of rope out from under the driving seat. It fitted easily into the pocket of his coat.

He was glad of the oblong of orange light in the doorway of the house to guide him up the shadowed path of the garden. He had the money ready, waved it expansively at her with a grin, and put it in the fruit bowl on the sideboard, as if he had been here many times before. 'There's ten quid extra for you to strut your stuff, Miss Whiplash!' he said with an excited giggle. With the benefit of his fantasies over the last few days and half a bottle of red wine, he had convinced himself that this buxom lady looked forward to the violence and the threat of physical damage as much as he did.

He undressed quickly, not bothering to fold his clothes, not noticing her movement behind him as she reached up the wall unobtrusively and pressed the button the police had installed after they had been round to warn her of the dangers.

She felt like a traitor immediately. This man hadn't done anything really dangerous last time, after all. Only said he fancied something a bit more violent, and called her Miss Whiplash. That wasn't so unusual: she had met a lot worse than that in her many years on the game. But the deed was done now. There was no turning back.

He wanted her to get the whip out, muttered to her that Catherine the Great used to beat her men on the bottom before she did it with them. She giggled a little at this unexpected piece of erudition from him; they watched each other self-consciously in the mirror on the wall by her bed.

She had put on black stockings and suspenders, and now she pretended to look for the whip in the drawer, though in truth she knew very well where it was. She had left the door

175

unlocked, and found now that she could not concentrate on the business of arousing the man in the way he wanted, because she was waiting for the sounds of the police arrival.

He was between her thighs when they entered the house, telling her to treat him roughly, chuckling with sexual excitement. There were only two of them, but they burst in like a posse, yelling to him not to move, telling him that he was under arrest, warning him that it might prejudice his defence if he withheld information which he might later use in his defence.

It was noisy but swift. David Strachan stood abject and bewildered, shamed in his nakedness, watching his arousal dying swiftly before his horrified eyes. Sally Aspin wanted to apologize to him, to tell him that it was nothing personal, that toms had been told to turn in all customers who wanted violent sex, as a precaution in the period following the murder of one of their kind.

But Sally said nothing. It was only after the bewildered man had been led away that she realized that he had left her sixty pounds and received nothing.

Eighteen

'Think I'll get one of those corner baths put into my place,' said Percy Peach ruminatively. 'There'd be room for two of us in one of those.'

'Wouldn't suit your lifestyle,' said Lucy Blake. 'We'd both be late for work if you had a bath like that, and that would really set the tongues wagging. I prefer my nice modern shower, where I can shut the door on you!' She felt a little more in control of her man when they were in her neat modern flat than in the icy bedroom of his fifties house.

'Too small for two, that little square box is,' said Percy regretfully. 'I can't get in there with you without leaving something sticking out, and you're lethal with that sliding door.'

'It's cosy and warm and reliable,' said Lucy primly, measuring the distance between Percy and the shower with an experienced eye.

'Just like me!' said Percy eagerly. 'Prove it to you again, if you like!'

'Boasting again. And I shan't call your bluff, in view of the danger to your ageing bones!' She dropped her bathrobe to the ground and leapt quickly into shower, ignoring the moan with which he greeted her sudden nudity.

Percy lay back on the pillows and enjoyed the vision of the gradually pinkening curves amidst the steam of the two-foot square glass box. Like Rubens through a filter lens, that was. He was glad that she hadn't called his bluff and come back to bed, though he would never have admitted it. It had been quite a night; he reviewed what he could remember of its rapidly evolving pleasures.

Lucy took care to cover most of herself with towel before

177

she emerged. She wasn't going to dress in front of him. That would lead to more erotic grunting and possibly to delays they could ill afford: they were already at the last minute. 'I'll get you some toast, if you make yourself respectable.' She threw on her dressing gown and hurried away to the kitchen.

DS Blake, demure in plain clothes, left first in her bulbous little blue Corsa. DCI Peach, immaculate in a grey suit, drove his Mondeo away a discreet five minutes later. The retired man in the adjoining flat gave him a curious glance as he shut the door of Lucy's flat. Envy, thought a happy but not entirely objective Percy Peach. He gave the man a sly wink from an otherwise immobile face.

It wouldn't do to beat his chest and yell his joy out loud.

Peach took DC Pickering with him in search of the man who had assaulted Jenny Pitt. It was by way of reward for the young man's perceptive gathering of the evidence in Bolton. Of course, he did not tell him that.

At eleven o'clock on a Wednesday morning, a seedy night club is seen at its worst. There was a scent of stale drink in the main rooms and, through the open door of the gents', the odour of vomit permeated even through the strong disinfectant which was being liberally spread around the floor.

'We're not at home to pigs!' The big man stood just inside the doorway of the club, with his huge hands held awkwardly away from his sides on arms that were a little too long; he looked like an unfriendly gorilla.

'Surprising, that, when you live in a pigsty.' Peach, warming to the chase, was past the man's ritual hostility and peering into the dark and seemingly empty regions behind him.

He strode past the long and now deserted bar, across a small dance floor and the poles where lap dancers pranced during the evenings, noting how shabby the décor looked in even the modicum of daylight afforded to it by the double doors which lay open behind him. He kicked open the door at the back of this main room, and was rewarded by the spectacle of a man hastily removing his feet from the desk inside.

'Nice of you to show such respect for the arm of the law!'

Peach said pleasantly, as the man half-rose and then slumped back into his chair.

'I was doing no such thing! Thought for a minute you were Mr Johnson,' the man protested. He reached out his left hand towards the phone, then thought better of it and folded his arms. You didn't need to phone the boss, just because the filth were here. Let them know who's in charge, behave as though you'd nothing to hide, and they couldn't pin a thing on you, the boss said.

And the boss should know: he was doing very well out of it. Ray Shepherd tried to give himself confidence by thinking how much more successful and well-heeled Joe Johnson was than the stocky little man in the smart grey suit who had just burst into his office.

Peach looked round the office, with its prints of dancers in erotic poses, its photograph of the club as a cinema in the fifties, its big empty desk in front of the leather chair presently occupied by Shepherd. He fastened his eyes on this central figure with genuine contempt. 'You've been beating up women again, Ray. We don't like that. Don't like it at all.'

Shepherd leaned back in the boss's chair and leered up at him, his thin face full of craft and composure. 'Don't know what you're talking about, I'm sure, DCI Peach.'

He enjoyed getting the rank right, showing the bouncy little pig that they were up to date on his promotion. The fuzz couldn't pin anything on him, he was sure. Just keep grinning and denying and watch the filth become frustrated. That was the tactic. Joe Johnson had built his empire upon it. And Joe Johnson controlled vice in this town; Joe Johnson now had clubs and casinos in other parts of the north-west and in the Midlands; Joe Johnson lived in a house a Chief Constable could never aspire to; Joe Johnson was a multi-millionaire and the police were plods; Joe Johnson ran this town and would protect his staff. Hold on to that, Ray Shepherd, and annoy them with your smiling.

Peach smiled back at him and said, 'Keep talking big, Shepherd. Do it in court, if you like. The judge won't be favourably impressed.'

He seemed very confident, though he couldn't possibly have any evidence, could he? Like all bullies, Ray Shepherd was shaken when anyone threatened him. He said, 'I told you, I don't even know what you're talking about.'

Peach nodded at Gordon Pickering, who said, 'Young lady by the name of Jenny Pitt. Pretty girl. Or she was until you called in and tried to knock her head off yesterday morning.'

'Never heard of the girl. You try to prove otherwise.'

Peach smiled at him, like a tiger taking its time over a large and succulent goat. 'We will, Mr Shepherd. Shouldn't have let yourself be seen going into that house, should you?' There were in fact no witnesses to the visit, other than Jenny Pitt herself, but he knew how to undermine men like this. Shepherd was a cut above the ignorant muscle men that Johnson had used on the way up, but Peach saw apprehension in his thin, watchful face, and exulted in it. This wasn't a formal interview, with the man cautioned and the tape running at the station.

'Wouldn't give much for your chances in an ID parade, with your looks – distinctive, I'd say they are, Ray, being a charitable sort of chap. No, when we add an identification to Jenny Pitt's evidence, I wouldn't give much for your chances.'

Shepherd would never have made an actor. His unease was tangible. A wiry arm lifted towards his face, then fell back to his side. His tongue flicked over the prominent front teeth to moisten the thin lips. 'She wouldn't give evidence. She wouldn't dare.'

He realized immediately that he had made a mistake. Peach underlined it by his delighted beam, then let the silence stretch for a moment to emphasize his satisfaction. 'Shows a surprising knowledge of this girl he's never met, wouldn't you say, DC Pickering?'

'Amazing, sir. At least it would be amazing, if we didn't know perfectly well that he beat her up yesterday morning.'

Shepherd flashed a look of hatred at the fresh-faced young detective. 'She won't talk anyway. And that'll be the end of it,' he said sullenly. Assurance was ebbing away from him by the second. He inched a hand towards the phone, wishing desperately that he could get the advice of Joe Johnson, then dropped his hand back again to his side.

Peach grinned when he saw the movement. 'You're on your own here, Ray Shepherd. Just the same as Jenny Pitt was when you beat her up. That's the trouble with people like Joe Johnson. They drop you like shit off a red-hot shovel when you're going down for a long stretch.'

'I'm not going down, Peach. There isn't the evidence. You won't get that Jenny Pitt to go into court.'

'Her injuries are being photographed at this very moment, Ray. In glorious technicolour. The blues and the greens and the yellows should be at their best on this bright morning – bright for us, anyway. Our chief photographer's a good lad. He'll make the most of the bruises on the body, when he prints and develops. And it looks as if you might have broken Jenny's cheekbone. Shame for her, but it will help the case.' Percy didn't mind stretching the truth a fraction, in a good cause like this.

'You won't get me for it.' But the apprehension in the thin face belied the words.

'It was DC Pickering here who put us on to you in the first place. Bright lad, he is, though I don't suppose someone like you would give him credit for it.'

Ray Shepherd glanced at Pickering contemptuously. 'Brains of a pig, I should think he has.'

'Intelligent animals, pigs. But I don't expect you've read *Animal Farm*.' Peach switched suddenly back to business. 'I've already noticed that you're left-handed, Shepherd. But it was DC Pickering here who worked out that the man who struck Jenny Pitt so hard with the back of his hand had to be left-handed. Smarter than your average cop, isn't he?'

'Doesn't mean it was me, does it? It could have been any—'

'And then there's the DNA, of course. Useful new addition, DNA, when we're dealing with thickos who forget all about it. Almost unfair, it seems sometimes. We could ask you for a sample now, but there's no real hurry. I think we'll leave all that to the Forensic boys when you're safely in custody.' The DCI smiled happily, even smugly.

181

His attitude had its effect on Shepherd. They could hear the confidence draining out of his voice as he said, 'You don't scare me, Peach. You won't get a DNA match with me.'

'You really think not? Well, I'm glad to say that I don't share your view on that, Mr Shepherd. You broke the skin on that girl's face with the back of your hand: I'm sure you left a small sample of your estimable self behind. I shall be very surprised if it doesn't show up in the blood samples DC Pickering collected from the poor girl's face last night.'

It was news to Gordon Pickering, but he managed a brilliant smile when Shepherd glanced instinctively at him. Peach registered this pleasing reaction without turning towards his DC. Having lured this dangerous fish into the complex meshes of his net, he was looking now for a much bigger catch. 'So you can look forward to at least an ABH charge, or possibly GBH, when we've assessed the injuries. With your record, a conviction for either of them should get you a nice few years inside.'

Now Peach did look at his companion; then he spoke as if they were in conference alone. 'The question is, DC Pickering, can we now nab this bugger for murder?'

'I should think it very possible, sir.'

'I'm glad you agree.' The two faces turned back in unison to look at the slim man behind the desk, studying him in unblinking silence, as though he were a specimen under a microscope.

The scrutiny was unnerving, even to a man who had endured many police interviews in the past. Ray Shepherd said uncertainly, 'I don't know what you're talking about.'

Peach dropped his smile as swiftly as if it had been a foul smell beneath his nose. 'Murder, Mr Shepherd. The unlawful killing of Sarah Dunne on the night of Friday, the fourteenth of November.'

'I didn't do that. I've never killed anyone. You're barking up the wrong tree there. That would have been . . .' His voice drained away, seeming to echo a little in the silent room as it went.

Peach's smile returned slowly, grimly, letting the speaker

182

realize the mistake he had made. 'Would have been who, Mr Shepherd?'

'I don't know who, do I?'

Peach watched him closely, savouring the fear in this man who lived his life by physical violence. Then he said in a low, even voice which made every syllable register, 'If you want to save your own miserable skin, Shepherd, your only chance is to co-operate absolutely with us. Even someone who has behaved as stupidly as you must see that, surely.'

'I'm not a grass.'

The sentiment Peach had heard before, a thousand times. The words that even the youthful Gordon Pickering was bored with by now. Peach shrugged. 'If you want to go down for the maximum, I'll be happy to arrange it. I don't like blokes who beat up helpless girls.'

'You know I can't grass. You know what Joe Johnson would do to anyone who grassed.'

Peach concealed his excitement, apparently coming near to a yawn before he said, 'All right, we'll throw the book at you, if you want to protect one of Johnson's other palookas. We'd like to have the right man, of course, but so long as we get a murder conviction, it will look just as good on our clear-up rates.'

'You won't make murder stick.' Yet the apprehension which now flooded into his vulpine features said otherwise.

'Oh, but I think we will, Shepherd. If I were a betting man, I'd estimate us as about five to one on. Of course, the odds might alter dramatically if you gave us a name.'

'That death was nothing to do with Mr Johnson.'

'Really? You'll understand if I treat that view with a certain scepticism.'

'It was nothing to do with us. I don't know who killed Sarah Dunne.'

Peach saw denial dropping down the wolfish features like a drawbridge. He said, 'Indulge me for a moment, Mr Shepherd – you'll have plenty of time on your hands, where you're going. So let us speculate. If someone in the Johnson organization had killed her, who might it have been? Assuming for a moment at least that it wasn't you?'

'It wasn't us. Wasn't any of us.'

Peach nodded slowly. 'Pity, that. You're a waste of space, Shepherd, and I'd like to see you put away for as long as possible, so a life sentence won't worry me. But the purist in me likes to get the right man, when it's murder. You could call it a weakness in me, and I expect—'

'Lubbock.' The tone was so low that it was no more than a mutter.

'Did you say something, Mr Shepherd?'

'I said Lubbock. It wasn't anyone in our set-up who killed her, but if it had been . . .' His voice trailed away unconvincingly, as if he could not bring himself to repeat the name.

'If it had been, it might have been Lubbock. I understand. Just hope for your sake that you're not setting us up.'

Shepherd shook his thin face miserably, unable to produce the words he needed to plead for discretion from them in following up this information.

Peach nodded to Pickering, who stepped forward and pronounced the words of arrest over the man who had been so contemptuous when they had entered the room.

'You'll be safe from any Johnson reprisals, where you're going,' said Peach sourly.

Father Devoy looked after the finances at St Matthew's church. It was the biggest Roman Catholic parish in the town, and the turnover was considerable.

On those nights when he put on the blue anorak and ventured out into the town, John Devoy had always taken the fifty pounds out of his own resources, but that was becoming less possible as his visits to the ladies of the streets became more frequent.

On the afternoon of Wednesday, the twenty-sixth of November, Father Devoy was wondering whether to extract fifty pounds from the parish coffers for the first time.

No one would notice. He would simply take fifty pounds in cash from the moneys which had been collected at the week-end masses. The old Canon wouldn't question it, wouldn't even consider that the highly regarded and hard-working

184

Father Devoy would be capable of such a thing. The theft, if theft it was, would go undetected.

It was the morality of the gutter: the question was not whether an action was right or wrong, but whether you could do it without being caught. He had always despised that stance, had even preached from the pulpit against it. John Devoy could scarcely believe that he had now sunk so low.

He was losing control of himself and his actions. He despised himself, but he despised also those Jezebels who were leading him on to his destruction. He'd warned that girl on Monday night of the evil she was doing, told her that she was destroying herself and the weak-willed men she led astray. But she hadn't paid any heed to him. Probably she'd laughed at him, when he'd gone away. Perhaps she'd even told her friends about him. Those friends with the short skirts and soft, supple, accessible bodies. Perhaps they'd all laughed at him together.

He didn't fight the urge to go out after them at nights any more, not the way he used to fight it. That was because he knew now when he began to wrestle with his conscience what the outcome would be. He would go in the end. And once you knew what the outcome of your inner turmoil was going to be, it made the argument much shorter. The days when he had prostrated himself before the Blessed Sacrament in the empty church and prayed for the strength to resist seemed suddenly to be a long way behind him, to belong to a different world.

Thoughts raced through his mind in rapid, feverish succession. Contradictory thoughts. Sometimes he saw himself as a lost soul, consigned to Hell by the deadly sin of Lust. Then this picture was subsumed into that of the missionary bringing salvation to those lost souls who paraded in the streets and sold their bodies to weak and fallible men.

There was a third image, one which his troubled brain identified vaguely with the Old Testament. What happened if the women failed to heed that message, if they treated the word of the Lord with contempt, as that girl had on Monday night? Divine retribution would surely fall upon them. Perhaps it was to be John Devoy in his torment who was to be the instrument of that retribution. It seemed that these women were failing to heed the lesson of the girl among their number who had been struck down twelve days ago. They had been back on the streets within days, sinning themselves, and also offering their bodies as the occasion of sin in others.

Father Devoy slipped the fifty pounds into the pocket of his trousers.

Nineteen

David Strachan was pale but determined. Brazen it out. Give them nothing. Let them know that they weren't going to get any co-operation from him. They'd have to prove his guilt, and they wouldn't find that easy if he kept his head. Correction: they'd find it impossible. He tried to adjust his mind-set to the appropriate position. This was Britain, where a man was innocent until proved guilty. The opposition had its hands tied and would soon get frustrated. The system was all on the side of the criminal.

He had never met Detective Chief Inspector Percy Peach.

Strachan had spent a troubled night on the hard bed in the police cell. He had used his one phone call to tell his wife that he had been arrested, that there had been some kind of mistake, that it was probably a case of mistaken identity. It looked as if he would be detained overnight, but he had no doubt that he would be released with apologies on Wednesday morning. He had expected Eileen to be curious, had prepared an elaborate tale for her, but she had been non-committal and low-key. She did not seem astonished by what had happened.

He had been given breakfast and a big mug of tea before eight o'clock. He expected to be interviewed early in the day. But two hours dragged by with no sign of any activity. Every twenty minutes or so, an eye would peer at him through a flap in the steel door, but he got no information when he asked what was going to happen to him.

It was half past ten before he was taken to an interview room, a small, bleak box of a place with green walls and minimal furniture. He was confronted there by a pretty woman with striking red-brown hair and an unsmiling man with a bald head and a very black moustache. When they

187

studied him without speaking, he smiled weakly at them, but received no response. The man said tersely, 'I'm DCI Peach and this is Detective Sergeant Blake. And you are David Strachan and in the deep doo-doo. Do you want a brief?'

'No. I don't need one. I've done noth—'

'Your decision, sir.' Peach gave just the faintest impression of surprise, and David was immediately wondering whether the decision he had taken in the first grey light of the day was the right one. 'But you'll understand that we shall be keeping a record of this conversation. People under arrest have a curious habit of forgetting quite what they said later in the day.'

David Strachan watched the cassette tape silently turning, recording his every syllable, waiting, it seemed to him over the next twenty minutes, to chronicle the errors he made under the relentless attack of the squat man who sat opposite him and who seemed now to be preparing to enjoy himself. He said, 'I don't know why I'm here. I don't know why I've been kept in a cell and treated like a common criminal for the last twelve hours.'

'Really, sir? Well, perhaps we can now give you some answers to those questions.' Peach gave the slightest nod to the woman beside him, without taking his eyes off the pale face two and a half feet from his own.

Lucy Blake spoke unemotionally but with extreme clarity. 'You are probably aware that twelve days ago a young woman was killed within a quarter of a mile of the house where you were arrested last night. Her name was Sarah Dunne and she was a prostitute. As part of the investigation into that crime, the known prostitutes in the area have been equipped with alarm buttons in the rooms where they practise their trade. They have been asked to draw our attention to anyone who threatens to turn violent in the course of a sexual encounter.'

So it was Sally herself who had shopped him. That experienced, accommodating woman, with the pneumatic curves which had so excited his imagination in the nights of the last week. Sally had taken him back to her flat, pretended that she was going to be Miss Whiplash, had taken his money, and then buzzed the police to come and get him.

David looked at the fresh, unlined face of this younger

woman who had told him of Sally's treachery and said, 'She didn't need to do that. I wouldn't have hurt her.'

'Remains to be seen, that. It's what we're here to find out. We'll see what story you have to tell us, Mr Strachan.' Peach's voice was harsh after the cool clarity of his companion. 'Where were you on the night of Friday, the fourteenth of November?'

He wanted to say that he was nowhere near here, that he was a hundred miles away, at home with Eileen, the lean wife who suddenly seemed a safe haven. But he was conscious of the recorder, turning slowly and silently, recording any mistake he might make now to be played back to him, perhaps to be used against him in some sceptical courtroom. 'I can't remember, off hand. I wasn't expecting to—'

'Were you in this area on that night, Mr Strachan?'

'I – I suppose I might have been. I'm a sales representative. It's my area, the north-west. Lancashire in particular. We do a lot of business in this region. There's quite a demand for computer hardware and—'

'Were you anywhere near Brunton on that Friday evening? It's only twelve days ago. It shouldn't be impossible for you to recall.'

He tried the apologetic tone. It usually seemed to work with the traffic police: you often got off with a warning if you seemed contrite. 'I'm afraid I really can't recall where I was, not immediately. It may come to me later. You must remember that I've had a very disturbing and embarrassing experience. My thoughts have been concentrated on what happened last night, only to find you now—'

'We could contact your factory in Wolverhampton, I suppose. Get them to consult their work schedules. Ask them to look at where you were supposed to be on that day. We haven't involved them so far, because we didn't wish to add to your embarrassment unless there was a real need. But now it appears that we're going to need their help.'

'I'd rather you didn't contact the office. I asked my wife to ring in and say I was sick, and if they now find that—'

'I see. Quick work, that was. Dishonest, but resourceful. Would you say that you were habitually dishonest, Mr Strachan?'

'No. It's no more than many—'

'And resourceful? I'd say a man who was going to kill women and go round threatening others would need to be dishonest and resourceful, if he was to get away with it for any length of time.'

'I haven't killed anyone.'

Peach regarded him evenly. 'You'll have to convince us of that.'

'I don't see why I should. Surely a man is innocent until proved guilty.'

Peach smiled at such naivety. 'I wouldn't advise you to take that attitude. Really I wouldn't. I've seen it get a lot of men into trouble. Men less deep in the doo-doo than you are at this moment.' He paused and pursed his lips. David Strachan wondered why this Torquemada of an opponent never seemed to blink. 'Where were you on the night of the fourteenth of November, Mr Strachan?'

'I was in this area. I'd been in Lancaster and Morecambe, trying to pin down orders from three firms in those towns. Although it was a Friday, I didn't finish work until quite late in the day.'

'And after you'd finished, you no doubt returned home for the weekend?'

He wanted to lie. It would have been so easy to agree. But they'd check it out. 'No. I – I was very tired. The M6 is busy on a Friday night.' It sounded feeble, even to him.

'When did you get home, Mr Strachan?'

'It must have been around midday on the Saturday. Between ten and a quarter past twelve, I think.' The ridiculous detail seemed suddenly important to him, as if by convincing them of such unimportant trivia he might get them to believe in other and greater things.

'So where did you spend the Friday night?'

'In Preston. At a bed and breakfast place I've used before. I can give you the address and telephone number, if you want them.'

'I'm sure you can. Can you also give us an account of your movements on that evening?'

He shook his head miserably. 'I went out for a meal in

Preston. Well, just outside, really, down near the Ribble. A Little Chef place, it is. You get used to them, when you're travelling. I'd been there before.' He looked up at them with a sudden desperate hope. 'They might remember me there, if you want to check it.'

'I suppose they might. I know the place: it's near Samlesbury, on the road to Brunton.' Peach paused to let that information sink in. 'What time were you there?'

'I can't be precise. But I suppose I went there at about half past seven. And I didn't hurry my meal. I sat and read the paper. I think I had a second coffee: I usually do, when I've time to kill. I must have been there for an hour at least.'

'So you left a restaurant about seven miles from Brunton at around half past eight on that evening. I have to tell you that our information from Forensic is that Sarah Dunne was killed some time between nine and eleven on that night.'

David felt that he had just sprung a trap of his own making upon himself. He said dully, 'Everything I've told you is true.'

'I'm inclined to believe you, Mr Strachan. To be more precise, I'm ready to believe your account of what you say you did that night, up to the time of half past eight. What happened after you left the Little Chef?'

'I drove back into Preston. Watched the telly in my room. Made myself a cup of tea with the kettle provided. Went to bed just after eleven o'clock.' He produced the phrases like an automaton, giving the impression that he did not expect them to be believed.

'You didn't go for a drink in a pub?'

'No. I'm not a big drinking man.'

'Yet you were drinking last night. Half a bottle of wine, you told the station sergeant. Working yourself up for something, were you?'

'No. Well, not for the kind of thing you're getting at, no.' He wanted to explain that he'd just clinched an important order in Preston, an order that might keep his job safe. That he'd been excited by the thought of high sexual jinks with Sally, with Miss Whiplash. But the words would not come, and they would surely have been the spur only for ridicule from this remorseless man who questioned him so quietly.

'So you claim that you left the Little Chef at around eight thirty and went back to your bed and breakfast house, watched television, and went quietly to bed at just after eleven.'

'Yes.'

'And can you provide us with the name of anyone who saw you between eight thirty and eleven on that night?'

'No. But it's what happened.'

A long pause, during which Peach stared steadily into the mobile and increasingly desperate features of the wretched man on the other side of the small, square table. 'Did you kill Sarah Dunne, Mr Strachan?'

'No. I wasn't even in Brunton that night.'

Lucy Blake said softly, 'Let's move on to last night. What were you proposing to do when you picked up Miss Aspin?'

For a moment, he didn't even knew who she meant. Then he realized that Aspin must be the second name of the well-rounded Sally. Somehow, he'd expected something more exotic. 'I was going to have sex with her. I paid her for it.' He looked at the table. It seemed more difficult to talk about the details of it, to explain himself properly, to this attractive young woman.

'Yes, Mr Strachan. You paid over the odds, in fact, according to Miss Aspin. Tell us why you did that, please.'

'I – I thought she deserved it. I'd been with her before, you see, and I wanted to reward her properly.' He looked hopefully into the young face, wondering how much she knew about the way these things went.

She gave him a faint, mirthless smile. 'You don't strike me as the sentimental type, Mr Strachan. I can't see you paying more than is needed to secure a woman for sex. You were paying in advance for extra services, weren't you?'

He glanced at Peach, silent now when he would have wanted him to be putting the questions, and found the near-black eyes in the round face studying him more intently than ever. David said in a voice they could barely hear. 'Yes. I gave her ten pounds extra because I was anticipating a little extra fun. Fun we never had, thanks to the intervention of a couple of heavy policemen.'

'And what kind of fun would it have been, Mr Strachan?'

The quiet but fiercely concentrated DS Blake was as implacable as her chief in the pursuit of the truth.

Strachan glanced miserably from one to the other. 'I was hoping for extra services. That's what you just called it, isn't it?'

'You tell me, Mr Strachan. What kind of extra services?'

'Well, I don't really know how to put it. Not just straight sex, you see. A bit of – well, aggression, I suppose you'd call it. I asked her to get the whip out, knock me about a bit. Nothing too vicious, you understand, but—'

'And what were you proposing to do to her, Mr Strachan? How was Miss Aspin going to suffer at your hands for her extra payment?'

'Well, I can't really be precise. I was calling her Miss Whiplash, you see. Bit of a joke. Hoping she'd strut about a bit and invite me to discipline her. I think that's what they call it.'

'Is that so? And what would this "discipline" have involved for Miss Aspin? Going to knock her about a bit, were you? Going to knock her about a lot, perhaps. Was she going to go the way that Sarah Dunne had gone?'

'No!' He screamed the word, wanting to make her stop, wanting to convince them that he couldn't have done it.

The two didn't even flinch at his shout, didn't make even that slight concession to the threat of hysteria. They listened to his frantic monosyllable echoing round the windowless cube of the interview room. Then Peach said quietly, 'Then why did you have a length of rope in your pocket?'

There was a long interval, at the end of which Peach said quietly into the recorder, 'For the purposes of the tape, Mr Strachan is shaking his head.'

David said nothing for another few seconds. When he spoke, his voice was hollow with despair. 'I don't mean I didn't have the rope. Of course I had it. I got it out from under the seat of the car and took it into the house with me.'

'So what were you proposing to do with it in the house?'

'I don't know. Not exactly. We were going to play-act a bit. Or that is what I hoped we were going to do. I thought she'd strut about with the whip, smack me once or twice with it, and then I'd – well, discipline her, like I said. Pretend to slap her. Show her the rope.'

Peach studied the man as dispassionately as ever in his anguish. 'You were going to put that rope round her neck, weren't you?'

He wanted to deny it, but he hadn't the energy left to fight them. 'Yes. I suppose so. I wasn't going to hurt her, though. Not really. I just thought that if all went well with the rest of it and we got excited, I'd put the piece of rope round her neck, threaten her a little, even tighten it gently, and then finish off by coming inside her with a big orgasm.' He stared at the scratched surface of the table.

'And you think you wouldn't have hurt her, wouldn't even have alarmed her, with a performance like that?'

He could hear the disbelief in Peach's voice, but he was too exhausted, too beaten down by the two of them, to fight back. He said miserably, 'It turns me on, that sort of thing. It would have got me excited. I wouldn't have hurt her.'

'You know how Sarah Dunne was killed.' It was a statement, not a question.

'No, I don't.'

Peach gave him a faint, disbelieving smile. 'She was killed with a ligature round her throat, Mr Strachan. She died in a few seconds. Someone pulled something tight round her neck from behind. Something very similar to your four-feet piece of rope.'

'It wasn't me. And I wouldn't have killed Sally. I only wanted a bit of fun that I couldn't get at home.'

'A bit of fun like that can quickly get out of hand. Is that what happened with Sarah Dunne?'

'No. I didn't even know the girl.'

Peach regarded him steadily, waiting for long seconds, until David Strachan could not forbear to lift his hunted eyes from the table and look at him.

'I think you should get yourself a brief, Mr Strachan. We shall be asking for a DNA sample, when you've had a little time in your cell.'

Twenty

ather John Devoy took the familiar dark-blue anorak from its peg in the caretaker's room behind the youth club. He had given up speculating now about the original owner. The garment had become the costume for that other persona which took him over when he ventured out at night on to the narrow streets of the old part of Brunton, the section of the town where vice hid its head in the shadows.

The anorak was too big for him, but usually he felt something comforting in its looseness about his shoulders. Tonight it seemed more than usually large, seemed to hang about him 'like a giant's robe upon a dwarfish thief'. The phrase came springing back at him from childhood. Probably from *Macbeth*, he thought. That memory must have been stored away in his subconscious, when he had thought it long gone. What other effects was that subconscious having upon him? He saw the priest who operated by day now as another and totally different person. He felt his world collapsing around him, like Macbeth's Scotland when the wood of Dunsinane began to move upon him.

He took a more circuitous route than usual towards the street he knew he was destined to tread, as if he hoped that even now there might be some intervention from the angels to save him from his sin. But no divine intercession, no sudden shaft of saving grace, no voice thundering in Damascene command from the dark clouds above him, interrupted Father Devoy's journey into the dark night of his soul.

The old cotton town of Brunton, with its deserted mills presiding like ruined monasteries over the drab industrial landscape, was not the place for miracles or for angels.

John Devoy flicked up the hood on the anorak over his

head and sank his hands deep into its pockets, as though its voluminous folds could save him from his fate. But his hand felt the fifty pounds in notes that he had taken from the parish funds earlier in the day; even his sense of touch reminded him of how deep he had trodden into evil.

He would spend his fifty pounds and his lust on the woman he had spoken to on Monday night, the one he had tried to warn about leading men into sin. And after he had lain with her, after she had sold her body to him for money, he would warn her again about the wretchedness of her life, about the danger she presented, with her soft curves and her whore's smile and her readiness to sell the sweetest intimacies of herself to vulnerable men.

And if she ignored his warnings as she had last night, he wouldn't let it go. Men were weak vessels, who must be protected from the occasions of sin, especially when those occasions presented themselves in this delectable, irresistible form. That other girl had died, almost two weeks ago; this one should take heed of that, if she was to avoid the same divine retribution.

The woman was on the usual street. He felt that he had known all along that she would be there, blonde and beguiling, in her appointed place. Tonight had an air of inevitability about it. Something, but he was not yet sure what, was coming to a conclusion.

Usually he had lurked in the shadows, waiting for his moment, and had then declared himself with an urgency which stemmed from his need for secrecy. But tonight he strolled quite openly along the street, meeting the smiling strumpet head-on, walking without hesitation towards the instrument of the Devil.

They spoke the dialogue as if playing out a pre-determined scene, his own lines rising effortlessly to his lips for his part in this strange drama. Toyah Burgess had been half-expecting him. She flashed him a wide glimpse of her white teeth through the darkness and said, 'You again. I hope you mean business and not preaching tonight!'

John Devoy scarcely registered that word from his other calling, the one he left behind in the presbytery. He said urgently, 'I want you! Want you badly! And I've got the money.'

'That's what I like to hear! That's what keeps the wheels of the world turning, for a simple girl like me.'

She thrust her arm through his, urged him along over the uneven stone flags, which glistened with wetness even on this moonless night.

He felt his lust rising immediately at her touch, even though it was only her fingers on his forearm through the thick padding of the anorak. He let his hand steal up to her breast, muttered again into her ear, 'I've got the money.'

'All in good time, big boy!' Toyah said automatically. She was wondering if this was what the touch of a murderer felt like, these familiar, unremarkable, questing fingers. She removed his hand from her breast and put it back on her forearm, placing her other hand on top of it and walking along in step, as if they were any normal, affectionate couple. Now that the moment had come, she did not feel afraid, for she knew she had protection, knew she was doing no more than playing out a minor but essential scene in what might eventually prove to be a great drama.

John Devoy found in his tension that his hearing seemed more acute. He listened to the sound of their footsteps on the pavement, moving in harmony, landing together in a silence which seemed more than usually profound. Far off, over the tops of many buildings, he heard the faint sound of a bus pulling away from the town's centre. His lines in the play seemed to have dried up now. He said uncertainly, 'I shouldn't be doing this and neither should you. If you won't promise to give up selling yourself like this, I'll have to—'

The men came from behind him, strong, unyielding, and certain of what they had to do. He heard a shrill yelp of pain as his wrist was forced up hard between his shoulderblades. It took him a second to realize that the sound had come from him.

Then Toyah Burgess was saying, 'There's no need to hurt him! Please don't hurt him more than you need to!' The concern in her voice must be for him, he thought. He could scarcely believe it possible, such was the depth of his self-loathing.

Then one of the men was shouting the words of arrest into his ear, warning him that he did not have to say anything but if he withheld information which he later intended to use in court, it could prejudice his defence.

They loaded him carefully into the police car which now drew up alongside them, watching him carefully for any sign of aggression, any attempt to elude their hands.

Father Devoy attempted neither resistance nor escape. His distress was submerged in an overwhelming tide of relief.

On the following morning, Thursday the twenty-seventh of November, DCI Peach climbed the stairs to Chief Super-intendent Tucker's penthouse office with a lightened heart. He could see the end of this one, now. But he would put money on the fact that Tommy Bloody Tucker hadn't a clue about it.

Tucker didn't look pleased to see him. 'I have a busy schedule today,' he said accusingly.

'Just keeping you briefed on the Sarah Dunne case, sir. As per your orders.'

'I see. Well, it appears the murderer probably won't be found on our patch, Peach. In view of the connection now established with the murders of those two prostitutes in the Midlands.'

'No connection, sir.' Percy gave just a hint of his satis-faction in delivering that information. Silly old sod hadn't listened to his radio or read his newspapers, as usual. Probably Brünnhilde Barbara only allowed him Wogan and Radio 2 in the mornings.

'I think you'll find there is, Peach. That phone call last Sat-urday night was authenticated as coming from Birmingham and—'

'Man's been arrested, sir. In Walsall. He's confessed to killing the two toms in Birmingham. But he wasn't anywhere near Lancashire on the night Sarah Dunne was killed. I've spoken to the CID Superintendent in Walsall. The man they have in custody was on a works outing in Walsall that night. With seventy-three witnesses, apparently.'

Tucker stared hard into the impassive round face on the other side of the desk, then took a deep breath. 'I was never really convinced about this theory of a serial killer, you know. You jump to conclusions rather too readily, if I may say so, Percy. Without weighing all the evidence. I feel now that I shouldn't really have allowed you to sell me this one.'

'I see, sir.' Percy fixed his gaze on his favourite spot six inches above Tucker's head and resolved not to allow himself the release of anger.

'I shan't make it public that you were mistaken about this, of course.'

'That's good to hear, sir.'

'Solidarity, that's the key to good management and a cohesive CID unit. I'm here to carry the can.'

'Yes, sir.'

'Paid for it, in fact. So we'll say no more about this particular wild goose chase.'

He'll have convinced himself in seconds that the serial killer really was my notion, thought Peach, making a mental note to get a videotape of Tucker's media briefing on the previous Tuesday. He said, 'That phone call trying to link our murder with the pair in the Midlands may still be relevant, sir.'

'Relevant?' Tucker spoke the word as if it were part of an obscure foreign tongue.

'Yes, sir. Someone made the phone call, even though it wasn't the Walsall killer. Someone with a genuine Birmingham accent, according to our forensic audiologist. And possibly, just possibly, someone wanting to throw us off the scent. To divert us from our local suspects towards the false trail in the Midlands.'

Tucker frowned as he digested this difficult idea. 'I suppose that is possible. But probably over-subtle. I think you'll find in due course that this was no more than a straightforward hoax caller.'

'That is possible, of course, sir.'

'Not only possible, but overwhelmingly the most likely

explanation. You get a lot of hoax calls, when a murder goes undetected for any length of time, you know.'

'Yes, sir.' Peach noted with renewed irritation his chief's capacity to move from the outrageous to the blindin' bleedin' obvious.

'Anyway, you'd better get on with bringing me up to date on this case. I've a busy schedule today, you know.'

'Yes, sir, you did mention that.' Peach banished his automaton's expression in favour of one of his sunniest smiles. 'Well, there's no sign at the moment that this crime is down to a Mason, sir.'

Tucker's brow clouded. 'Your prejudice against Freemasonry is neither amusing nor original, Peach. I've told you before, a Mason is most unlikely—'

'Four times as likely to commit a serious crime as an ordinary member of the public, in the Brunton area, sir. You know my research.'

'I couldn't not know of it. You remind me of it at every opportunity.'

'Most interesting little monograph, it should make, sir. When I've the time to write it up and table the statistics. I'll give you full credit for help with the research, sir. Solidarity, as you say, is the secret of our success.'

'How near are you to an arrest?' Tucker jutted his jaw aggressively. Put the little sod in his place. Press the nose above that objectionable black moustache firmly against the grindstone.

'Quite near, sir. I wouldn't like to say how near. Mustn't jump to conclusions too readily, as you reminded me earlier.' He looked over his shoulder, as if to check that they were not overheard, then leant forward and spoke confidentially across the big desk. 'We pulled in a Catholic priest last night!'

The public relations man that was always just beneath the smooth surface of Thomas Bulstrode Tucker's skin leapt out as suddenly as a rearing stallion. 'A Catholic priest? This could tear the town apart.'

'Been giving some of our ladies of the night a real good regular seeing-to over the last few months, apparently,' said Percy gleefully.

'Peach, for Heaven's sake be cautious!'

The DCI chuckled. 'That's rather good, sir. For Heaven's sake! But we've no need to be careful, sir. The man's confessed to paying for it and getting it, apparently. Of course, I've still to interrogate him. Going to do that as soon as I've finished here, sir.'

'Then go carefully. When religion is involved, there's no knowing what—'

'Thought I'd take DS Blake in with me, sir. Get her to flash a bit of gusset, if he clams up on us.'

Tucker blanched visibly: an interesting sight, Percy thought. 'You'll do no such thing, Peach. Handle this with kid gloves.'

Peach looked disappointed. 'Really, sir? I was thinking more in fishnet tights terms. Man's shown where his weakness lies, so we might as well exploit it, I thought. But if you'd like to do the interview yourself, sir, I'm sure we'd all be delighted to—'

'No, Peach! You know my policy on these things. Not to interfere. To show confidence in my staff. To maintain—'

'Maintain an overview, sir. Yes, I understand. Just like to flash a bit of female thigh at a man, when he's shown a fancy for it. But you're the boss, sir, as always.' He nodded dolefully.

Anyone who had seen Peach in action would have known that the last thing he would have done was to use female lingerie in these circumstances. Anyone who knew Lucy Blake would have known how she would react to the very suggestion. But it was so long since Thomas Bulstrode Tucker had seen his staff working at the crime-face that he was easily deceived. He said weakly, 'Is this Roman Catholic priest your only suspect?'

'No, sir. We've still got our policeman in the frame.' Peach grinned happily at the prospect of charging down another politically dangerous avenue.

Tucker gave a sickly grin. 'The Sergeant from Morecambe, was it?'

'The Inspector from Blackpool, sir. Traffic Police. Name of Thomas Boyd. Stolid sort of chap to look at, sir. Wouldn't have thought he had it in him, if you'll pardon the expression.'

'Go carefully, Peach. That's an order. This is a sensitive area, when it involves a senior officer from another force. Haven't you been able to eliminate him yet?'

Peach shook his head vigorously and happily. 'Far from it, sir. Inspector Boyd was spotted cruising the streets in our area on Tuesday night. Looking for a certain lady of the streets to offer a little violence, I reckon. He ran into one of our patrols and drove off without dropping his trousers. But he remains in the frame.' He smiled and nodded his satisfaction with this happy situation.

'Along with others.' Tucker tried to speak firmly and assert himself.

'Yes, sir. There's Joe Johnson, for a start.'

'Our local Napoleon of Crime.' Tucker produced the phrase as if it were original. Then he went on more gloomily, 'If Johnson's involved, we won't get him. He's too big now, has too many influential friends. You know the problem: no one will give evidence against him. He's got the local crime scene sewn up and everyone's scared of him.'

'True enough, sir. And he's bigger than local, now. He's got casinos and clubs in Cumbria, the north-east and the Midlands, as well as Lancashire. Some of them are no doubt legitimate businesses.'

'We're not going to get him then, are we? Let's hope Joe Johnson has nothing to do with this murder.'

'Let's hope he *has*, sir! And that we can pin it on him!' Peach spoke with unusual vehemence, his passion for taking villains for once outweighing his contempt for Tommy Bloody Tucker.

Tucker shook his head. 'You've got to be realistic, Peach. Of course, I'd like to catch the man myself, but now that he's becoming almost respectable, the moment may have passed.'

'He'll be joining the Masons, if we leave it long enough,' said Percy grimly.

Tucker decided not to rise to this. 'Have we any other possibilities?'

'Yes, sir. Man by the name of David Strachan. Commercial traveller, sets up computer systems for firms and provides

202

the necessary software. His firm's in Birmingham, but the north-west is his area.'

'That phone call on Saturday was from Birmingham. The one trying to tie our murder in with the Midlands murders. The one you said might be designed to throw us off the trail.' Tucker came as near to excitement as he ever permitted himself to get.

'Yes, sir. We've taken a recording of Strachan's voice. The forensic audiologist is testing it against the tape of that call which came in on Saturday night.' Peach looked at his watch and said with a proper sense of drama, 'Perhaps at this very minute.'

'I have a feeling this might be our man, Peach. You'll tell me it's early days, but you get a feeling for these things when you've been in this detection business as long as I have.' He steepled his fingers and nodded sagely.

Percy decided that his chief watched too much television. Not surprising, really: he'd bugger all else to do. He fed him another titbit. 'Strachan patronized our local toms, sir. One in particular: mature blonde lady, name of Sally Aspin. Don't suppose you know her, sir?'

'Of course I don't, Peach! I'm not in the habit of patronizing our local prostitutes, am I?'

'No, sir, I suppose not. Bit of research, perhaps, I was thinking. Anyway, this chap Strachan likes a bit of rough play. Paid extra for it. Called the buxom Sally Miss Whiplash, I believe.' He shook his head sadly at the frailty of mankind.

'He sounds more and more like our man, you know. Is there anything else you can offer?'

'Well, sir, he admitted when we interviewed him that he proposed to offer a little violence himself, when he was sufficiently excited. And he had a piece of rope in his pocket which he admitted he wanted to put round his partner's neck at some stage in the exchange.'

'This is a clincher, Peach! You mark my words, a clincher!'

'You don't think this could be a normal sexual practice, sir? I mean, my experience is very limited, but they tell me the combination of sex and violence excites some men. I wanted to consult you about this, sir. I thought perhaps that with your

203

wider experience of connubial exchanges you could offer me some guidance as to the range of . . .' He spread his arms slowly and helplessly, opening the curtains on the delicious vision of Brünnhilde Barbara pursuing a sexually excited Tommy Bloody Tucker around the bedroom with a whip.

'No! What on earth do you think I am, Peach?'

Percy resisted temptation once again. 'A man of rich and varied experience, sir, in private as well as public life.'

'In sexual matters, Peach, I am a novice.'

'You surprise me, sir. You're sure this is not just the becoming modesty for which you are noted throughout the station?'

'Indeed it is not, Peach. I have no idea how the mind of a man like this – this commercial representative—'

'David Strachan, sir.'

'Thank you. How the mind of a man like David Strachan works. But I'm pretty sure he's our man.'

Peach decided not to draw attention to any contradiction here. 'He's given us a DNA sample, sir. It's being compared by Forensic with samples taken from the body of Sarah Dunne.'

'Good. If there's a match, I shall charge the man myself.'

Peach went back down the stairs hoping that that sad creature David Strachan was not guilty of murder. With Tommy Bloody Tucker gunning for him, there must be a very good chance that he was innocent.

Twenty-One

John Devoy presented a wretched figure to the succession of officers who checked on him in his cell at twenty-minute intervals. He sat with his face in his hands on the edge of the bunk, seeming not to alter his position over several hours. When he was eventually taken up to an interview room, he moved like an automaton, heeding the constable's commands but never looking up at him.

Peach took Lucy Blake in with him to question the man, but his attitude was very different from the one he had suggested to Tucker only minutes earlier. He studied the priest for a moment before he said, 'You will understand that we need to record this exchange, Father Devoy. Do you wish to have legal representation?'

'No.'

'It might be advisable.'

'It wouldn't make any difference. A lawyer would advise caution, and I don't want to be cautious. I'm finished.'

'That sounds very like despair. Isn't that still the worst sin of all, for someone like you?'

Devoy lifted his eyes from the desk, seemed to take note of them for the first time. He glanced at Lucy Blake curiously, as if he had not realized until this moment that she was in the small, square room, then returned his attention to the man who had spoken to him. 'You are of the faith?'

Peach smiled, recognizing an expression he had not heard for many years. 'No, I have lost it. I was brought up a Catholic. But I don't attend church any more.'

'But you remember that Despair is the ultimate sin, and remind me of it. There is a kind of charity in that, Chief Inspector, and I thank you for it. But it is difficult for me

205

to see any hope at the moment.' He surprised himself with a weak smile. 'There. We have touched on Faith, Hope and Charity already. Perhaps redemption is still possible, for you at least.'

Having secured the attention of a man who had seemed atrophied by his guilt, Peach hardened towards his more normal interviewing mode. 'You're in a lot of trouble, Father Devoy.'

'A hell of a lot, you might say. That might be the appropriate term, in my case.'

'We deal with this world, Father, not with some hypothetical other world. And you were brought in here because of threatening behaviour.'

'And for consorting with a known prostitute.'

'No. That is not an offence, in itself.'

The priest was so steeped in the idea of sin, so sunk in his own guilt, that he seemed not to understand this. Eventually he shook his head and said. 'I have given way to lust and spent my seed with harlots. As a minister of the church, I could scarcely have done worse.'

'Perhaps. We in the police service see worse crimes than lust, every day, Father Devoy. But we are not here to debate theology. No doubt that aspect of your conduct will be pursued in other places and by other people. DS Blake and I are pursuing an inquiry into the worst crime of all. Murder.'

Devoy nodded. 'The primal and worst sin. Cain and Abel.' He looked up suddenly. 'But what have I to do with murder?'

'That's what we're here to establish. You threatened violence against Miss Toyah Burgess.'

His face was blank for a moment before recognition dawned. 'Is that the girl I was with when your men arrested me?'

'Yes. Were you planning to harm her?'

'I was planning to have sex with her. I had the price she charges for her body in the pocket of my anorak.'

'We know that. The money was taken from you by the custody sergeant last night. If you are released from custody, it will be returned to you.' Peach spoke as if he were instructing not a man in his forties but an adolescent in his first brush with the law. He reminded himself again that the strange man on the other side of the square table might be a killer.

He had to do that, because this man of the cloth, who felt himself drowning in his sin, carried a kind of wild innocence about him. The first murderer Peach had ever seen, when he was still a young policeman on the beat, had been clothed in this same air of detachment from the world, even after he had put twenty-three stab wounds into the body of the bully who had tormented him.

John Devoy said, as if speaking through a medium, 'That fifty pounds wasn't my own money. It belongs to the parish.'

'It can go back to the parish, then. That's theft avoided,' said Peach acerbically. 'I'm not interested in the money, or in what you intended to do with Toyah Burgess in the sack, Father Devoy. I'm interested in the threats of violence which you offered to her.'

'She was using her body as—'

'Last night wasn't the first time you had accosted her, was it?'

'I've been with prostitutes before, if that is what you mean. It was my own money then, but whenever I could—'

'We're not interested in the sex, Father Devoy. Please try to understand that. Why do you think our officers were waiting to arrest you last night?'

'I – I don't know. I haven't even thought about it. I'm a priest who was consorting with harlots. Isn't that enough?'

'That isn't why you were brought here under arrest. That isn't why we're interviewing you now. Two weeks ago tomorrow, a young girl acting as a prostitute was murdered very near to where you were arrested last night.'

'Sarah Dunne, yes. She was a Roman Catholic. But she came from Bolton or greater Manchester, I think. She wasn't buried here.'

'She hasn't been buried anywhere, yet. Her body hasn't been released. It is still part of the evidence in a murder case.' Peach heard the irritation creeping into his voice. He nodded to Lucy Blake.

She said softly, 'You'd seen Toyah Burgess before, hadn't you, Father? And you'd spoken to her, as recently as Monday night.'

Devoy looked at her as if he had not expected her to speak. 'Yes. How do you know that?'

'And what did you say to her on that evening? Did you ask her to have sex with you?'

'No.' It was suddenly important to John Devoy that this woman understood that. The Blessed Virgin loomed large in his culture, and if beautiful young women were not to be objects of lust, then they must be respected figures of authority. 'I went to warn her that she must leave the path of evil. That if she persisted upon it, she would go to Hell herself and take vulnerable men with her.'

The phrases which had been familiar to Percy Peach as echoes of his childhood were alien to Lucy Blake. This strange, disturbed man seemed to her in need of psychiatric help, seemed to be divorced from the real world. He might be pathetic, but was he also very dangerous? She said gently, 'So you didn't suggest on Monday night that she had sex with you?'

'No. I took no money with me on Monday. I went out into the world of Satan to try to rescue one of his victims before it was too late.' He put his head on one side like a bird, appeared to weigh his words and his motives, and then nodded his head sharply two or three times.

The sudden, odd, uncoordinated movements of his body convinced her that he was very near to breaking point. She said, 'You threatened Miss Burgess on Monday night, didn't you?'

He stared at her with wide bright eyes, then nodded sharply again, as if digesting a new idea. 'You could call it a threat, I suppose. I told her that the wages of sin are death. There is surely no greater threat than the fires of Hell.'

It was a long time since Lucy had heard anyone talk about the fires of Hell. She said, 'You offered her a more personal threat, didn't you, Father Devoy?'

'I told her she was spending the glories of her body where they should not be spent. That she was spreading her own corruption amongst others. Amongst—'

'You laid hands upon her, didn't you?'

'Amongst fallible men. I told her she was taking fallible men with her into perdition.' He spoke as if he had not even heard her interruption.

'Did you lay hands upon her, Father Devoy?'

Perhaps it was the repetition of his title that brought him back to the reality of the claustrophobic little room and the two persistent questioners. 'I may have done. I wanted to convince her that she was the occasion of sin in others. Men are weak vessels, at the best of times. We are not proof against the temptations of women like her.'

'She had a scarf around her neck. Did you get hold of it?'

'Temptation must be removed from our paths, if we are to survive and attain the Kingdom of Heaven.'

Peach, noting his companion's increasing confusion with the man's language, took over the interrogation again. 'Answer the question, please. Did you or did you not lay hands on Miss Burgess?'

'She represented a dangerous occasion of sin. If she were removed from the streets, a dangerous occasion of sin would be removed from the paths of men. She was acting as an instrument of the Devil.'

Peach regarded him sardonically. 'If I remember the Church's teaching about dangerous occasions of sin, Father Devoy, it was that they should be avoided. You were hardly avoiding such occasions when you pursued known prostitutes and paid them for their favours.'

The priest's glittering eyes had been fixed above their heads. Now they dropped, first to Peach's impassive face and then to the small square table between them. 'It is true. I am the worst kind of sinner, the shepherd who abuses the trust of his flock.'

Peach wanted to tell him to drop all this flummery and answer basic questions. But he sensed that there was an illness in this strange man, or at least an oddness that he must indulge, if he was to get through to the truth within a disturbed mind. He said quietly, 'Miss Burgess had a chiffon scarf around her neck when you accosted her on Monday night. Did you seize the ends of it and draw it tight around her neck?'

'Is that what the woman says I did?'

'Answer the question please.'

'I – I suppose I may have done that. I was agitated. I was trying to convince her that she must see the error of her ways. I was telling her how she was encouraging men to commit mortal sin.'

'So you seized her scarf and tightened it about her neck.'

'I probably did, yes, in my agitation. I was anxious to save her soul from Satan. Anxious to save the souls of the men she was leading into evil.'

'So you were a little careless of her body.'

'I suppose I may have been. I did not mean to hurt her.'

Peach regarded him steadily, trying to work out exactly what was happening behind those finely cut but now very mobile features. 'You frightened her badly. She feels that if a car had not come along the street at that moment on Monday night, you might well have done her serious harm; might in fact have tightened that chiffon scarf around her neck until it strangled her.'

Devoy said nothing for several long seconds. Then he said, 'I was very agitated. Very anxious to convince her of the evil path she was treading. But I don't think I would have done serious harm to her body.'

It was Peach's turn to pause now, weighing the man's words, estimating his sincerity as Devoy made this extra-ordinary attempt to evaluate his own conduct. Then he said slowly, 'Let's come back to last night. You weren't trying to warn her off then. You were only too anxious to pay her and sample her wares.'

'Yes. That is my own vice and wickedness. That is why I am finished as a priest.' There was no self-pity in him, but only the deepest of self-loathing.

'And when you had finished the sex, what would you have done then?'

'I don't know. Remonstrated with her, I suppose. I know that it's illogical to lie with her and then complain about her conduct, but I think I would have tried again to show her that hers was an evil calling, when I had spent my seed within her.' He gave a mirthless smile at the contradictions in his conduct.

Peach studied him, waiting to see if he would crack, would venture further into the exposure of this other self who had torn him apart. But Devoy kept his gaze fixed upon the scratched table between them, until eventually Peach said, 'And what about that other girl, Sarah Dunne? Were you on the streets that night? Were you anxious to avail yourself of that young body? To warn her that she might be the occasion of sin for men like you?'

'No. I didn't venture out on that Friday night.'

'Is there any witness to that?'

A pause, in which he might have been thinking, or might not. He looked blank and defeated, near to collapse. 'No. No witness. I was in my own room in the presbytery at St Matthew's.'

Peach said quietly, 'Sarah Dunne was killed by someone who drew her scarf tight about her neck until it throttled her. That was exactly the method with which you threatened Toyah Burgess on Monday night. Father Devoy, did you kill Sarah Dunne?'

'No.'

'We would like you to give us a DNA sample, Father Devoy. It will be compared with samples taken from the body of Sarah Dunne. Do you understand the implications of this?'

'Yes. I have no objection.'

They thought those would be his last words, but when they indicated that the interview was over, he said, 'I shall have to give the Bishop all the details of this.'

It seemed as if that was a worse horror for him than all that had gone before.

Twenty-Two

The United Kingdom regards itself as a country where the law generally prevails. Yet for a fortunate few who escape the law, crime is a very profitable business.

An estimated four hundred crime barons in the country control some four hundred and forty million pounds of ill-gotten gains. The top thirty-nine among these are worth around two hundred million pounds. Joe Johnson had recently joined the ranks of this select – and infamous – group.

These men are shrewd enough to diversify their wealth into legal businesses as they become more affluent. The Proceeds of Crime Act of 2002, which did away with the need to tie a criminal's cash to a particular crime, has made it much easier for the police to seize money derived from criminal activity. Yet these most successful criminals, by developing legal sources of income to go alongside their darker projects, make it very difficult for the police to prove that vast sums of money actually came from criminal activities. A crooked accountant can do wonders with the books of a private company.

Joe Johnson got most of his income from drugs and prostitution and then laundered it through the books of legal but less profitable activities. His clubs and casinos were sometimes seedy, but they were properly licensed and perfectly legal. And they provided the perfect cover for his darker and immensely more profitable enterprises.

Chief Superintendent Tucker might have been pusillanimous in his contention that Johnson had now moved beyond the reach of arrest, but he was stating no more than a commonly held police view about such men. The situation was a shame, but it was a fact. Bloody-minded people like Chief Inspector Peach, who thought they could still imprison such men, were flying in the face of the facts.

Johnson had an Achilles' heel, however. As he climbed the ranks of crime, he continued to employ most of the hoodlums who had started with him in the days when brawn had been the all-important tool, and he had climbed on the back of the fear he instilled. Some of them were little more than crude 'heavies', neither as intelligent nor as quick on their feet as the man who employed them. They were loyal and they were cheap.

But for a man making millions each year from crime, economy is not always the best policy.

Ray Shepherd had been one of Johnson's later employees, a thin, steely man who knew the way to operate and had his boss's confidence. But he was a sadist, a man who enjoyed inflicting violence. Even in an organization like Johnson's, sadism got in the way of objectivity, and made him a liability as an employee. Moreover, like all cowards, Ray Shepherd had been easily scared when he came under threat. Faced with arrest for his assault on young Jenny Pitt, he had lost his nerve in the face of Peach's mixture of bluff and unflinching hostility. He had given his tormentor the name of Lubbock.

It took a little time to locate the man. He was still employed by Johnson, but he had been working for the last two days as a doorman at a small club in Carlisle: a bouncer, part of the muscle such places needed. Hidden away, in Percy Peach's view; the DCI had a suspicious mind.

Peach took Brendan Murphy with him and directed the young DC to drive the hundred miles up the M6 'like the clappers'. They found Lubbock lying on his bed in his room at his back-street lodgings. They had an interesting conversation about his whereabouts and his actions over the preceding thirteen days.

Deprived of the use of his fists, Lubbock was a pathetic opponent for Peach. They arrested him and deposited him in the local nick, where his miserable body would be safe from the attentions of his employer.

Lubbock was not allowed to phone Joe Johnson. By five o'clock, Peach and Murphy were back in Brunton.

*   *   *

213

It seemed to Peach appropriate that the last act should be played out in the big house where Johnson had so patronized them six days earlier. He took Lucy Blake with him and arrived unannounced at six thirty on that Thursday evening.

'Hurst Leigh' seemed to loom even larger above them against the night sky. Even the unflappable Peach sounded tense as he spoke their names into the microphone in the gatepost, and Lucy Blake realized for the first time just how much this meant to him.

There was a pause before Johnson's voice, harsh and distorted, rasped at them through the metal grill. 'Come back in the morning. I don't ruin my evenings by talking to pigs.'

'You will on this occasion. Unless you want the place surrounded by wailing police sirens and the neighbours out to watch the show.'

'This is harassment.'

'Maybe. I don't think a magistrate would see it as that.'

There was no further word through the grill, but the wrought-iron gates eased slowly back to allow them entry. The maid was in a black uniform: Johnson liked the trimmings of opulence. She said, 'Mr Johnson says he hopes this won't take long, because it's most inconvenient. He's waiting for you in his study.'

'Thank you. We know the way.' Peach led the way, walking so fast that Blake had almost to run to keep up with him.

He burst through the heavy oak door without knocking, and found Johnson speaking on the phone. The big man glared at him, then said into the mouthpiece, 'I can't talk any more now. I'll get back to you.' Then he said to the intruder, 'Manners as good as ever, Peach. The maid would have brought you up. And she'd have knocked before she came in.'

'Surprised you don't employ a butler, with your pretensions.' Peach looked round at the leather Chesterfield, the long, low table of luxuriant house plants beneath the heavily curtained Georgian window, the alpine prints on either side of the bookcase with its leather-bound, never-opened volumes. He nodded at the one jarring note in this carefully designed good taste, the framed cinema poster of Don Corleone snarling at his Mafia henchmen in *The Godfather*. 'Fancy yourself as the head of a criminal dynasty, do you?'

'I'm not in the mood to waste my time, Peach. Tell me why you're here, and then get out of my house.'

'We're here about the murder of Sarah Dunne on the night of the fourteenth of November.'

'A death about which I know nothing, as I told you when last we spoke.'

'You did. You also told us that she had been killed near Alexandra Street, a fact we didn't even know ourselves at that time.'

The big man smiled. 'I didn't kill this Sarah Dunne. I can account for my whereabouts for every minute of that Friday evening. Not that I intend to do so.'

'Or we to ask you. We don't believe you killed her yourself. Our contention is that you gave the orders for the girl to be killed, because she was challenging your monopoly of prostitution in the town, and because you wanted to scare anyone else who proposed to follow her example.'

'That isn't true, of course. Even if it was, you'd never be able to prove it.' Johnson sat down on the swivel chair behind the leather-topped desk, leaving them standing in front of it. He eyed Lucy Blake insolently and appreciatively from top to toe, as if considering her as an addition to the ranks of harlotry.

Peach had been prepared for this and more. He was angry, but it was a cold, controlled anger, disciplined by his conviction that he would arrest this man, eventually. He said, 'Ray Shepherd is already under lock and key. He will be charged with inflicting Actual Bodily Harm on Jenny Pitt.'

Johnson raised his eyebrows a little, narrowed his smile just a fraction. 'I can't comment on that, as the incident had nothing to do with me. If convicted, Shepherd will naturally be dismissed from my employment.'

'Jenny Pitt was warned off by you thirty-six hours before

215

she was assaulted. You told her on Sunday evening that if she intended to practise prostitution in this town she would need your protection.'

'Really? I don't expect for a moment that you have any witnesses to support that contention.'

'Ray Shepherd will no doubt be put away for several years, with his previous record. He will also state in court that he was acting on your orders when he beat up Miss Pitt.'

Johnson allowed himself a snigger. 'Oh, I doubt that, DCI Peach. I doubt that very much.'

'When you are facing a murder charge yourself, Joe Johnson, you will find that support and loyalty drop away alarmingly.'

For the first time, real anger flickered across the coarse features above the immaculate suit. His stocky opponent's certainty was beginning to get to him. Peach noted the reaction and began to play his trumps. 'You made mistakes when we were here last Friday. One of them was to draw my attention to the News Review section of the *Sunday Times* and the article there about the hunt for the Yorkshire Ripper, Peter Sutcliffe.'

'I always enjoy factual accounts of police incompetence. That was a full and very good account.'

'I don't dispute that. I went to the press files and read it myself. The article reminded me of one of the crucial things which threw the man in charge of the Ripper hunt off the scent. That was a taped message from a man with a north-eastern accent who claimed to be the Ripper. For two years the murder team were attempting to "find the Geordie", when the Ripper did not come from the north-east at all.'

'Yes, I remember that. As I say, I'm a bit of a connoisseur of police ineptitude.'

'So that when we had a phone call from a man with a strong Birmingham accent a day later, I was inclined to treat it with a certain degree of scepticism.'

'A view not shared by your Chief Superintendent, if I remember what I saw of his press conference on television.'

'I also thought that I knew where the idea had come from.'

Peach stared hard into the face of a man who was not used to being challenged.

'I don't do accents, Peach. That isn't one of my many talents.'

'No. As usual, you get other people to do your dirty work. The call was made from a phone booth in Birmingham, and the local accent was genuine. You own a casino within two hundred yards of where that call came from. My belief is that it was made on your orders, when you realized after our visit that we had you in the frame for the Sarah Dunne murder.'

The smile this time was a little forced, but Johnson was perfectly calm as he said, 'Circumstantial, Peach, highly circumstantial. You'd never make it stick in court.'

'Perhaps not. But when people are charged with being an accessory to murder, they often become very anxious to explain their conduct. It's my belief that we'll find and punish the man who made that phone call, in due course. But we won't need him to give you a life sentence.'

Peach's certainty was now visibly affecting Johnson. The skin seemed to tighten a little around his forehead and temples, making the lines of his old scars a little whiter and more noticeable. He rose from his chair as he said, 'I think I've had enough of this. I've been patient with your wild theories for quite long enough.' He leered slowly down the curves of Lucy Blake and said, 'I'll be very happy to offer my hospitality to DS Blake, if she likes to stay, but I think it's time you were on your way, Peach.'

'You should really have got rid of Lubbock, of course.' Peach threw the name like a quiet stiletto at his man's ribs, and watched him sink back into his chair as if he had been physically wounded.

Johnson kept his voice even as he said, 'I have no idea what you're talking about. I believe I have employed – perhaps still do employ – a man called Lubbock. I have many employees nowadays.' His attempt to indicate the width of his empire by a wide wave of his arm fell flat because the limb seemed suddenly enfeebled.

'I suppose you felt that if you looked after him, gave him some sort of employment, you could keep him under scrutiny and ensure his loyalty. So you sent him off the scene as soon as he'd killed Sarah Dunne. He didn't seem to have enjoyed his week in Morecambe, by the way. Not much to do at the seaside in November, especially for a man as limited as Len Lubbock.'

Joe Johnson had been severely shaken by the very mention of Lubbock's name. Now, with the implication that Peach had sought him out and interviewed him, his world was beginning to collapse about his ears. 'If Lubbock did anything to harm this Sarah Dunne, he wasn't acting on my orders.'

'Not what he says, Joe. He's singing like a canary, is Len Lubbock. Old-fashioned heavy, you see. You should have got rid of him a long time ago. He was all right for a bit of old-fashioned violence when you were on the way up, but now he's landed the two of you with a murder rap. And he scares easily; you should employ a better class of villain, but I'm glad you didn't. And just in case you're thinking of stopping his song, he's safely caged, where you can't get at him.'

'He was never ordered to kill the girl.' For the first time, Johnson spoke in a dull monotone.

They paused, allowing the sense of defeat in his words to take its full effect in the incongruous setting of the silent, opulent room. Peach grinned down into the whitening face of the man in the chair behind the desk. The fact that they had been left standing now seemed to give him physical dominance. 'We'll argue that out in court, no doubt. Lubbock has already admitted to strangling Sarah Dunne with her own scarf. I expect we'll match his DNA with hairs we found on the girl's body. He's quite clear that he was acting on your orders.'

He nodded to Lucy Blake, who stepped forward and pronounced the words of arrest. Joe Johnson slouched between two uniformed officers to the patrol car waiting outside.

Lucy Blake was silent in the face of Peach's elation as they drove back to the station in Brunton. The town was rid of an evil man, but she could still see the dead, seventeen-year-old face of poor, pathetic Sarah Dunne.